PRAISE FOR *DEATH FLIGHT*

'Gripping, intriguing, action-packed and powerful, I raced through this hard-hitting thriller in just two days!' Philippa East

'Jarringly authentic, pulsatingly engrossing, a granular frontline reporter's eye – her finest thriller yet' Peter Hain

'A tense political thriller that veritably thrums with menace. Clever, ambitious and utterly compulsive, it takes complex themes and weaves them into a gripping premise. I can't wait to see what's next for our intrepid reporter, Jonny Murphy' Kia Abdullah

'*Death Flight* is a must-read, high-octane political thriller that does not let up, so you better get your sleep in early. Sarah Sultoon's visceral portrayal of Argentina's meltdown brings to life the most heinous historical crimes with razor-sharp characterisation and first-hand political insights to produce a heart-stopping and deeply touching read. Superb.' Eve Smith

'A heady ride of reality-fused fiction … inhabited by characters that really get under your skin – characters who are living out a dilemma rooted in heart-rending fact' Michael J. Malone

'With Argentina back in the headlines, this is a timely thriller exploring one of the darkest chapters in the country's history … a gripping read' Martin Patience, *BBC News*

'A nonstop, breathless, harrowing, who-can-we-trust thriller, all the more powerful for being based on real tragic events' Anthony Dunford

'A charged, breakneck, high-danger investigation, set against a time of social, financial and political unrest, that had me completely hooked from start to finish … a shocking story with its foundations in truth' Jen Med's Book Reviews

'Solidly plotted, well executed and lots of twists and turns' Surjit's Books Blog

PRAISE FOR SARAH SULTOON

WINNER of the Crime Fiction Lover Best Debut Award
LONGLISTED for the CWA John Creasey (New Blood) Dagger

'A first-class political thriller' Steve Cavanagh

'An extraordinary piece of writing from a political-thriller writer at the very top of her game' Victoria Selman

'*Dirt* is both a fantastic page-turner and an intriguing look at a complex and dangerous world. Sarah Sultoon creates intelligent, memorable characters and fascinating stories. Journo noir at its finest!' Holly Watt

'A bitingly sharp, pacy thriller. Devilishly good. I inhaled it' Freya Berry

'A compelling thriller that weaves a complex tale of political tensions on the Israeli border with volatile secrets in a kibbutz, escalating to a shocking finale' Eve Smith

'Shocking and visceral, this novel deals with the horrors of war ... a brave, important and utterly compelling book' S.J. Watson

'Raw, authentic, powerful ... you won't see the end coming!' E.C. Scullion

'As searing an authentic thriller as you are likely to read ... Passionate, disturbing storytelling at its best' James Brabazon

'Brilliantly conveys both the exhilaration and the unspeakable horror of life on the international news frontline' Jo Turner

'A powerful story of the brutality of front-line journalism. Authentic, provocative and terrifyingly relevant. It will stay with you' Will Carver

'A brave and thought-provoking debut novel ... sensitive handling, tight plotting and authentic storytelling make for a compelling read' Adam Hamdy

DEATH FLIGHT

ABOUT THE AUTHOR

Sarah Sultoon is a journalist and writer, whose work as an international news executive at CNN has taken her all over the world, from the seats of power in both Westminster and Washington to the frontlines of Iraq and Afghanistan. She has extensive experience in conflict zones, winning three Peabody awards for her work on the war in Syria, an Emmy for her contribution to the coverage of Europe's migrant crisis in 2015, and a number of Royal Television Society gongs. As passionate about fiction as nonfiction, she completed a Masters of Studies in Creative Writing at the University of Cambridge, adding to an undergraduate language degree in French and Spanish, and Masters of Philosophy in History, Film and Television. When not reading or writing she can usually be found somewhere outside, either running, swimming or throwing a ball for her three children and dog while she imagines what might happen if...

Her debut thriller, *The Source*, was a Capital Crime Book Club pick, won the Crime Fiction Lover Best Debut Award, was nominated for the CWA's New Blood Dagger, was a number one bestseller on Kindle and is currently in production with Lime Pictures. It was followed by the critically acclaimed *The Shot* and *Dirt*. Follow Sarah on X/Twitter @SultoonSarah and Instagram @sarahsultoon.

Also by Sarah Sultoon and available from Orenda Books
The Source
The Shot
Dirt

DEATH FLIGHT

Sarah Sultoon

**ORENDA
BOOKS**

Orenda Books
16 Carson Road
West Dulwich
London SE21 8HU
www.orendabooks.co.uk

First published in the United Kingdom by Orenda Books, 2024
Copyright © Sarah Sultoon, 2024

A catalogue record for this book is available from the British Library.

ISBN 978-1-916788-01-5
eISBN 978-1-916788-02-2

Typeset in Garamond by typesetter.org.uk

Printed and bound by CPI Group (UK) Ltd, Croydon CR0 4YY

For sales and distribution, please contact info@orendabooks.co.uk

DEATH FLIGHT

Prologue

La Plata, Argentina
November 1998

The body was almost invisible at first, the same colour as the dawn sea, nudged up the wide sands by the gentle swell of the water. Was it blue, grey or white? That it was a curious combination of all three hardly mattered once it became obvious what it actually was.

A female torso. Bloated and headless. Only identifiable as a torso because it still had arms, even if the hands on the ends were missing their fingers. Ragged stumps where there had once been legs, sawn off rather than sewn up, no doubt as to how brutally they'd been removed. No identifying marks save the faded outline of a tattoo over the long-silenced heart.

The men looking on all appeared the same at first, too. Smudged fatigues, tall jackboots, flat caps. Four military officers marching in step along the deserted beach, any differences between them as camouflaged as their uniforms. Only when they paused to regard the water's edge did any variations in their posture emerge. Was one standing prouder than the next, or was it that another was recoiling? Suddenly, they didn't seem aligned at all.

The coast wind was blowing hard enough to whip away any sharp intakes of breath. The early-morning light was still murky enough to justify any squinting and blinking in disbelief. But nothing could justify the orders and instructions that followed, centred on one man in particular, who was hunching lower and lower as if to hide his shame. The only voices crying foul were those of the seagulls, wailing as they circled in the clouds overhead.

Could the Flights of Death have joined these birds in the skies once again? The abominable legacy of Argentina's Dirty War, supposedly ended fifteen years earlier, a military repression unprecedented in scale. Planes loaded with human cargo. Thousands of shackled prisoners disposed of mid-air. Dead bodies destined to disappear forever in the icy depths of the sea. It was only thanks to the inescapable rhythm of the tides that some remains were ever found. But the former military regime was yet to be fully brought to justice.

Only when the jackboots finally marched away did the gulls swoop and feast. But by then there was little left to enjoy.

Chapter One

His coffee cup rattles in its saucer as the dancers spin. Thick white china, too small for its earthy measure of espresso – a *cortado*, they call it, bigger than its Italian cousin; no, *better*, the Argentinians insist, always with a knowing wink, despite the fact they're yet to manufacture a satisfactory cup to put it in. Another aromatic splash trembles over the brim but Jonny Murphy is miles away, transfixed by the couple whirling across the cobblestones directly in front of his table. Beyond, the candy-striped corrugated-iron houses that distinguish the Buenos Aires district of La Boca from anywhere else in the world shimmer in the afternoon sun, blocks of colour popping between the dancers with every clack of their patent heels. Half his coffee is pooled in the saucer by the time the performance ends, still Jonny stands to applaud, an appreciatory ripple through the jacaranda trees dripping blossom overhead.

Street tango. This most-famed symbol of Argentinian culture was forced underground during military rule along with all forms of artistic and intellectual expression. It's a moment of joyous abandon every time it reclaims its rightful place even fifteen years later. And Jonny Murphy has a whole lot of time for moments like these. He's still clapping long after his companion has sat down.

'Shall I get you another one?' Paloma arches an eyebrow at his spilled coffee.

Jonny frowns as he notices the thick black camera strap still slung undisturbed over the back of her folding chair.

'You didn't take any pictures? How could you not?'

She regards him from under a pair of heavy black eyelashes. 'Since when do you think we are going to earn any money from a lifestyle feature?'

'Since when are we going to earn any money, full stop,' Jonny mumbles, staring down the lane, brightly coloured little houses blurring into one. They both work in news – he's a reporter, she's a photographer – but they are struggling even when they join forces. The currency of freelance journalism is ephemeral at the best of times, but with Argentina's economy rapidly tipping into decline, it is fast becoming as devalued as the peso.

Paloma sighs, snapping open her battered tin of blonde leaf. 'Ironic, isn't it? We can barely cover our costs even when we're covering a financial crisis.'

'Not sure that's entirely ironic.' Jonny shoves his chair back under their table a little too hard. 'Unlike the fact that everyone on the newsdesk apparently has the memory of a fucking goldfish. I still have to explain almost every word I file on the bloody thing. What don't they understand? Debt is astronomic, inflation is off the chart, it's only thanks to the International Monetary Fund that the financial system is still functioning, and I haven't even got started on unemployment. "Follow the money" is all I've been told to do since I got here and that was almost a year ago. Even the newsdesk interns should get the basics by now.'

'It's all those big words you're using,' Paloma replies with a grin. '"The *International Tribune's* Jonny Murphy" is quite a mouthful, too.'

Jonny despairs at the blush instantly heating up his neck. 'Well, then the desk should try giving me more than three column inches to explain it in. Sometimes I think it would be easier if I was filing for a daily rag.'

'It would be a thousand times worse, is the truth. You're lucky to have the backing of a major international newspaper. We wouldn't stand a chance with any of the other stories we pitch otherwise. You're not just some nobody from New Mexico with bleak pictures of deserts in her portfolio. You've got an international profile. You can make a case for investigating something other than the financial crisis once in a while, even without a lead.'

Jonny sighs, even as his heart rate ticks up at the mention of their lead. The *Trib* may be the most widely circulated English-language newspaper in the world. But the truth is his profile is nowhere near high enough to warrant the kind of trust and investment this particular lead is going to need. He's spent most of his two years as a reporter trying to reinvent himself after his first journalism gig in the Middle East came to an abrupt end. He only got that gig in the first place courtesy of his fluent Hebrew – his Israeli single mother still insisted on speaking it at home long after they moved to the UK when he was a baby. As for Paloma – she has way more experience of Buenos Aires than he does, but is still scraping together a living off the back of flogging the odd good shot. The fact that she speaks the language this time is more use to him than it is to her. She doesn't need to speak to shoot.

He looks pointedly at her camera. 'Well we haven't got enough to actually pitch anything yet. Let alone successfully.'

Paloma's cigarette sparks with a hiss. 'And wasting a roll of film on pavement tango isn't going to help with that.'

Disheartened, Jonny waves for the bill rather than reply. He knows no journalist is stationed in Buenos Aires these days for the beauty shots. And he and Paloma are secretly looking into a far uglier matter. It's been fifteen years since Argentina broke free from a military dictatorship so brutal it went to unimaginable lengths to hide the evidence of its crimes. Lengths that have, so far, made it impossible to assemble enough proof to bring justice to bear, despite the growing clamour from politicians, journalists and human-rights groups the world over. The Dirty War, the repression was called, so named for the scale of its depravity. Jonny eyes the two burly men banked in a nearby doorway, arms folded, eyes darting around until the small packages openly changing hands in front of them are safely stowed and the scooter paused conspicuously ahead fires up and zooms away. Is it any wonder that former military commanders are still free to mix in Argentinian society regardless of accusations so horrific the details are almost unprintable? This exhibitionist city – its riotous colours, its intoxicating smells, its raucous and infectious energy – just demands to be seen. Even its underbelly operates in plain sight.

He drops a couple of crumpled banknotes on the table. 'I need to get back if we're going to have a chance of following up any leads tomorrow. There's loads more phone calls that I still need to make.'

There go those eyelashes again. Jonny briefly wonders if Paloma can actually see anything properly with them hanging in the way. She probably wouldn't bother looking so hard if she could.

'Fine. So let's go. But you don't get another coffee.'

Jonny tries not to watch her readying to leave. Paloma seems to be able to make even the simplest of tasks look elegant and sophisticated.

'I've got some sausages back at the ranch instead if you're interested,' he adds hopefully. 'My calls will only take a few minutes.'

'Thanks but I didn't realise it was so late. My film should be ready by now. The technician said twenty-four hours on the nose. If I hurry I can make it before the shop closes.'

Jonny brightens at the prospect, looking up. 'So bring it over afterwards, if you want. It'll help with working out what to do next if we can go through the pictures together.'

Paloma shakes her head, slinging the camera strap firmly around her body. Jonny commands his gaze away from how it cleaves across her chest.

'You know how I hate having someone ogling over my shoulder. I'll call you later, when I've had a chance to look. You can fill me in on the plan for tomorrow then too.'

Ogling? Jonny fixes his gaze on the pavement as he musters up a weak nod. He'd settle for enough money shots on that roll of film to give their investigation some momentum.

'Oh, and...' She pauses. 'Sausages?'

'I meant *choripanes*,' he replies lamely, regretting having mentioned them. 'You know, the ones like chorizo hot dogs—'

'My favourite,' Paloma interrupts archly. 'Save them for tomorrow, OK? Who knows, we might have something to actually celebrate then.'

Jonny settles for another meek nod rather than try and say anything else. Paloma falls in step beside him as they walk towards the bus station.

'It's amazing how much it's changed around here,' she muses, gesturing towards the football ground a few blocks ahead.

'How old were you?' Jonny gazes at the stadium's iconic silhouette. Boca Juniors, one of Argentina's so-called Big Five and one of the best-known football clubs in the world. 'When you first visited with your parents, I mean? I know you came loads.'

'Two or three, I think? There's a cool photo of me in a baby football shirt in front of the stadium. I only really remember the later trips. We never went anywhere else, so they all kind of blur into one.'

'Wow.' Jonny pictures Paloma as a baby – all inquisitive dark eyes and frown in the unmistakable navy-and-yellow Boca Juniors football kit. 'And visiting during the war, too. Hard to believe the military were happy to allow tourists in and out. Your parents were committed, huh.'

'To what?' Paloma flicks a glance at him.

'To Boca Juniors, obviously. You'd have to be, all the way from New Mexico.'

'It was a national shirt. Argentina all the way. But yes, I guess you're right. We lived in DC then, I don't remember anything about that either. They had US government jobs at the time. There won't have been much that fazed them.'

'I'm sure,' Jonny replies, still wondering. 'I suppose I just can't imagine holidaying here while the repression was in full swing.'

'It's a big place. It takes two full days and nights of driving to get from here to Tierra Del Fuego. And that isn't even the length of the whole country. It takes almost as long to get to the resorts in the Andes mountains. I keep telling you – you need to get out more.'

'Tierra Del Fuego.' Jonny tries and fails to pronounce the words properly. 'The land of fire?'

'It's actually covered in ice that far south, but yes. It's not much further to get to the Antarctic itself. But you don't have to go all that way to do some exploring. Get out there – dress it up as work. You know the financial crisis is worse in the provinces. When I was a kid we spent most of our time over in the mountains by the lakes. They call it Little Switzerland.'

Jonny snorts. 'Well the crisis is hardly biting down there. That place isn't known as Little Switzerland just because of its alpine lakes and twee chocolate shops.'

Paloma throws him another look. 'So you've been?'

'To Switzerland?'

She swats him. 'You know what I mean. I guess when I found out it was better known for all the Nazi war criminals who hid there for years I didn't want to stay there either. But my parents couldn't wait to get out of Buenos Aires. They wouldn't even leave the airport after a while. We would just hang around until the next available connecting flight out west. They were always so busy at home, we hardly spent any time together outside of those holidays. But then all they wanted to do was go for long walks on their own. And still they wouldn't let me stay behind in the city. It drove me nuts.'

'Is that why you won't leave the place too now, like me?'

'Nice try, buster. Stick to broadening your own horizons.'

'Speaking of horizons.' Jonny pauses by the stadium, distracted by the sight of the spectator stands stretching perilously high into the sky. 'Are those the new bits, then? Those top tiers? They're insanely tall. They can't be legal in this day and age.'

'You've obviously not been living here long enough if you think they would need to be legal to get built anyway.'

'But you said everything had changed so much around here.'

She waves a dismissive hand. 'I just meant that it used to be so much more rundown. The poorest, most deprived neighbourhood in the city. Sure, it's still shady as hell, but at least it doesn't look like it now.'

Jonny tries and fails not to eye her bulky camera case. Paloma rolls her eyes.

'What? I haven't said anything.'

'You didn't have to.'

'I just wish you wouldn't carry it so visibly, that's all.'

'Don't be so paranoid.'

Jonny blanches. A fancy, expensive piece of equipment on display in times like these? In a location that, by her own admission, is still hiding its reputation as one of the most deprived parts of the city behind its fancy colours? Worse, in a country where only fifteen years ago the former military regime lumped journalists into the same category as the underground revolutionaries waging a guerrilla war? Too influential to be trusted. Too much power to mislead the public. Dissidents by a different name.

'Paranoid?' he repeats.

'Yes. Five minutes ago you were disappointed I hadn't taken yet another shot of dancing in the street. Now you're wishing I'd left the camera behind.'

'OK, OK, OK.' Jonny holds up his hands. 'I just don't like

flaunting it, that's all. Especially not around here. Carry it in a different bag or something...'

'Lugging around an enticingly bulging rucksack doesn't sound like a better idea.'

'It wouldn't take much to make it look less like a very expensive camera.'

'What about when I actually have to get it out? I can hardly hide the lens.'

Jonny sighs, fingering the notebook and pen stashed safe below the wallet in his trouser pocket. 'Look, I realise that sometimes it isn't as easy for you to do the job as it is for me. That I get to be a bumbling Englishman apologising for every question, whereas you have to stick a camera in people's faces. But money is getting tighter and tighter around here. Weren't we just talking about exactly that? The only stories I can get into the bloody paper are the ones about a full-blown financial crisis, which, by the way—'

'—don't necessarily lend themselves to good pictures,' Paloma finishes. 'I don't need reminding that I'm the one with more to prove than you at the moment.'

They start to walk again. Jonny finds himself shivering even as they leave the shadow of the stadium behind them. He can't help but ask. 'Are you honestly sure you'll be OK getting home by yourself?'

Now shadows of a different kind are passing across Paloma's face.

'I can look out for myself, Jonny. I'm used to taking risks, you know. Sometimes I have to, to get the job done properly.'

He scuffs a boot into a crack in the pavement. Instantly he's reliving the moment they met, at his first *cacerolazo* – an exclusively South American form of popular protest involving the deafening bashing of saucepans. Thousands of Argentinians had taken the contents of their kitchens to the streets that day to demonstrate their frustration at the government's kamikaze handling of its economy. A few pots and pans had slammed directly into Paloma's face while she was busy proving herself on a story about the financial crisis which did, in fact, lend itself to good pictures. There was so much blood pouring down her face by the end of it that he could see it even from his stupid safe distance away. The fact that those pictures eventually trebled the impact of his reporting is one he still feels uncomfortable with. She's the one with the scars as a result, not him.

'Don't remind me.'

Her tone softens. She runs an unconscious finger down the angry red mark on the side of her face. 'It wasn't your fault. How could it be? We'd never met before, I didn't even know you were there at first.'

Jonny tries not to stare. 'That's not what I'm talking about right now. This particular film of yours isn't full of pictures of kitchen utensils. Whoever has developed it now knows precisely what's on it. And it isn't exactly pretty, is it? All I'm saying is that maybe both of us should go and pick it up instead of you going in by yourself. Just in case there's an issue. Then I can see you safely to your door afterwards.'

'It's in the opposite direction.'

'That's my problem, not yours.'

'And what about all those calls you have to make? The pictures on that film are worth nothing without some more interviews, and you know that.'

Jonny sighs. A tin can clatters as it rolls into their path on a draught of purple petals. The interruption seems to be enough to make Paloma relent.

'How about I call you as soon as I'm back home? You do your job, I do mine. And we can have your *choripanes* tomorrow when we put all the pieces together.'

She flashes a smile and Jonny's resolve instantly crumples. He makes a show of checking his watch to save face.

'Fine, then,' he mutters, still uncomfortable. She won't be

travelling in the dark, at least. But this particular film of Paloma's can't fall into the wrong hands. The problem is they are a long way from working out exactly who is incriminated by its most horrifying content.

Almost at the bus station, Jonny only realises he's lagging when a warm hand tugs at his. Usually they would take the same route from here – Paloma's apartment unit in the Congreso neighbourhood is a few bus stops before Jonny's. He finds himself reflecting on how soon his lease is up for at least the eightieth time. There are vacant apartments in her building. Can he make a reasonable case for moving in there, since they are almost always working on something together? A reporter needs a photographer and a photographer needs a reporter, otherwise their work is only ever two halves of a whole. And with that the dream takes hold – apartment doors a floor apart, fairy lights strung over their identical wrought-iron balconies, the smell of *choripanes* beckoning from his open window up to hers – Jonny sways on his feet just imagining it until he gets a very real whiff of the acrid fumes belching from the vehicles inside the terminal.

He pauses, reluctantly pulling his hand from hers. 'You'll call me?'

Paloma nods. 'And I'll be careful. Go on.'

Joining the back of the horde boarding his bus, Jonny has to resist the urge to look back. But by the time he's squeezed inside, the vehicle's small oblong windows are already thickly misted over – the tell-tale mark of at least a dozen too many passengers, as usual. Peering through the fog, Jonny is sure he can spot Paloma's bus idling a few stands down. At least she won't have long to wait, he thinks, squinting. Has she already boarded? But all he can make out is a blur as his vehicle pulls away, yawing on its way out of the terminus and into the traffic.

Jonny steadies himself with a hand on the metal bar overhead and tries to pick out some words from the streams of rapid

Spanish humming all round him. Once Jonny prided himself on his grasp of languages, fluent in both Hebrew and English. But his mother tongue, as he used to call it, now only serves as a reminder of all he has lost. His first job in the Middle East wasn't just Jonny's first journalism gig, it was also a ticket into his past. By the time Jonny actually arrived in Jerusalem, having only just finished school in the UK, his Israeli mother had been dead for over ten years. But she'd been dead to her own parents for far longer than that – over something she never had the guts to tell Jonny she'd done.

He fidgets in the crowded aisle. Is that why, after more than a year scraping together a living in Buenos Aires, literally thousands of miles away from anything to do with his past, Jonny is still resolutely bad at speaking the local language? Because he associates speaking anything other than English with his mother's betrayal? All he was ever told about their move to the UK was that it had to happen. That they had to start again after his mother brought unthinkable shame upon her family by marrying his father who, incidentally, also abandoned them both when Jonny was a baby. He sighs as he considers the real reason, so much more twisted than that. The fact is that Jonny was never meant to be alone – he wasn't even in the fucking womb alone: he once had a twin sister who his mother willingly gave up to his father on the condition he left her and Jonny behind for good. And now Jonny is the one left alone, with no way of finding this fabled twin sister, with no memories of ever having a sibling in the first place – unlike his mother, who couldn't live with the guilt in the end. She took her own life, he thinks, reliving a conversation that, almost fifteen years later, still makes no sense to him. As a bewildered and terrified nine-year-old boy, he hadn't realised what the social workers meant when they came to break the news to him. They had to explain she had killed herself before he understood.

He's stuck so far in the past that he misses the clamour building behind him until a rough hand jerks at his collar.

Jonny looks down at another tug on his sleeve – it's a woman, in traditional Bolivian dress, unmistakable with its vividly coloured shawls and bell-shaped petticoats crowned incongruously with a shiny-black bowler hat. The bus lurches the moment he feels for his wallet – yep, still stashed safe in his pocket – as if to physically reprimand him. Quite right too: was Jonny's first instinct really to assume that as an indigenous woman she could only be out to rob him? The woman tips her face towards him, hat still somehow balanced perfectly on her head even though she's craning her neck. But the next thing that happens is so unexpected that he has to crane his own, bending down to catch her every word.

'*Subversivos*,' she whispers urgently. 'You understand? *Subversivos*.'

The bus lurches again before Jonny can reply, his mind spinning along with it.

'*Subversivos*,' she repeats. 'They…' she trails off, eyes darting, makes the sign of people walking with her tiny fingers.

'Follow?' Jonny finds himself whispering. He can't believe what he's hearing. The woman nods back, so vigorously that the hat should slip, but it doesn't, polished dome blazing with conviction.

Jonny reels even as the bus steadies. Does this woman honestly mean to tell him he is being followed? Who is she? How on earth would she know? And what the fuck is the Spanish word for 'follow'? He thinks of the notebook in his pocket, the scribbles that would surely make sense to no one but him unless paired with the pictures on the roll of film currently coming into focus in a deliberately random darkroom.

By the time he's collected himself the woman is hunched away from him, an impossibly small mound in a sea of people, showing only the top of her bowler hat.

'I don't understand,' he whispers as if she can hear him, but the hat doesn't flinch. '*No ... No entiendo.* I'm being followed? How do you know that?'

And now she's just gazing at him with an expression as nonplussed as he'd have expected from a native Bolivian woman being harangued by a sweaty Englishman on a packed public bus.

He raises his voice, he can't help himself. 'Do you understand me? What do you mean?'

But not even a flicker of recognition crosses her impassive face. An elbow now, digging into his ribs. Is it any wonder? Jonny knows he's making a scene. Then another, followed by a shove. A swarthy man, as squat as he is burly, forcing himself between them. A stream of invective that Jonny doesn't need to understand to know exactly what it means: Lower your voice. Leave her alone.

'I'm sorry,' he gabbles, straining to see over the man's shoulder to find the hat has already been swallowed up by the rest of the crowd on the bus. The man glares at him, more unmistakable invective, puts in a shoulder for good measure. Jonny holds up his hands, finally musters up some comprehensible Spanish, manages to edge round the man towards the doors sighing open as the bus pulls into a stop. Up ahead, the bowler hat finally reappears, its patent shine bobbing in the gaggle dispersing across the pavement.

'Wait!' Jonny cries out, stumbling off the bus into a jolt of petrol. She's moving quickly now, are there more hats in the crowd? He concentrates on following a flash of brightly coloured shawl. Ducking off the pavement and into the adjacent square, he realises the bus had made it as far as Plaza Miserere. Good, his unit is only a short walk away; but it's almost impossible to locate anyone amidst the jumble of street-market stands.

Breathing hard, he pulls up short, scanning the plaza for the shiny-black bowler hat he knows will have long disappeared. While it isn't exactly common to find native Bolivian women in some parts of the city, Plaza Miserere is one place they can blend in. It's usually impossible not to spot their distinctive hats and skirts – sometimes even a live chicken flies out from under a tumble of petticoats. But here, jostling with the street vendors that come from all over the South American continent, even birds don't register. Plaza Miserere is one place where the only people that can't disappear are people like him.

Jonny drops on to a bench parked in the shade of a giant rubber tree. This woman was as identifiable as she was forgettable. Which means she took a risk, a big one. There is a certain amount she must have known – but how? And why? He rubs his temples as if he can physically push the different theories scudding through his head into a single, coherent whole. A sudden draught of candied peanuts wafts up his nose, so sweet he can almost feel the sugar rush coursing through his body.

Digging into his pocket for some change, he finally realises what is missing.

His wallet is still there.

But his notebook is gone.

Chapter Two

Even though it is pointless, Jonny retraces his steps: back out of the plaza on to one of the city's main arterial avenues, pavements littered with discarded cigarettes, crushed tin cans and bottle-tops – everything except his damned reporter's notebook with its distinctive buff cover, the one that gives him a pathetic thrill every time he notes the word 'reporter' on the front. He kicks at a crack underfoot, digging around in his empty pocket as if he can physically reconstitute its pages.

His notebook had to have been deliberately filched, otherwise why would his wallet still be in place? Is it possible it was a mistake, made by an incompetent petty thief? Jonny pulls into a doorway, turning the wallet between his fingers. In the cramped space and dim light of the bus, he supposes they could have felt the same. And it is more likely that someone rooted around for the first thing they could find and came up with something completely useless. If so his precious notebook is probably disintegrating somewhere in the drains halfway to the bay by now.

A sudden, sharp rattle from behind prompts him to stash the wallet again, but it's only two elderly gentlemen squeezing past with folding chairs and a camping table, ready to set up on the pavement for a game of draughts. Something snags in Jonny's mind as he watches them chunter back and forth. That mystery Bolivian woman knew to speak to him in English. Jonny's been in Buenos Aires long enough to know that most people dressed so traditionally usually speak one of the many indigenous languages of the South American continent over the Spanish of their colonisers, and certainly over English. That woman clearly had a point to make. So was she the one who took the notebook? Was that her play all along? Distract him while she went into his pocket for something far more valuable to her than his stupid wallet?

Jonny dashes past the elderly gentlemen and sprints back into the plaza, trying to remember exactly what he wrote down. There were names and dates, different theories and possibilities. Feeling suddenly winded, he stumbles back to the bench under the rubber tree. But just as he sits, he remembers.

She said Jonny was being followed. And if she was right, he's done nothing over the past few minutes other than meander around in stupid, misguided circles.

Suddenly grateful for his wallet over his notebook, Jonny hurries to a curio stand, bursting with vibrantly coloured knitted hats and scarves. Grabbing a random handful, he proffers a clutch of crumpled peso notes to the vendor, and despite the heat of the late-spring afternoon – spring in November, Jonny still can't get used to it – he jams a knitted hat on his head and wraps himself in a scarf. Cornering the sprawling train station on the plaza's northern tip, the smell of candied peanuts gives way to the acrid belch of fuel. Jonny speeds round the last few corners to the heavy wrought-iron gates of his apartment unit a few blocks away.

The familiar chorus of street patois greets him as Jonny fumbles for his keys – yep, still safely in his pocket with his wallet. He'd hand over the keys in a flash if he could just find his precious notebook. The usual cluster of men are crouched on the pavement outside searing something unidentifiable on a small, makeshift grill. When Jonny last asked, this group had numbered a Colombian, a Peruvian, two Bolivianos and a Paraguayan. At the time he'd been sure they were making it up as they went along just to mess with him. He'd even played the dumb gringo, given them a laugh at his own expense – these were men he'd rather have on his side than not, parked on the street outside his apartment block every day and night. But now he finds himself wondering whether they're not just using this stretch of pavement as a kitchen, but are here for another reason. Fitting his key into the lock, the heavy iron security gate clangs opens into the small shared courtyard. Checking behind him, to make sure no one's looking through the gate, Jonny is finally able to rip off his knits, taking the iron staircase two steps at a time, up to his small studio on the top floor and dropping his pile of fabric just inside the door.

The phone line rings out for a full minute after Jonny's picked up the receiver and dialled Paloma's number. She's not there yet, of course; the shop where she left her film to be developed is in the opposite direction to where they both live. He peels off his sweat-soaked shirt, flinging it on to the bare floorboards in frustration. The open window doesn't do him the courtesy of ushering in even a puff of fresh air. Squeaking open the tap, he draws a glass of water, trying to steady himself for long enough to consider what he knows.

It's been nearly two weeks since Jonny started investigating something other than Argentina's looming financial crisis. Nearly two weeks since the grisly discovery of a woman's body washed up on a city beach – no, Jonny is already correcting himself, dropping into one of his two rickety dining chairs. That's only what they were told. What *Paloma* was told. He kicks at a table leg, instantly regretting it as water slops all over the place. Jonny is the reporter in this relationship. By now he should be the one fluent enough to do some of the talking instead of letting his Mexican-American colleague translate for him all the time.

He takes a gulp of water, starts again. What he knows is that it's been nearly two weeks since the body was found – or since Paloma and Jonny found out about it. Body *parts*, rather than an intact corpse. Headless, the police-issue crime-scene photograph had confirmed, with no fingerprints because there were no fingers left either, the only identifying mark a faded tattoo of a bird on the chest. Jonny twists round to consult the map pinned on the wall behind him, running a sweaty fingertip the short distance down the coast from Buenos Aires to the beach in question at the community of La Plata, known as the city's southernmost suburb.

The horrifying crime-scene photograph reassembles in Jonny's mind with inescapable clarity. These beaches are not virgin sands. Argentina's Dirty War saw to that some fifteen years ago. He reaches over to his tiny bookcase to consult the threadbare historical textbook he seems to spend all his time re-reading. Argentina's military dictatorship terrorised the country for almost a decade, propped up by the might of the United States, more terrified of the rise of Communism than the rest of the South American continent put together. Death squads stalked the streets with impunity. Thousands of alleged political dissidents were arrested, tortured and killed – many on the so-called Flights of Death.

Los Vuelos de Muerte, Jonny thinks, the sweat on his back turning cold. Whole planeloads of prisoners spirited away, drugged and hogtied, to be flung out into the open skies over the sea. Where better to hide the evidence of a killing machine as brutally efficient as Argentina's former military dictatorship than the icy depths of the Atlantic Ocean? No one would ever have been able to prove what really happened were it not for the ocean tides inexorably moving some human remains back on to dry land. But the burden of proof is still the size of the Andes. Thousands of bodies simply disappeared.

Jonny considers this, flipping back and forth through the well-thumbed pages. The Dirty War ended fifteen years ago. He doesn't need a textbook to tell him that bodies don't survive intact in water for that long. And there are plenty of other reasons why a corpse might find its way into the water in a city like Buenos Aires. Drugs. Gangs. Money. Revenge. People getting angry. People getting even. People sending messages in the vilest of ways.

Jonny's finger stills on a random page. The echoes of the Dirty War in this case seem far too convincing not to be at least partly deliberate. The similarities to the most inflammatory period of Argentinian history are, in fact, glaringly obvious. And yet this latest discovery hasn't hit even the local news headlines. Why? He flicks to a more recent chapter, reminds himself how influential the military remained even once the war had ended. Democracy was only restored after the economy collapsed. But the incoming president had to waive the prosecution of crimes committed by the former military regime to hold off another coup. The amnesty is still in place, leaving commanders accused of the most heinous of crimes free to mix in Argentinian society.

Jonny snaps the book shut. Is that the reason local journalists are keeping the news off the front pages? Human remains showing up on a popular city beach is a top story whichever way it is spun. But Jonny's been scouring the papers for days now and come up blank. Evidence of an attempted disappearance fifteen years after the end of the Dirty War would mean elements of the former military junta are still operating underground, with state-sponsored impunity, sending gruesome messages of their own. That's the real news story here. But Jonny has to prove it.

Dropping the book on the table, he paces back to the window. In order to get anywhere with this he needs to identify the victim. The police haven't made any headway yet, or at least, aren't willing to tell Paloma and Jonny if they have. In fact they were hustled out of the local police station after barely ten minutes of looking through the state's official files on missing people. How exactly is he expecting to do it alone? Drugs. Gangs. Money. Revenge – these are the fearsome criminal enterprises he'll have to discount from the equation, and that's only if he's right.

Jonny digs around for his notebook only to turn his empty pocket inside out with a howl. Despite the growing campaign for justice, the Dirty War is still a difficult matter to research openly.

International outrage at the continued whitewash is one thing. But asking questions with the Argentinian military still at such close hand is quite another. And for those answering, it is clear there is still danger. The complex where most alleged dissidents were imprisoned and tortured remains operational as a military training facility in a fancy Buenos Aires suburb. The woman Paloma and Jonny quietly met with earlier even admitted to using a fake name, despite discussing her missing children for hours on end. The yellowing photos shaking in her gnarly brown hand flash into Jonny's mind – her daughter Mercedes, only seventeen years old when she was arrested on a street corner on a charge of consorting with the wrong people. The same for Pablo, her son, six years older and labelled a dissident just for being an academic. And now he's lost his record of their entire conversation.

Jonny eyes the movements on the street below the window, trying to remember every last detail scribbled into his missing notebook. Who could be interested in the scant information he has so far accumulated about this most recent body on the beach? And why? That's not all that's bothering him. Paloma and Jonny can't be the only ones the local police tipped off about the corpse. The information practically landed in Paloma's lap. And all so-called exclusive news leaks come with an agenda attached to them, especially when handed out to junior reporters like Jonny Murphy from the *International Tribune*.

There Jonny pauses, mind barrelling back to an altogether darker place. Is he still just an amateur, being successfully played all over again? It wouldn't be the first time, would it? His first gig in the Middle East may be in his past now. But all the secrets he unearthed there are still as clear to him as yesterday, and are the real reasons his stint there came to such an abrupt end: the rogue intelligence he witnessed operating with impunity on one of the hottest international borders in the world. An unthinkable scoop, were it not for the fact it implicated members of Jonny's own family – the Israeli grandparents he'd spent years trying to locate after his mother died. Those sacred oaths of journalism – holding power to account, remaining objective, following the facts to wherever they lead – Jonny kept them all until he found out the truth and proceeded to bury the entire thing.

And for what? He's still alone. He still has no means to find his long-lost twin sister. And he's still scared that someone might find out the extent of what he hid, which is why he's playing catch up on his career on the literal other side of the world to everything he's ever known and loved.

He shakes his head, turning inside to pore over the map again only to come up against the date on the calendar pinned up next to it. Time to write another one of his fucking airletters. Jonny has to send news to his grandparents every week. He's still relying on the money they send him by return. He protected them, and now they're protecting him. Debt letters, he thinks bitterly, eyeing the neat blue stack of them on top of his bookcase. They really should come in red.

Jonny sighs, gazing back down at the pavement only to meet a street dweller's baleful eye.

And then the phone rings.

Chapter Three

Jonny answers in both Spanish and English, almost within the same word. Clammy hand slipping on the plastic receiver, he repeatedly barks his nonsense. Nothing. Unless that is the faint whistle of breathing on the other end? He recoils as the dial tone suddenly blares, harsh and insistent.

Wrong number, he thinks. Of course that happens in Buenos Aires as often as anywhere else. It's easy enough for a finger to tremble, for memory to slip. Isn't it? He replaces the receiver with a soft click; only for it to ring again almost immediately.

'Hello?' Jonny's shouting now, plastic receiver giving an indignant squeak as he squeezes it. '*Hola?*'

A beat of silence – yes, definitely silence, unless Jonny counts the scooter backfiring on the street below. And then the unmistakable rattle of a sigh – he peers out of his window, suddenly torn between the mystery of who is on the end of the silent telephone line and who might be riding the motorbike he can see disappearing around the street's far corner. In the direction of Plaza Miserere, he notes as he barks down the phone again, but now it's only the dial tone answering him.

Jonny curses, most definitely in English this time, slamming the phone back into its cradle. Not even baleful eyes meet his searching gaze from the pavement below; they're focused on their pavement *parillada*. He scrabbles for his lost notebook again, ripping at the sweaty lining of his empty pocket. Who has this apartment's telephone number? What numbers are so similar that they might be confused with his? Finally a useful idea: why not try calling an almost identical number to see who picks up? But just as his hand touches the receiver again, it rings. And this time there is no mistaking the voice on the other end.

'You won't believe it,' he gabbles at Paloma while she gabbles at him just as urgently. She's trying to catch her breath, gasping every few words.

'I've got the pictures, but—'

'Someone stole my notebook—'

'They're all there, except—'

'I'm pretty sure I know who it was, but—'

'A frame is missing—'

They both stop in the same breath.

'Missing?' Jonny asks just as Paloma says, 'Stolen?'

'Hang on a second,' Jonny says, the sweat still glistening on his naked chest turning colder. 'You mean one of your pictures is gone? Which one?'

'Yes,' Paloma replies. 'There's no doubt about it. I counted, I don't know, probably twenty times, just to be sure. There aren't enough prints.'

Jonny mentally flicks through their last roll of film, snapped in a hurry during their first visit to the police station in La Plata. The crime-scene photographs, the police report, the pictures of pictures – torn and aged mugshots, spread out on a grimy table top in front of them. Evidence of people who are still missing. And now one of those pictures is missing too.

'It can't be a coincidence,' he mutters, pulling at the frayed lining of his pocket, which still hangs inside out down his trouser leg. 'She must have been telling the truth.'

'She? Who? What are you talking about?'

Jonny starts to pace, words suddenly faltering as he processes the events of the last couple of hours. 'Listen, did anyone follow you? Home, I mean – from the camera shop. Or before that? Actually, it doesn't matter. Meet me—' Jonny catches himself before he says the location out loud. 'You know where. I'll explain when you get there. Do you know what I'm talking about? Where I'm talking about, I mean.'

Paloma exhales into the receiver rather than reply. But Jonny is heartened. The fact she's chosen not to say anything else is almost all the understanding he needs to pass, unspoken, between them. Finally feeling able to sit down, he collapses heavily into a chair, instantly regretting it as his forgotten glass of water topples over, rolls off the table and smashes all over the floor.

'What was that?' There's a tremor in Paloma's voice.

'Nothing.'

Jonny tries to swipe away the worst of the mess with his boot. Now he's down to his last glass. He doesn't even have a toothbrush mug to make up a pair. Which, he supposes, is no great shakes, since he's always on his own up here. He winces, broken glass gritty underfoot. What would a woman like Paloma possibly want from an inexperienced idiot like him – other than work of course?

'Just me being a clumsy idiot,' he adds hurriedly. 'I'll be twenty minutes, tops. We can talk then.'

'It might not be open, you know.'

'Of course it will.' Jonny checks the time, picturing their preferred restaurant's shadowy, humid interior. 'And don't bring anything with you, OK?'

'What, like my appetite?'

Jonny grunts despite the fact his stomach is twisting too. They don't meet at that particular restaurant to eat. They meet there to talk in private when they need to. He pushes away the thought they could just as easily talk in private in one of their tiny apartments. He'd rather not reflect on why that never seems to happen. 'You know what I mean. Leave everything of value behind. I'll see you there.'

Paloma returns agreement through her teeth. Jonny slots the receiver back into its cradle. Crunching through the rest of the broken glass on the floor, he retrieves a clean shirt. He's still stuffing an arm into a sleeve when he steps back outside on to the iron walkway.

A picture and his notebook are now missing, he thinks, speeding over to the narrow spiral staircase linking his unit's upper floors with its internal courtyard. And that woman said he was being followed – he pulls up short, retraces his steps, finds the pile of garish cloth heaped just inside his front door. Shaking out the brightly coloured shawl from the rest, Jonny drapes it over his shoulders before starting off again. There's an attempted cover-up of a sort under way, but of what? And by whom?

Outside, night is beginning to fall, helped by the high-rise buildings on either side of the narrow street, which is barely more than an alleyway. Jonny tightens the unfamiliar shawl around himself. Usually he feels nothing but comfortable here, luxuriating in the shade of the buildings, the muttered greetings from the various groups who make their home on the pavement. But tonight the façades feel oppressive, the sidelong glances watchful. He shivers into his shawl despite the lingering heat of the evening before turning on to the main road.

'*Subversivos*,' Jonny repeats under his breath as he walks. That's what the Bolivian woman had said. She'd explicitly used the umbrella term given by the former military regime to anyone thought to be displaying politically dissident tendencies during the Dirty War. Journalists, academics, artists, all were labelled as dangerous as the underground revolutionaries doing the actual fighting. So is it another journalist on Jonny's tail? Has someone else been tipped off about his investigation?

He picks up his pace, mentally ticking off the blocks he knows he needs to cover before he reaches Paloma at their preferred meeting place – a *tenedor libre*, that exclusively South American all-inclusive, open-all-hours buffet, conspicuous only for the fact that across the entire continent no one actually seems to eat anything until long after ten p.m. The smell of meat the wrong side of charred reaches Jonny just before he gets to the top of the dark, steep stairwell. Paloma is already downstairs, hunched in the far corner over an untouched bowl of noodles. Sliding into the booth opposite her, Jonny hurriedly pulls off his shawl.

'Don't ask,' he mumbles as she raises her eyebrows. 'I'll be back in a second.'

He walks back to the bank of trestle tables laden with lukewarm hotplates in the centre of the fetid dining room to grab a couple of slices of pizza. By the time he sits back down, Paloma is visibly agitated.

'This was inside the photo sleeve,' she says in a low voice. 'I only found it after you rang off.' Jonny spots the edge of a crumpled piece of paper in the closed fist she's tapping between them on the tiled tabletop.

'What is that ... a message?' Jonny mutters, picking up a piece of pizza only to wave it in the air. 'And it was in with the pictures?'

Paloma nods, letting her fingers relax a little around the scrap of paper. 'Sort of. I didn't notice at first, I was too busy counting the actual prints. Someone must have put it there at the same time as stealing one.'

Jonny holds his pizza in front of his mouth as he whispers: 'So what does it say? And which photo is missing?'

Paloma just shakes her head. Her fist moves under the table and he reaches towards it with his free hand. The small, scrunched-up ball of paper moves into his palm. He bites into his pizza with relief, instantly regretting it as a crust like cardboard sticks inside of his mouth.

'Mmmmm,' he grunts pointlessly, chewing and chewing. 'How's yours?'

Paloma picks up a fork, makes a show of twirling up noodles. 'It's a map,' she whispers. 'At least I think it is. There are scribbled street names, I don't know where they're supposed to be. We'll have to find a way to look it up, somehow.'

Jonny feels his mouth hang open, has to jam more pizza into it. His notebook has gone missing, Paloma's film has been tampered with, he's apparently being followed, and now someone has scribbled them a map? Swallowing hard, he is finally able to explain himself and the events of the last couple of hours in a series of short, sharp whispers – warnings from a mystery Bolivian woman, a contretemps on a packed public bus, his notebook disappeared by the end of it.

Paloma stirs her noodles as she thinks.

'Maybe she was going for your wallet,' she finally says.

'I thought so at first,' he replies, suddenly back on the overcrowded bus, jammed so tight he can barely distinguish accidental jostle from deliberate shove. 'But given what's happened with your pictures, don't you think it's too much of a coincidence?'

Her fork stills.

'I guess so,' she answers after a moment.

'But a notebook?' Jonny muses, trying to put it together. 'Full of English? When the only pieces of paper worth anything around here at the moment are money? It still doesn't make sense. Which of your prints was gone?'

'One of the mugshots from the missing-persons' official archive. The pictures I snapped just before we left the station. I can't say which one – it's not like we looked at them for very long. But it must be as the copies of the crime-scene photos are all still there. I'll never be able to forget those.'

'All those people would look so different by now, too.' Jonny ponders the strange irony of mugshots of such young faces becoming yellow with age. 'We should have insisted on staying a bit longer. We barely had ten minutes with the archive files.'

Paloma sighs. 'We could have stayed all day and it wouldn't

have made any difference. Thousands of people are still missing. We already know exactly when most of those cases date back to, and bodies don't survive in water for that long. We can't make this into something it's not.'

But Jonny is still preoccupied. 'Yet my notes have disappeared, so has one of your pictures, a complete stranger warned me I was being followed, and there's apparently a map in my hand.' He taps his fist on the table, precious piece of paper still balled into it. 'All of that adds up to something, not nothing. Also, why lift a mugshot of a missing person and not the one of a crime scene? It doesn't smell right.'

Paloma wrinkles her nose reflexively. 'I hate that expression. We're talking about people who've lost their kids. We actually interviewed someone whose daughter was only seventeen when she disappeared. I mean, seventeen. How do you ever get over that?'

'Her name was Mercedes,' Jonny says, trying and failing to take the edge out of his voice as he thinks about his own long-lost twin sister. But Paloma doesn't notice.

'Mercedes,' she echoes softly. 'And Pablo, right? Her brother disappeared too.'

'And we'll make sure their stories are heard regardless. I won't stop until I have, I can promise you that. We can even pitch a whole magazine feature on the missing if we get enough good personal photos and testimonies to match. That's the only way to get the *Trib* as interested as we are. All they care about at the moment are dollars and cents – literally. But we're not going to turn away just because...' He trails off as he checks his watch. 'Bollocks. I didn't realise it was already so late. I should have made those bloody phone calls this afternoon.'

'To the Mothers of Plaza de Mayo, you mean?'

'Yes,' Jonny replies. 'It's even more important we meet them now. Don't start, I know what you're going to say. This latest discovery can't have anything to do with their missing children. But we need to understand what happened in the first place to establish whether there can possibly be any connection this long after the end of the war.'

He hangs his head, tips of his ears tingling in shame. Paloma is right. They're talking about people who've lost their kids. And these are mothers whose children have disappeared. A group of women united by unspeakable tragedy. Named for the public square where they march every week, right under the nose of Argentina's presidential palace. These women have been demonstrating for almost twenty years, even when it was illegal to gather in groups of more than two, their trademark pristine-white headscarves fluttering like symbols of surrender when in fact they are symbols of anything but. Jonny needs their testimony now more than ever. He shouldn't have let himself get sidetracked for anything.

'Listen, it's never too late in the day around here,' Paloma says, as if she can read his mind. 'Let's go try them now. It's not like we're actually going to eat anything.'

She pushes back her bowl. Galvanised, Jonny follows suit, switching the ball of paper in his sweaty hand for the remaining banknotes crumpled in his pocket. He hurries after Paloma to the stairwell, the murmurs of male appreciation that seem to follow Paloma everywhere she goes rippling through the dank dining room. Once in the open air, he keeps his cloth shawl resolutely wadded in his fist.

Paloma turns to him, clear night sky bright and optimistic with stars overhead. Caught off guard, Jonny can't help but smile for a moment. He could certainly do without losing his notebook, without looking over his shoulder at every turn. And he could certainly do without having to carry around this stupid fucking cloak, but no matter. If people are after him – whoever they are – he must be doing something right. And to be doing it with someone like Paloma ... Jonny catches himself before his smile turns into an idiotic grin.

He notices her tugging at something over her shoulder – her handbag, black leather strap looped tightly round her body as usual. An unmistakable expression crosses her face – miles from what he was hoping for. It's so unexpected he frowns and has to look again.

It comes when he tries to step towards her.

The hard, implacable jab of a pistol into the small of his back.

Chapter Four

Jonny's hands curl reflexively into fists, a flood of adrenaline surging through his body. Their assailants are clustered around them with military precision – there are at least four of them, squaring their every corner, casting darkness all around them. They're in the middle of the pavement, halfway between the shopfronts and the road – won't there be passersby? Surely he can shout, draw someone's attention? But the idea explodes as rapidly as it forms with another harsh shove of the pistol into the small of his back.

'Give it to them,' he mouths, willing Paloma to just hold up her hands, or pass over her bag, or take off one of the myriad pieces of jewellery she always seems to be wearing, which usually seem effortlessly quirky and stylish but now just feel impossibly misguided. Jonny curses inwardly. The financial crisis is pushing street muggings from commonplace to expected, and it's getting worse with every day, yet they chose to exchange the risk of being overheard on the phone for meeting in a deliberately shady corner of the city at night? Like the nondescript landline in either of their tiny apartments might contain an actual phone tap.

'Your bag,' he mouths again, but multiple shadows are blocking out the twinkling night sky that had thrown an entirely different light on their tableau a few seconds earlier. All Jonny can see now are the glimmering whites of Paloma's eyes above the meaty hand clamped over her mouth and—

His breath catches.

...The quicksilver flash of a blade at her throat.

A whimper escapes – his? Cold steel jabs at his back again. The knife is moving now, sawing at the leather strap perilously close to Paloma's neck, spiriting the bag and its contents away. Jonny holds his breath, their assailants have got what they came for, surely? His hand twitches towards the wallet in his pocket. What will it take for the pistol to leave his back, for the blade to leave her throat?

And then his world is suddenly plunged into darkness.

Rough fabric rasps at his face as a hood is wrenched over his head.

Jonny cries out, reeling, arms pinned tightly by his sides. All his senses desert him inside the implacable darkness of the hood. He's suddenly everywhere and nowhere, unbalanced by total disorientation and overwhelming panic. Hauled forward, his feet scrabble for purchase, but it's no use, he's off the ground, being carried into a sudden squeal of brakes, an acrid bolt of burning rubber. Screaming Paloma's name into a mouthful of hessian, only a fist to the side of his head answers back. A hefty click and crunch as a heavy door opens and he is bundled into a vehicle like a rag doll, supported only by the figures at his either side – who? And where is she? He cries out again, only for something far harder than a fist to slam relentlessly into his gut.

Jonny's head pitches forward, lolling slack on his neck. The vehicle is moving now, flinging his winded body from side to side, something squeaking with every roll – leather seats? Is he in a car? Fragments of thoughts clatter in his head, breaking into single words: who? Where? Why? Another waft of burning rubber makes him gag inside the hood, the vehicle travelling at increasing speed, every movement feeling ever more erratic. He closes his eyes, willing that he just go under, that his consciousness drops below the surface.

And then … Jonny gasps as the hood is yanked off his head, a draught of cool, fresh air hitting his lungs like another punch.

Jonny gulps, dimly registering his surroundings: he's in the back seat of a car, a man to his either side, holding him upright. He immediately realises the disorientating rushing in his ears is actually just the sound of air flowing through the vehicle, both windows cracked open as the car speeds along a smooth, wide highway. He squints at the night sky shimmering through the windscreen ahead. How long have they been on the move? Did he lose consciousness under the hood? They must already be some way out of the city to be on a highway without traffic. He strains to pick out details in the dark, grappling to reset his internal compass without moving so much that he antagonises anyone.

A cold object is suddenly thrust into his lap.

Jonny blinks at its form slowly taking shape in the dark – a pristine plastic bottle of mineral water? The blow to his head must have been even harder than it felt.

'Drink,' an equally incongruous voice commands, in English.

Jonny gives his head a little shake, eyeing the men on either side. They both stare resolutely ahead. Fidgeting as he frees his arms, he risks a look over his shoulder – nope, nothing and no one. So who is sitting up front? Panic licks at his throat as he realises it is most definitely not Paloma. And unless she is cowering in the boot, she is most definitely nowhere else to be found inside this car.

Just the thought of Paloma tied up, terrified and gasping for breath inside a locked sedan car boot, sends his mind and body back into a horrified spin.

He fumbles with the plastic cap, bottle slipping between his fingers.

'You must have questions,' the voice muses, in perfect if heavily accented English.

Jonny leans forward only to recoil in shock.

For there, in the front passenger seat, is the small but perfectly formed figure of an elderly man, so tiny his outline has been almost completely obscured by the curves of the upholstery.

Jonny clenches at the unopened bottle for support. Pathetic, he suddenly rages. Is clutching pointlessly at some useless plastic all he can compel his body to do in the form of self-defence? He's been forced into a car, blindfolded and at gunpoint, with no idea with whom or where he's being taken. And what of the woman he has left with a knife to her throat on a street corner in one of the dodgiest parts of an increasingly desperate city? Since these men surrounded them on that pavement all he has been able to do is freeze, gag and wail. Finally he locates his voice, uses it.

'Where is she?'

The man lets out a brittle little laugh. 'She's safe. On that you can trust me.'

Something tugs at Jonny's consciousness – the awkward, inverted cadence of the man's English – but he can't quite surface its significance.

'Who are you? Where are you taking me? And what have you done with her?'

'I told you, your companion is safe. You will be reunited when we are finished.'

The rhythmic click of an indicator seems loud in the car as it smoothly changes lanes and accelerates.

'You must have questions,' the man repeats once the manoeuvre is complete. 'After all, this is what you suspected, yes?'

Jonny is floored. His head moves dumbly on his neck, taking in his surroundings as if he's seeing them for the first time. He's in a car. A nice car, at that – smooth chassis, leather upholstery, low, melodic purr of a well-oiled engine. He was hooded and forced inside at gunpoint, but with his belongings still in his pockets – he feels for his wallet, yep, still there – so these people must want him, and not anything he's carrying. But the men flanking him are now only threatening by blocking his exits, nothing else. They are, in actual fact, behaving as if he isn't there. They're travelling calmly on a highway rather than barrelling off into a side road, twisting deeper and deeper into the rabbit hole of a deprived neighbourhood as he might have originally feared. There are no hoods, no weapons, no objects of intimidation on display at all, and the elderly man up front—

Jonny gasps, finally realising what the glimmers in the dark really are. The shiny medals and pristine buttons of a military uniform.

The unmistakable wings of the air force.

'We don't have much time,' the man adds. 'So ask me while you still can.'

Jonny's mind spins with the highway lights scudding past, glinting off the battalion of buttons lined up either side of the man's chest.

'Did you … I mean, are you—?'

'Yes.' The man cuts him off. 'I am a pilot. I flew planes during the war. I was under orders. I carried them out. But I regret it. I have regretted it every day since. That is why you are here.'

Chapter Five

'Tell me what you think. Then I will tell you if you are right. That is all I can do, you understand.'

A statement, not a question. The landscape, or lack of it, scuds past in an unidentifiable blur. Jonny exhales, a curious mixture of relief and disappointment. That's why they put him in a hood. That's why he's been boxed into a moving car. He can't work out where he's going nor who he's with, but it is for his own protection as much as anything else.

'How do I know I can trust you?'

'You don't,' the man replies. 'But what other choice do you have?'

'Is that what you told all your other prisoners too? That they could trust you? That you were flying them to their freedom? Not just to fling them out of the plane once you were far enough over the sea?'

The questions he's long prepared suddenly stick in Jonny's throat, words so bitter he can almost taste them. He swallows, again and again, but the lump just grows more acrid.

For that wasn't the only alleged deception of the so-called Flights of Death. But he can't bear to voice the others. Some prisoners were said to have been so weak from torture they had to be helped on board by military doctors, doctors that even went on to give them an injection, saying it was a vaccine to protect them from diseases in their new home. Those same doctors went on to strip them, tie their hands and feet for good measure, before shoving them out into the open air.

'Yes,' the man answers softly. 'But in truth, it wasn't necessary.

By then, they were broken. They couldn't fight, even if they had wanted to. And neither could we.'

'Because—' Jonny has to stop, clear his throat, start again. 'Because you had already tortured them almost to death?'

'At the detention centres. Yes. And because we lived beside them there too—'

'Lived beside them?' Jonny parrots. 'What do you mean?'

'Our quarters were directly below the cells. Prisoners and commanders would pass each other on the stairs on the way back and forth to the torture chambers. We were expected to eat lunch in between sessions. Like it was just another day at the office. Or we would end up on the wrong floor. We would be imprisoned for dissent ourselves.'

Jonny shakes his head. 'I don't understand.'

'You can't,' the man replies softly. 'No one can. It is incomprehensible. But that is how it happened. Week after week, month after month. We were prisoners too.'

'No, you weren't.' Jonny's retort comes out a little louder than he intended. 'You may have been under orders, but only criminals could actually have carried them out. And if your conscience started getting in the way why not just finish them off in the detention centres? Why fly them out to sea?'

When the man turns, matching the agility and speed of the car's well-oiled engine, his eyes glitter as brightly as the buttons on the front his starched uniform.

'To make them disappear.'

'To make them disappear,' Jonny echoes softly, mesmerised by the gleam in the man's eyes – are they sparkling with tears? The Disappeared. *Los Desaparecidos*. The thousands of bodies that still haven't been recovered, making it ever harder to prove what happened to them in the first place.

This is the thought that snaps him back to the pages of his lost notebook.

'A body was found on the beach in La Plata two weeks ago,' he says. 'What do you know about that?'

The man cocks his head. 'Well, what does it look like?'

Jonny balks, his picture of the crime scene swimming into gruesome focus inside his head. 'Look like?'

'A body washes up on an Argentinian beach without a head, legs or fingerprints. What does it look like, to you?'

'Well,' Jonny ventures, 'I guess it looks like someone was trying very hard to make sure the body cannot be identified.'

'Why do you say that?'

'No face or fingerprints. No head, so no dental records, and no hair – you can even work stuff out from that these days. The fact the body washed up at all is a stroke of bad luck for whoever did it.'

'What else does it look like?'

'Well, it could be a drug cartel killing. Those guys aren't exactly known to show mercy, are they?'

'True.' The man nods. 'But how do you send your opposition a message without being clear where it is coming from?'

An overhead highway light suddenly illuminates in a quicksilver flash the salty tracks streaked over the man's cheeks. Rather than finding a portrait of evil in the front seat, Jonny is astonished to find a picture of despair – and a far younger picture than he was expecting. He takes in the forehead lined with anguish rather than age, the slump as opposed to a hunch in the shoulders, the elegant hands clutched together in the lap. This man must have been little more than a teenager when he flew those planes.

Jonny stares into those glittering eyes as a beat passes between them.

'I think we both know what it really looks like,' he finally says. 'Especially you. It looks exactly like an attempted disappearance. And it looks like the victim was never intended to be identified, let alone found.'

An elegant finger trembles as the man lifts it to his eye, wipes a tear away with an infinitesimal nod. Jonny only realises he's been holding his breath when it all comes streaming out in one go. Answering questions on record about the original death flights is headline enough. But linking them with this most recent discovery of human remains on a city beach is an even bigger deal. Suddenly Jonny can barely conceive of it.

'Just so I'm clear,' he begins again. 'You're telling me that fifteen years after the end of the Dirty War, someone – no, some people – have gone to the trouble of deliberately dismembering someone and then shoving the pieces out of a plane? Or making it look exactly like they have? Why? Do you even know who the victim is?'

'You will have to find that out for yourself. You are already looking in the right places. I would not have found you otherwise.'

'So you didn't fly this particular plane, is what you're saying—'

'No!' Jonny flinches as a fist suddenly shoots towards the dashboard. 'No. I did not.'

'So how do you know exactly what happened here?'

'It is not enough that I am telling you I once did?'

Jonny finds himself grappling again with the prospect of an almost unthinkable scoop. Getting a former Argentinian military pilot on record testifying to the horrors of the Dirty War is worth multiple international front pages. The current political amnesty might protect this man from prosecution and jail time, but it's hardly an invitation to provide the details of every unspeakable crime. And the current military leadership views any expression of responsibility or regret as the ultimate betrayal. Most former commanders would rather die than break the oath of silence. So why is this man admitting it to him? And what has it got to do with the body on the beach?

'It's more than enough,' he replies hesitantly. 'I'm sure you know that it'll be the first time that any military officer has done so publicly. You said you regretted it, and you've regretted it every day since. Is that why you've finally decided to speak out?'

'No,' the man replies softly. 'In fact I do not wish to do that at all.'

Jonny blanches. 'Why, because you'll be put on trial for genocide? You said that's why I was here. You said exactly that.'

The man lets out a brittle little laugh. 'And you think that once you've printed your story, justice will prevail, because in the end, it always does? Tell me, Jonny Murphy from the *International Tribune* – yes of course I know your name. How many flights do you think it takes to disappear thousands of people? How many planes, how many pilots, how many guards, how many torturers? Hundreds? Thousands?'

'It takes an army,' Jonny replies quietly. 'That's the worst part of all. You were part of a state-sponsored military machine made to silence people.'

'So why do you think I am talking to you about it?'

'Well, if you think I am going to print your last will and testament, I'm afraid you've come to the wrong place.'

'Indeed, that is not what I want from the *International Tribune*.'

So what do you want, then? Jonny wonders. And why are you telling me? A little voice adds in his inner ear. A black thought slithers out from the darkest corners of his mind. This man clearly knows a whole lot more about Jonny than Jonny knows about him. This man knows exactly what Jonny has been doing, where he has been doing it, and who he's been doing it with. So what *else* does he know about Jonny? Has he come to Jonny because he knows he hasn't been wholly truthful in the past?

'Sometimes machines break,' the man is continuing. 'You just have to find out why.'

'This isn't about some kind of mechanical failure,' Jonny shoots back, trying to recover himself. 'This involves real people, actual human beings, not component parts—'

'*Claro,*' the man interrupts softly, eyes shining. And suddenly something altogether different snags inside Jonny's mind. The man sighs, so long and deep, a little thrum echoes around the inside of the car.

'*Ya esta,*' he adds. 'That's enough. My job here is done.'

'Oh no.' Jonny shakes his head. 'We're not even close to being done—'

But then the rest of his sentence dead-ends into nothing as a blow thuds into the side of his head.

Chapter Six

The first thing he registers is the smell. The whiff of char. The heady scent of barbecue.

Somewhere deep in his subconscious, Jonny wonders if he's dreaming. It's the grill that does it. And it's the dream he has all the time, watching a family picnic from high on a clifftop. The action is all lit in colour, warmed by the sun – shouldn't Jonny be able to join in too? After all he's only a few feet away, teetering on the precipice, like he's standing on the edge of the world. It's a journey that should take seconds, but for Jonny is still taking a lifetime. All he's ever wanted is somehow always just beyond his reach. His own family. His own sense of belonging. His own sense of meaning something, and meaning the same to someone else.

But then Jonny registers the second thing. The hand repeatedly smacking him around the face. And when he finally opens his eyes, all he can make out are faces – three, maybe four – clustered overhead. Anxious expressions, dark knotted eyebrows.

Jonny grunts, even the blinking is an effort. His endlessly recurring dream seems to have taken a nightmare turn. He flails a hand around to try and shield himself from more blows. There's bolt of harsh light – is that a street lamp overhead? Is he lying on a pavement? The faces fall away as Jonny rolls to his side, pain thudding through his skull with every movement. The landscape spins into a nauseating blur as he heaves himself to sitting. And when his world finally settles, the first things to come into focus are the distinctive wrought-iron loops and curls of his front gate.

Jonny's gasp turns into a whimper at the sudden use of his bruised face muscles. He's on the pavement in front of his apartment building. He must have been unloaded almost directly into the perennial street barbecue outside. The cluster of men who seem to reside here day and night shift back on to their haunches, regarding him with a curious mix of suspicion and concern.

Jonny gingerly assesses the lump vibrating on the side of his head. How long has he been out? He must have been dumped unconscious by—. Another gasp and whimper, as previous events clatter back into his mind. Something is thrust under his nose exuding an earthy belch of steam – a gourd of *yerba mate*, shiny silver straw gleaming incongruously between the dirty fingers proffering it to him. Despite the pain and confusion, a seed of warmth starts to bud inside Jonny. He sips, letting the warmth penetrate to the depths of his torso. A murmur of satisfaction ripples around the group.

Jonny tries to catch the eye of the hobo next to him as he passes the drink on. Who brought him back here? And when? The lump on the side of his head throbs as if to remind him how pointless his questions are. It is painfully obvious he has been out cold for some time. The people who snatched him off the street are pros. His unconscious form will have changed hands, not to mention cars, at least once, if not multiple times. His entire skeleton feels as if it has been taken to pieces and reassembled incorrectly.

Another grunt as Jonny rolls on to his knees. Instantly, two of the men cluster to his either side, hooking hands under his armpits to help him up. Even mumbled thanks are out of the question as Jonny stumbles, legs threatening to buckle with every movement. One of the men props him up against the gate, while the other shoves a hand into Jonny's trouser pocket. He tries to stop a moan of protest escaping, but it's no use, his bones are rattling inside their joints, but how is anyone supposed to know that other than him? Instantly both men fall back, expressions hardening into irritated resignation. Jonny's keys are flung into the centre of his chest with a thud before they both turn away.

Jonny sags against the gate, disgusted with himself. If any of these men witnessed anything useful, they're hardly likely to tell him about it now. He hunches to retrieve his fallen keys, wincing as he turns to unlock the gate, heading into the dark internal courtyard without another sound.

The climb up the stairs to his apartment door is just one agonising step after another. Jonny may have a few more facts at hand now, but none of them are adding up. That Bolivian woman warned him about *subversivos*. She specifically used the term given to anyone displaying politically dissident tendencies against the former Argentinian military regime. She can't have meant a former military pilot, then, a member of that former regime – unless she somehow knew the man wanted to turn? Is that what she meant? Talk about the ultimate subversion. Or was she referencing something else entirely? Or was the whole episode just a distraction while her meathead comrade went for his wallet only to filch something far more significant?

Head spinning, Jonny levers himself up another step. He tries to organise his thoughts as precisely as he tries to place his feet. What had the pilot said about the body itself? That it was an attempted disappearance – or deliberately staged to look like one. That Jonny would have to confirm the identity of the victim for himself. That he was already looking in the right places. That the pilot wouldn't have found him otherwise.

So where has Jonny been looking? He cups a hand over the lump on his head to stop himself from scratching it. The original tip-off about the body came from local police in La Plata. Access to the missing-persons' archive too. Getting relatives of the disappeared to talk hasn't exactly been straightforward. And as for connecting the two? Jonny flashes on to the photos they saw, torn and yellow with age. How could any of them possibly be relevant fifteen years after the end of the war? Even Paloma, the photographer herself, has started to resist taking pictures of pictures – resistance that Jonny is finding increasingly difficult to explain, let alone appreciate.

'Paloma,' he whispers, bracing himself against the banister, fresh jolt of agony coursing through his skull at the thought. How can he have forgotten about her until now? Where is she? And has she been harmed? If those men have so much as touched a single hair on her head ... Jonny is suddenly suffused with a flood of panic and rage so intense that he's inside his apartment and punching numbers into his phone's keypad without being entirely sure how he finally got there, mind jangling with loose threads, connections he can't make, words he still can't fucking understand. By now all he is sure of is he can't trust anyone.

Mercifully, Paloma answers the phone almost as soon as the line starts to ring.

'Jonny? Is that you? Are you OK?'

He props himself against the wall, sagging with relief at the sound of her voice.

'What happened? Where have you been? I've been going out of my mind—'

'Don't worry,' he stops her. 'Really. I'm OK, I promise. I need to tell you everything, but I'll catch you up with it all in the morning, understand? I just called to make sure you were alright—'

'What?' Paloma's shock crackles through the receiver. 'In the morning? What do you mean, in the morning? You were snatched off the street at gunpoint, you've been missing for hours, I've been losing it over here, and now—'

'But I'm OK,' Jonny stops her again. The idea that their phones might be tapped would have felt fanciful before. Since he's been ambushed, it feels anything but. The pilot knew far too much about both him and his work to assume anything else. 'Please just tell me that you're OK too?'

'What the hell are you talking about?' Paloma is shouting now. 'I'm not the one who was bundled into a moving car with a hood over my head. I lost my bag but I'm fine other than going crazy over what was happening to you. I thought ... I thought you were dead...'

'I told you, I'll catch you up in the morning, I promise. I don't want to talk about it on the phone right now, if you get what I mean.'

Paloma lets out an audible gasp. 'Oh my God, you're ... you're not alone? Are you still being threatened now? Is someone holding you up at gunpoint inside your apartment?'

Jonny shakes his head. 'No, no, no, nothing like that. No. There's no one else here. And I'm fine. I wouldn't be on the phone to you if I wasn't—'

'Then just tell me what happened before I completely lose my mind.'

'Not now, Paloma. Don't you understand? Those men weren't just robbers. They were after a lot more than your bag. They knew exactly who I was. We were followed. Deliberately. By very dangerous people. We need to be even more careful now about everything we do, everything we say.'

And who we say it to, he reminds himself. Paloma's behaviour was already starting to confuse him. He can't let his guard down completely with her now, either.

A beat of uneasy silence passes between them.

'Do you mean ... do you mean those men knew about our ... about our work?'

'Exactly,' Jonny replies, sagging with relief all over again. 'Like I said, we need to be really fucking careful from here on in, Paloma. I'm so relieved that you're OK.'

She sighs, a low thrum through the receiver. 'Well, I'm glad that you are, too. Are you sure that you're really—'

'Yes,' he cuts her off. 'I promise you. I'm fine. Just lumps and bumps, nothing critical. What happened to you after they got me into the car?'

'They just dropped me. Literally dropped me, I didn't realise my legs had gone until they let me go and ran. Someone helped me up, I don't know who it was. I was screaming for you.'

'Did you see where they went?'

'No clue. I was just concentrating on where the others were taking you. I tried to run into the road but it was impossible. I'm sorry, Jonny. The car just disappeared.'

'Don't worry. What could you have done? All that matters is that you're alright—'

'And that you are too. I was thinking the worst, you know? What could they possibly want with you when they already had my bag.'

'So how did you get home? Didn't you lose your keys?'

Paloma suddenly goes quiet. Jonny frowns.

'Paloma? Are you still there?'

She answers in her small voice again. 'Don't be angry, OK?'

'Why would I be angry?' Jonny wonders, trailing off as he realises exactly why. She must have left her door open – all her doors, by the looks of it. All her cameras unattended. All their pictures lying around for anyone to see. He told her to leave everything of value behind. He didn't mean leave it unprotected and on display. The bump on his head resumes operations with a thump, firing a fresh burst of adrenaline into his bloodstream.

'I know.' Paloma's low voice is laden with guilt. 'And you're right. You've been right all along. It's all I've been saying to myself since you disappeared. I should have taken the whole thing more seriously. I promise I'll be more careful. I swear I'll never leave it unlocked again.'

But Jonny can't reply, his mind stuck in a hellscape involving masked, armed men lying in wait for Paloma anytime she returns home, in the dark, defenceless and alone. And now in the increasingly more likely event that dangerous people are actually listening to their calls, she's told them that she can no longer lock herself in.

'The first thing I did when I got back was barricade myself inside, close all the windows. It's so hot in here I can hardly breathe. Nothing's been taken, everything is exactly as I left it.'

'You're sure you've checked everywhere?' This time his reply comes out as brusquely as he intended. They're living in an increasingly desperate city, the peso is losing its value by the day. The financial crisis has been their literal bread and butter for weeks now, the only news story making headlines internationally. The most basic of precautions are not just common sense, they're a matter of survival. And Paloma can't even seem to see that.

'Yes. I'm fine, Jonny. I promise. There's no one else here. Unless they're a ghost.'

'Well, there are plenty of those around,' he mutters to himself, turning on the spot, reflexively checking the confines of his own unit, as unremarkable as ever, until his gaze snags on the battered clock against the wall.

'Did you call the police? Or call anyone else at all? What did you tell them?' Jonny checks the time on the clock with that of his watch. Can it really be gone three a.m.? He must have been out for hours. Was he drugged? Instantly he is picturing dark skies, unconscious cargo, black water.

'Of course I did. There were guns, you were dragged into a car. I wasn't going to sit around waiting for you to show up in a ditch somewhere. But all I could really tell them about was being robbed myself. If they had a dollar for every time someone said that these days they'd be millionaires.'

'So what *did* they say? When you reported it? What did you say, I mean.'

'That a gringo had been abducted. And that I was robbed in the process.'

'But no one has come around to take your statement, or

whatever they do in this country? Or get you to show them where it happened?'

'No. Well, not yet, anyway.'

'Did you give them my name? Or tell them what I was doing here?'

'Yes and no...'

Jonny has to pull the phone away from his ear for a moment as his head starts to spin again. He was officially reported missing almost six hours ago and no one has followed up since? A foreigner forced into a car at gunpoint looks a whole lot like a kidnapping, doesn't it? In a city so beset with financial problems? Or is it so equally beset by drug problems that this looks like just another day at the office? He lifts the phone back to his ear.

'Well, you better call off the dogs.'

'No way,' Paloma exclaims back. 'I mean I'll call in that you've turned up, but—'

'What? You don't even know what happened.'

Jonny finds himself yanking the receiver away again before she can question him any further. It couldn't be more obvious that they both need protection, but Jonny still can't be sure from what. They have been followed. Their possessions have been stolen – her pictures, his notebook. But they haven't been warned off. In fact, quite the opposite – they've been given clues. And they've been given them deliberately. They've even been given an actual map. Although they're yet to figure out exactly where it leads. When he finally puts the phone to his ear again there is only breathy silence on the other end.

'Thank you for looking out for me,' Jonny begins. 'There's nothing else we can do about it for now. And I'm OK, I really am. Try and get some sleep, and we'll talk first thing.'

'Sleep? Are you kidding me? How can I possibly—'

'Look, just try and rest. It will all look different in the morning, I promise. I'll see you then.'

Another beat of silence passes between them. He pictures their preferred coffee stop, conjures the smell of the beans, sets the scene in his head as if he can project it down the line via telepathy. Coffee, clatter, conversation. A low hubbub to drown everything out.

'And bring your camera,' he adds. 'We've got a ton of work to do.'

Paloma sighs. 'Well, I hope at least you get some sleep.'

'I hope you do too. *Y que suenes con los angelitos*. Or something like that, anyway.'

Finally her voice softens. 'You're full of surprises, you know that, Jonny Murphy?'

'Just don't test me in a real conversation. I'll see you in the morning.'

'Sweet dreams to you too,' she answers, before ringing off. Jonny lets the dial tone blare in his ear for a moment. As usual, the direct translation would be far more appropriate, he thinks. It's the only reason he can ever remember the expression to start with: *May you dream with the angels*.

Hanging up, he limps over to his bookshelf, wincing as he shoves it away from the wall, checking the floorboards beneath are undisturbed. He reaches into his pocket, removes his wallet, finds the small ball of paper crammed underneath – the map that Paloma had found tucked inside her photo sleeve. Smoothing it out with a shaky hand, he commits the pencil drawing and its scribbles to memory before folding it neatly into a flat, tiny square.

Kneeling, he runs a sweaty fingertip over the two newer screws, still slightly too shiny for his liking, most definitely out of place to anyone who knows where to look. Easing the tiny square of paper into a crack between the boards, he heaves the bookshelf back into place. A few staggered steps later, ceiling lamp still blazing overhead, he is finally able to collapse into his bed. His unconscious mind only ever quiets under the brightest of lights.

He is asleep in seconds. At last his dreams fill with vacant, infinite dark.

Chapter Seven

Jonny waits for the sharp hiss of the coffee machine before starting to fill Paloma in. Only salient details. Just enough to answer her most burning questions.

'So. Last night. I thought we were just being robbed too at first. But everything changed once I was in the car. It turns out I was only dragged inside so one of the other passengers could talk to me.'

Paloma's eyes widen. Jonny drops his voice another notch.

'And it was a pilot. A military pilot. He was even wearing his uniform. Said he flew some of the original death flights. Confirmed the months of torture alleged to have gone on beforehand. I know, it's unbelievable,' he finishes, as Paloma just stares in shock.

When she replies, she's almost having to choke the words out. 'How ... how did he know where to find you?'

'I don't know,' Jonny replies grimly, 'and I don't know his name either. He knocked me out before I had a chance to ask.'

Paloma is aghast. 'Knocked you out? Oh my God, what? I thought you said that you were OK—'

'I am.' Jonny reaches for his coffee, thick white china cup appearing steaming on top of the glass counter. 'I've just got a bit of a headache, honestly. This'll sort me right out.'

Paloma shakes her head. 'I don't understand. A former death-flight pilot breaks his silence on something so horrific out of ... of nowhere?'

'Not exactly.' Holding his cup with one hand, he beckons her over to a small table with the other. 'It must be something to do with the body on the beach. That must be how he knew about us in the first place. Because he knew exactly what I was talking about when I asked him about it. Not only that – he confirmed it was deliberately staged to look like an attempted disappearance. But he just answered in riddles when I asked why, or how he knew. Then one of his honchos laid me out before I had a chance to ask anything else. When I came to I was on the pavement outside my apartment. I have no idea what happened in the intervening few hours. Now we've just got to work out who he is and try and find him again.'

Paloma shakes her head again, blinking at him wild-eyed. She's still standing, hovering by her chair; it's as if she can't bring herself to actually sit down.

'I don't see how. Did you even see his face?'

Jonny nods, taking a sip of coffee. 'He was far younger than I was expecting, too.'

'Than you were expecting?' Paloma parrots back, finally pulling out her chair. 'What were you expecting? Don't tell me you expected any of this.'

'You know what I mean.' Jonny drains the rest of his coffee in a scalding gulp. 'My point is, we have to find out who he is and talk to him again to be able to report anything at all. And I'm pretty sure I know where we can make a start.'

He reaches into his pocket, pulls out a map of the city and unfolds it on to the table.

'When I first thought of it I wondered if it was why we've been given the other map. You know...' He taps a fist on the table rather than say it out loud, so that Paloma recalls the scrap of paper she'd shown him clutched barely twelve hours earlier. 'But that drawing is completely different. It's all loops and circles, crosses and dashes.'

'So?' Paloma prompts.

Leaning forward, Jonny drops his voice as low as it will go, tapping a finger on the map between them. 'We need to get inside the former prison complex. I can't believe we haven't thought of it before. Forget about the police station in La Plata. That's just the nearest precinct to where the body was found. But the place where most of the missing were held and tortured before they were flown away is barely ten miles from here. We need to get inside.'

Paloma blanches. 'No, Jonny. No way. We can't.'

'Of course we can. Look where it is. It's literally up the road.'

'What difference does it make where it is? It's fifteen years too late.'

'And yet it's still operating as a military training facility. In fucking Belgrano, of all places. Like it's completely normal to find a former torture complex sitting in between a bunch of swanky houses and shops.'

'That's where you think we should start?' She reaches over with a warm hand, running fingers purposefully through his hair. Jonny's heart starts to race, but it's only for the briefest of moments, because he realises what she is actually doing. 'Honestly, I think we should start by getting you properly checked out.'

'Stop it, OK?' He half-heartedly bats her hand away. 'I'm fine.'

'You are most definitely not fine. Those men must have knocked half your brain out.'

'He said the guards' quarters were below the cells,' Jonny continues regardless. 'That they were all imprisoned together for months, just on different floors of the building. That commanders would pass prisoners they'd just tortured going in opposite directions on the stairs. Like it was just another day at the office. If he lived there himself for months, who knows what we might find left there now?'

Paloma looks nervous. 'Come on, Jonny. We can't just pitch up and try the bell. You said it yourself, it's a military training facility.'

'I know that.' Jonny smacks the map closed, shoving it back into his pocket. 'Obviously we need to figure out how we're actually going to pull it off – we'll need a distraction as well as a cover story to get past the gates. We've got to get to the Plaza de Mayo now in any case. I just meant—'

'Are you serious? That's where you want to go now? Just head on down to the Plaza de Mayo as if nothing remotely dodgy has happened since we last discussed it?'

'Yes, I'm serious. We have to keep investigating, and we can only trust people with similar goals to us. And I'd say they don't get much more similar than the group of women demanding to know what's become of their missing children who have been marching outside the presidential palace every Thursday for the last twenty years.'

'You honestly think we can just turn up and talk to whoever we want? That we won't attract even the least bit of controversial attention?'

Jonny tries and fails to keep a note of irritation out of his voice. 'So what if we do? These woman marched even when it was illegal to gather in groups of two.'

'You know what I mean. You said we needed to be more careful. I'm just trying to make up for lost time. You were snatched off the street last night by someone potentially instrumental in disappearing some of these missing people.'

Jonny pushes back his chair as if it might bring an end to the debate but can't quite bring himself to get up until she does. 'Look, if these women aren't worried about doing it, then neither am I. You don't have to come if you don't want to.'

Paloma's expression is caught somewhere between mutinous and hurt. 'Well you can't do it on your own.'

'I don't want to, either,' Jonny concedes, inwardly cursing for at least the eightieth time his resistance to learning Spanish. 'You should have heard me on the phone this morning. I had my dictionary out and everything – it was still painful. And you were right, by the way. It's never too late – or early – in the day around here. I called first thing and someone answered the phone straight away. It's not just going to be the mothers today, either. The grandmothers are going to be there too.'

And suddenly Jonny doesn't care whether she comes with him or not, picturing the Mothers of Plaza de Mayo's trademark white headscarves teeming like doves in front of the presidential palace. Is there anything more powerful than a group of mothers demanding answers on behalf of their disappeared children? It turns out there is. Try being cheated out of both children and grandchildren. The grandmothers are the angriest of all. And Jonny Murphy knows a whole lot about angry grandparents and disappeared children. If he can't find his own answers, he can damn well try and find some for other people like him. His mind's echo chamber suddenly clamours with his own personal questions, the ones he asks in those stupid fucking airletters but never gets answers to.

'Let's go, come on.' He makes a show of looking at his watch. 'I know you'll want to scour the place for the best composition, find exactly the right jacaranda bush. Or rubber tree. Or whatever. Let's just go.'

He walks out without glancing back at her. Paloma has to hurry to catch him up.

'All I meant was that we should maybe just take a breath. Last night wasn't exactly easy for me either, you know.' There's an audible crack in her voice. Jonny slows, instantly suffused with the heat of regret.

'Look, I know this is my fault. I'm the one asking the dodgy questions. But we can't just stop asking them because they've got us noticed. We're obviously on to something. That's the whole point. We can't let ourselves be intimidated.'

'That's not what I'm saying.' Paloma tangles with her sleeve. 'I just think we should lie low for a while, is all. Look at some more routine stuff. Stop making waves.'

'Which is exactly what we're doing. We're going to the Plaza de Mayo like a gazillion other people do on any given day. We're going to talk to a group of women who couldn't be better known. It's really not particularly controversial behaviour.'

He rounds the corner into the square itself only to stop dead immediately. The Plaza de Mayo is a sight arresting enough even without the benefit of historical background. But in the full context of its political significance – named for the May revolution that heralded Argentinian independence from Spain – it is breathtaking. Paloma pulls up next to him as they gaze at the Casa Rosada, the presidential palace at the far eastern end of the square, morning sun lighting its pink stucco an otherworldly shade of crimson blush. Not so routine, then, Jonny says to himself.

'They're already here, look.' Paloma waves at the group of women in the distance, white scarves pinned over their heads. Crossing the square, Jonny's hand is outstretched, but Paloma arrives first. The women greet her like she is already one of their own, clasping her hands and smiling. When Paloma turns back to him, he is heartened. She finally looks as animated as he feels.

'It's probably better if I translate from the start,' she says, ushering the group over to a bench in the shade of a jacaranda tree radiant with purple blossom. 'It'll be more fluent overall. Is that OK with you? I'll do it regularly so you can chime in with questions.'

'Of course,' Jonny replies. 'We need as much detail as we can get.'

And what detail it is. Every name they're told comes with an unforgettable face. Every faded photograph they're shown gives voice to an avalanche of memory. Basking in the rosy splendour of the Casa Rosada, Jonny feels as if these conversations are reconstituting people with each word. These are mothers breathing life into their missing children just by talking about them.

'This is Soledad,' Paloma translates as a woman sits down between them. 'Her daughter's name was Julia. She was an academic, pregnant with her first child when she was snatched from the street just outside her university building. Soledad's mother is here too.' She points into the crowd.

Soledad, Jonny thinks, wincing. Again, the direct translation is painfully appropriate. Solitude. Nothing compares to the agonised isolation of losing a child.

'And this is Maria.' A small, elderly lady takes the seat next to Soledad. 'Maria is a founder member. There were only fourteen of them at first. Mothers united by their quest to find their missing children. They first met when the dictatorship was at its most repressive, when public gatherings were forbidden. So they partnered in groups of two, walking, much as they'll do today, in pairs, round and round the square. The goal was to be seen. Not just to be heard, but to be seen. So they couldn't be ignored.'

To be seen, Jonny says to himself. To prove they would not disappear without a fight. Overwhelmed by the lack of answers, by the mockery and contempt with which they were received by public office, these women grew in number until they were impossible to ignore.

'They continued even after three of them were disappeared themselves,' Paloma continues as if she's picking up his mental thread. 'They vowed they would never stop looking. They would remain visible for as long as it took.'

Jonny tries not to picture the more harrowing details that follow. How these women were snatched by a naval squad from their homes, from their churches, even from hospitals – locations usually revered as sanctuaries – to never be seen again. The sudden touch of a small, determined hand on his arm makes him flinch in fear.

'We held on to what we said at the beginning,' Maria states in halting English. 'We must keep going. No matter what happens.'

'Do you think enough is being done to bring those responsible to justice?'

A frown crosses Paloma's face, Maria starting to reply before she's finished translating.

'What is it?' Jonny asks her, but Maria is still talking, a rapid, incomprehensible stream.

'That they will never bring everyone to justice,' Paloma finally answers.

'And?' Jonny prompts. Paloma is still frowning as their back-and-forth continues, a draught of purple petals whipping distractingly from the branch overhead.

'Hang on,' Paloma mutters, Maria standing and beckoning her over to a huddle a few feet away. Paloma narrowly misses swatting Jonny in the face with her camera case as she stands up herself to follow.

'Sorry,' she says, flustered.

'What are they saying?'

'I told you. That they will never be able to bring everyone to justice,' Paloma repeats, staring at the women gesturing to each other – or is it at the Casa Rosada beyond? The sun is higher in the sky now, washing its façade a crystalline sugar-pink.

'You already said that,' Jonny snaps.

'Sorry.' Paloma pulls her camera out of the case, squints into the viewfinder.

'That too. Don't tell me – you've never seen a more perfect composition?'

But all he gets in response is a volley of shutter-fly.

Jonny scratches his head, stepping towards the women.

'*Permiso*,' he says tentatively. 'Excuse me...'

The gaggle of women opens up immediately. Jonny replies in kind, summoning all the Spanish he's got, pencil poised at the top of a new page.

'Is there anything left that the government can do for you now?'

An elderly woman steps forward. Jonny's pencil stills with her answer – in perfect, if heavily accented, English.

'Yes.' The rest of the group echoes her sentiments with a determined, co-ordinated nod. 'They know where the babies are. And we want them back. We want our grandchildren back.'

Chapter Eight

Jonny eyes Paloma still furiously snapping off frames in the opposite direction. Is he really surprised to learn that some of these women speak English? The Dirty War was backed by the United States. Paloma knows that better than anyone. They called it Operation Condor, she once explained to him with a snort. They even had the gall to name it after the largest vulture in South America. In the twenty years that have passed since, these women must have had to deal in a whole lot of English. He turns back to the elderly woman in front of him with a renewed sense of purpose.

'Would you mind telling me your name?'

'You can call me Abuela,' the woman replies, using the Spanish word for grandmother. 'That way I am speaking for all of us. For we are all mothers here. Only some of us are also grandmothers.'

'Thank you, Abuela. Thank you all. Sharing these stories must be so painful.' He gazes around the rest of the group amid a gentle ripple of laughter. Purple petals are settling on their white headscarves like jewels.

'Yes.' Abuela nods. 'But our suffering is part of God's plan. It is not so for our children.'

Jonny makes a show of scribbling rather than nodding back. Thousands of Catholics were persecuted during the Dirty War, to a deafening silence from the Church itself. He knows the military employed its own chaplains to hear confessions to sins of the worst kind. Was that supposed to remove the need for justice? He looks up to find only conviction and determination shining in Abuela's dark eyes, filing the question away. It is not for these women to answer for the Church.

'We want to know where their babies are,' she continues. 'Where *our* babies are. This government will never bring everyone to justice. But there is still time for the babies.'

Jonny's pencil stills. 'Forgive me for asking. I know how painful this must be for you. But what do you mean by babies? Do you mean what the regime is alleged to have done to pregnant prisoners?'

Abuela suddenly starts shouting. 'We know this happened, do you understand? It is not an allegation.'

'Of course, of course.' Jonny holds up his hands, but Abuela is not mollified in the least.

'My daughter was pregnant when she disappeared. Hundreds of women were pregnant when they were taken. Some were little more than girls themselves. We still don't know what happened to them or their babies. The sea has returned some bodies. But there are no babies among them. So where have they gone? Where have all the babies gone?'

'What do you think really happened?' Jonny prompts, as gently as he can.

'You tell me,' Abuela shoots back. 'How many people do you think it takes to disappear thousands and thousands of people without trace?'

Jonny starts, hand stealing to the lump on his head. He's been asked the same question far too recently for comfort. 'It takes a machine,' he replies softly. 'A killing machine.'

'And how do you keep a machine running smoothly? How do you make sure the people operating its essential parts keep doing their jobs, day in, day out?'

'I … I don't know,' Jonny stammers. Except he does. The truth is Jonny knows full well that some people will do unimaginable things to keep the peace. He thinks about his long-lost twin sister, allowed to leave with his father so he'd stop abusing his mother, only for her to kill herself out of guilt. *Sometimes machines break*. But it's emotions that make human beings finally break, not mechanical failure.

'You give them whatever they want. And our babies paid the ultimate price. They took our babies. They took our babies for themselves, and gave them away to military families to be raised as the next generation of loyal soldiers. Not as the children they were supposed to be. The children of students, artists, musicians, academics. Young families who should still have their whole lives ahead of them.'

Jonny wipes an eye, the spectre of newly born babies being torn from their captive mothers' arms to be given away to military families almost too much to bear. To be redistributed like pieces of military equipment.

'You say there is still time,' he begins again. 'For what, exactly? Retribution? Justice?'

Abuela waves a dismissive hand. 'There will never be true justice. Too many commanders have already escaped to Europe, to America. Now they are protected by, by...' She trails off, clicking her fingers.

'Extradition treaties? Overseas legal arrangements?'

'Exactly. Yes. But this is why there is still time. These governments are protecting maniacs, allowing mass murderers to live freely in their societies. So, in return, let us make use of their scientific advances.'

'Forensic genetics? DNA analysis? Is that what you mean?'

'*Sí*. This is what we want. We have been trying to do it since the end of the war. Our babies are still here, somewhere, living as other people. And we need to find them. They deserve to know who they really are. They need to know what happened to their real parents. To our children.'

At that, Abuela's eyes start to glimmer. Her hand trembles as she wipes away a tear. She suddenly looks as old as her years, shrunken and hunched below her pristine-white headscarf, the wisps of hair almost the same colour escaping from underneath.

'But that will take another kind of machine,' she finishes. 'With every day that passes, we lose more time. And some of us don't have much time left.'

'So you haven't made any progress? Or you have?' Jonny regrets the question almost as soon as it is out of his mouth, feeling the spell break between them. Abuela covers her eyes with a shaking hand. The women close ranks around her, hunching as they comfort one another.

Jonny's pencil scratches at his notebook, trying to hide his frustration. He steps away, gives them room to grieve, walking over to Paloma. She's looking at the ground, turning her lens cap over and over in one hand.

'What now?' she asks, still staring down. The clumps of mashed-up purple petals on the flagstones between them suddenly look like lurid litter.

Jonny stabs at the page with his pencil. 'Can you have another go? Try and get her to open up again. Ask if there is anything we can do beyond raising awareness of their cause. Just try a different tack. She might respond if you do it this time.'

Paloma shakes her head. 'But it's just insulting. We already know exactly what we can do. Get them a feature-length spread in an international news magazine. Garner as much international attention as possible.'

Jonny fumes. These women have spent the best part of twenty years campaigning for information. Jonny and Paloma have only spent the best part of two weeks. They need details of every single missing person. Anything that might be traced back to the grisly discovery in La Plata in some way. Anything that might be connected to the former military pilot who went to the trouble of knocking Jonny out last night. Uncomfortable questions, but that doesn't mean they shouldn't be asked. What is Paloma afraid of this time? He leaves her ruminating on her lens cap, stepping back towards the women.

'Thank you for trusting me with your stories,' he says. 'You don't have to be a parent – or grandparent – to imagine your pain. What happened to your children was the most grievous of crimes.'

'Thank you,' Abuela replies softly. 'Please, take our cause to Washington, to Madrid. Make our voices heard around the world.'

'May we take some more pictures of you all?' Jonny gestures towards Paloma. 'We want you to be seen, as well as heard.'

Paloma finally takes her cue. Jonny steps aside, lets the hubbub wash over him. After a few moments, Abuela makes way for Maria and a group of younger women to have their photos taken. She comes to rest beside him in a pool of shade. Beyond, the Casa Rosada's rosy glow makes it seem as if the landscape itself is looking on and smiling.

'Abuela,' he asks conversationally. 'There was something you said earlier. Do you know the names of any of the military officers still believed to be in hiding, even the ones that have escaped abroad?'

She nods, brow furrowing. 'But we cannot be sure, of course. And we will never trust a government again. Even now military training is still permitted in the place where our children were tortured to death.'

'The Naval School of Mechanics?' Jonny pictures the former prison complex barely ten miles up the road.

Abuela replies with the Spanish acronym. 'The ESMA. Yes. That is why we need scientists from overseas. We have no hope of justice from this government. The pressure from the military is still too great.'

'Of course, of course. But are you able to share any of those names with me? I will be asking many more questions of the government, and of the scientific community...'

He trails off as Abuela leans closer, dark eyes burning like coals. Closer, and closer, until he can hear the names being whispered into his ear.

'You never know what might help,' he murmurs, scribbling down every word. But this time he's writing in a language that only he can understand.

By the time Abuela has finished, Paloma is back by his side. 'I'm done,' she says, tucking the camera back into her case.

'As am I.' Jonny smiles as Abuela gives his arm a little pat before turning back to the rest of the crowd.

'What's all that?' Paloma frowns as she spots his notebook, covered in scrawl. Jonny flips it closed, shoving it back into a trouser pocket.

'I wrote everything down in Hebrew.' He pulls the pencil from behind his ear, stashes it alongside his notebook. 'Nothing else can fall into the wrong hands.'

Chapter Nine

Jonny empties a bag of candied peanuts directly into his mouth. Behind Paloma, women are still gathering in the distance – some with placards, others with megaphones, all bathed in a luminescent glow from the sunlight reflecting off their white headscarves. He sways on his feet, sugar rush coupled with the new information in his pocket suddenly making him feel as high as the birds swooping overhead. Is that an Andean condor biding its time in the Buenos Aires haze? The vulture making its grand reappearance fifteen years after Operation Condor was finally laid to dust? He crumples the empty paper bag, tries to stop himself getting carried away.

When he looks down, Paloma is holding her bag of peanuts in one hand, and a single peanut between the fingers of the other with distaste.

'I was hungry,' he says hurriedly. 'Aren't they amazing?'

Paloma's expression darkens.

'The women, not the peanuts. The mothers,' he adds. 'The grandmothers, too. Or did you think I meant the birds?'

But Paloma just frowns down at her peanut.

'Do you think you got enough decent shots?' Jonny ploughs on. 'I suppose it's impossible to take a bad picture around here, isn't it? We can stick around for the march too, if you think it's worth it?'

She shakes her head. The air is so sweet with sugar from the street vendor nearby Jonny can still taste it, but it seems to be having the opposite effect on Paloma. He leans towards her, whispering out of the side of his mouth.

'She gave me names. Military names.' Jonny jerks his head in Abuela's direction, only for Paloma's expression to furrow further.

'And you wrote them all down in Hebrew too. I can barely read your writing to start with. Isn't everything already incomprehensible enough?'

Unease prickles up Jonny's back even though he'd deliberately chosen a language he was sure she wouldn't be able to read. 'Well, they could be a whole lot of use if they match anything we find inside the ESMA.'

Paloma throws up her hands, scattering peanuts over the ground.

'Look, just think about what we already know,' Jonny tries again. 'A mutilated body washed up on a beach. A former military commander kidnapping me to confirm the whole thing was staged deliberately. A stolen snapshot of a missing person's mugshot—'

Paloma groans, rubbing her temples. Nettled, Jonny turns away. Reflecting on what they already know is also making him reflect on how little he really knows about her. His earlier comment plays back in his mind. *We can only trust people with similar goals to us.* He's starting to wonder whether that still includes Paloma.

'You can hang around for the march if you want. But I'm going to get going.' He jams his hands into his pockets, willing himself to just start walking and leave her behind, but somehow cannot make his feet obey even the simplest of instructions.

'You said—' Paloma checks herself, steps closer. Jonny tenses – if he can't bring himself to turn away from her does he honestly think he can make any difference to the blush he knows is about to stain his neck, right below where Paloma is about to whisper in his ear?

'Names, you said?'

'Yes.' He lowers his voice another inch. 'Military names. The former officers still known to be living here. I know the whole thing feels impossible. But working out who the pilot is seems more feasible than identifying the victim on the beach. The police haven't even done it yet – and probably can't without a whole lot of forensic assistance, which, judging by what Abuela just said, doesn't feel particularly forthcoming.'

'So you think identifying the pilot will help us to identify the victim?'

'It's a start, isn't it? And we need to find the pilot himself again too. The details he gave me about the original death flights are a massive story in their own right. No one has gone on record about them before. And whoever this latest victim is obviously hasn't been preserved in the Atlantic for years. But it must be connected in some way to the death flights. We've got an even bigger scoop on our hands if we can find out how. Not only will we have confirmed details of Dirty War atrocities for the first time, we will be exposing how elements of the former military junta are still operating underground fifteen years later.'

Paloma whistles. Jonny's chest hitches as her breath tickles his ear. He manages to continue but in little more than a croak. 'Look, we have to start somewhere.'

'We may as well be blindfolded though.'

'Not if we can get inside the ESMA. I may not know where to find him now, but I know exactly where he lived back then. We might even find out more about the babies—'

'No.' Paloma cuts him off. 'That's one thing we can at least discount immediately.'

Jonny pauses, frowning. 'Listen, I really don't think we can discount anything.'

'Yes, we can. Those babies are adults now.'

'Maybe that's it,' Jonny murmurs to himself. 'Maybe the victim was one of those babies—'

'Stop it. This isn't something we can just stand around speculating about.'

'Speculating?' Jonny parrots in horror. 'You think I'm

speculating? I'm the one trying to figure out what really happened. You don't even want to know.'

Paloma's groan turns into a yawn. 'I'm sorry, I'm just so tired. I don't want to think about what happened to those babies right now. I don't want to think about anything like that at all, really. It's just horrific.'

Jonny sighs only to start yawning too, the last of his sugar rush fizzing away.

'Let me walk you back, come on.' He makes to leave, looking over his shoulder. There's a crowd forming around the street vendors behind them. 'There's plenty I can work on by myself for now. So long as you promise to barricade your door behind you. And get the locks changed too, pronto.'

Finally Paloma smiles, hitching the camera case round to her front as they start to walk. Jonny waves in Abuela's direction even though it's impossible to pick out one white headscarf from the next at this distance. Just wearing one means something, he thinks. These women only started doing so when it became important – no, essential – to be able to instantly recognise supporters in a crowd. His hand turns from wave to salute before Paloma reaches for his arm.

'Here,' she says, pressing what's left of her bag of peanuts into Jonny's hand. 'You're still hungry, I bet.' Then she gestures at the growing crowd. 'And we're not queuing for any more in this heat.'

Jonny frowns, are all these people just waiting for candied peanuts? There must be other stalls behind the big steel drum that he just can't see. Quickening, they move past the street vendors, but find themselves at the back of a crowd blocking the entire pavement leading off the far end of the square.

'What is going on?' Paloma is by his side now, straining to see over the heads of the crowd in front.

Jonny turns, scans the other exits to the square, notes similar numbers streaming from queues backing out of each. They are in the heart of the city, the focal point for politics, tourism, commerce, you name it. Crowds aren't unusual, but at just before ten in the morning? And Argentinians aren't exactly known for waiting patiently. On cue, a scuffle breaks out a few heads in front, small-scale pushing and shoving. Paloma shields her camera case with one hand, shading her eyes with the other.

Out of nowhere the crowd suddenly surges, Jonny realising too late that they are caught right in the middle, the absolute worst place to be inside a multiplying mob. Paloma stumbles as they are thrust forward, Jonny's head spins on his neck, when did all these people cluster behind them? Every expression anxious, every forehead furrowed, crowd spilling from pavement to road, horns blaring with every step. The urgency behind him hits with a shove to his back and elbow to the ribs, atmosphere turning more febrile by the second.

Paloma shouts, swept from his side by another surge, crowd corralling them towards the same target, becoming clearer and clearer with every fevered step.

Somewhere overhead, a clock chimes like a starting gun.

Jonny reels, lifted off his feet by a final desperate rush towards a giant, gleaming set of implacably closed glass doors. The realisation hits him with equal velocity.

'It's the banks,' he yells, as if Paloma will hear him over the roar. 'The banks are about to open! But I don't know—'

The rest of his question dies into the sudden, cataclysmic boom of breaking glass.

Chapter Ten

Jonny fights to stay upright as the crowd presses forward like a wave. Another unearthly crack rents the air – has the mob breached the doors? His arms fly up to protect his head, mind filling with images of the last time he and Paloma were caught in a riot, the unspeakable amounts of blood pouring down her face. Sirens are suddenly screaming through the air, cacophonous, the clock still chiming overhead – yep, it's most definitely ten o'clock, which is when the city's banks open, so why are people being kept out? His head whirls on his neck, desperate to make sure Paloma is still standing, hoping it's her dark hair he can see flying a few feet away. But his shouts just add to the dissonance enveloping them.

A loud pop – a flare, it must be, lurid pink smoke streaming into the sky overhead. Jonny struggles to keep his arms up, gulps air that tastes acrid and foul. Banks across Argentina, especially in Buenos Aires, have been under pressure for months. He's filed a dozen different versions of the same story. It's called capital flight – the increasingly rapid liquidation of bank accounts in order to transfer financial operations abroad by companies running scared of total economic meltdown. And it's not just companies – families with any form of life savings have been spooked into converting them into American dollars to avoid losing it all if the Argentinian currency collapses. Which of course has already begun. So is this its chaotic conclusion? They're right downtown too, outside the biggest bank branches of all. Jonny stumbles as the crowd presses forward, pressure building at his back. This isn't the story he wants to cover. But he's got no choice. He's suddenly right in the middle of it.

Elbows out, he turns his body sideways, careful to stay with the forward motion of the crowd, to remain upright at all costs. The mob is seething now, projectiles are being launched overhead, but for all its pushing and shoving, it is barely moving. Jonny scans the far side of the street. Is there a doorway somewhere that he can shelter in? Sidestepping and shuffling, he inches forward … then spots part of the façade ahead that is jutting out. There must be a doorway or entrance to an alley below, somewhere he can get out of the crush.

Clasping his head, he pushes forward, the crowd's perpendicular motion helping him move like a riptide, cutting a diagonal path through the mob to the far edge. The kerb almost catches him out but the squeeze is so tight now, he's able to prop himself between bodies as he moves. One last shove and the shade of the doorway is upon him, exactly as he'd foreseen – a deep recess, a dark corridor of some kind in the middle. It's only when he is finally able to pause, gasping as he leans against the cool stone, that he realises how much he is shaking.

Jonny knuckles his hot eyes, letting the dark consume him for a moment. He's a journalist, he should feel nothing but exhilarated to find himself in the right place at the right time. There is no doubt a news story is unfolding – a literal run on the banks is taking place on the pavement less than two feet away. It is the only logical conclusion to months of misguided financial measures. And what is he doing about it? What is Jonny Murphy, the *International Tribune*'s man in Buenos Aires, doing to make this scoop his own? Voluntarily watching from the side lines, while Paloma puts herself in harm's way again to get the best possible pictures.

He digs the heel of a hand into his eye again. For the real source of his pain is everywhere other than in this stinking, damp doorway. It's just increasingly poking its way to the surface at the most inopportune of moments. As if working out what really happened to someone else's mother, brother or sister is ever going to make him feel any better about losing his own. He kicks at the ground, tells himself he's sending an invisible message. Isn't it true that twins can feel each other's pain? Is she, his long-lost twin sister, in the same pain as he is? But another kick and all that happens is he cries out. Clamping a hand over his nose and mouth, he finally heads into the dark behind him. The passage turns a corner to reveal a stairwell at the far end. Breaking into a run, charging up the steps and straight into Paloma, hovering at the top, wild-eyed.

'Where the hell have you been?'

'Me?' Jonny staggers a little at the sight of her, blessedly unharmed save for the fury blazing in her eyes.

'Why were you just standing around in a mob like that?'

'Standing around?' Jonny parrots back, surprise fermenting to disbelief. 'I was trying—'

'To get yourself to safety? By waiting it out in the middle of a crowd?'

'I was trying to work out what was going on. And I was also looking for you—'

He gasps as Paloma shoves him.

'You're an idiot, you know that? I assumed you'd be following me but when I got to the doorway all I could see was your stupid head still sticking out of the middle. You're lucky that everyone in this country is so fucking short. You'd never have made it otherwise.'

He catches hold of her hand as it flails. 'Stop hitting me, would you?'

Paloma struggles. 'Let go of me.'

'What, so you can hit me again?' Still, Jonny drops her hand, bracing for another shove. But to his astonishment Paloma flings herself into his arms instead, bursting into tears.

Now Jonny is reeling for altogether different reasons. The unmistakable warmth of another human being willingly pressing themselves against him is so intoxicating that he sways on his feet, even as his self-preservation instinct is screaming that he back away immediately. Paloma is the first person he's met that seems to share similar instincts to him. The tug of a profession that requires a lack of commitment to everything else except the facts, and where they might lead. A way of living based on forming connections in sometimes the most unthinkable of circumstances and places. And now she's behaving as if she feels the same connection to him too. Jonny feels a tear opening up inside his chest, as desperate to prolong the moment as he is to pull away. He doesn't want to be suspicious of her, but he is. He has to be. The rational part of his brain is insisting on it.

'I was really worried,' she chokes out between sobs. 'After everything that happened to you last night, too. And after the last time ... you know.' Jonny nods, trying and failing not to picture the moment they first met and the sickening amount of blood on her face. 'I ... I just ... I just couldn't bring myself to go back into it once I was safely out.'

'It's OK. We're both OK, look. And I'm glad you didn't. Try and pull me out, I mean. If something had happened to you again on my account...' He trails off rather than finish his thought out loud.

'I could say the same to you,' Paloma sniffs.

'How do you mean?' Jonny wonders, letting his head rest on top of hers for the briefest of moments. Why does Paloma think that she's the one putting him at risk? If anything, he feels like she's been trying to slow him down. His skin prickles with a curious mix of relief and regret as she pulls away to peer over her shoulder.

'Just that it's a really nasty mob,' she finally replies, still looking in the direction of the commotion. 'It's going to get a lot worse, too.'

'Why, what have you heard?'

'Apparently the government has frozen everyone's bank accounts. That's all I could make out between the yelling. I don't know if it's actually true or not.'

'What?' Instantly Jonny is snapped back into action. 'Blocked people's personal bank accounts?'

'Yep. It's going to get really messy.'

But Jonny is already hurrying down the tiny passageway. 'Where does this alleyway come out?'

'I don't know,' Paloma pants, catching him up. 'But there will be mobs outside all the banks in the country. Everyone will be trying to get whatever's left of their money out.'

She frowns as he pulls up short just before the alley opens out on to the street, rooting around for the notebook in his pocket. 'This is it, Jonny. This is the professional breakthrough we need – we won't be short of work for weeks.'

'Just give me a minute.' He flips open his notebook, rips out the page in Hebrew.

'Good.' Paloma nods approvingly, pulling her camera from its case. 'This is the only story in town. And we're right in the middle of it – come on.'

Jonny folds the page carefully into his pocket, tries to keep his expression neutral. The crisis that has been simmering for months is obviously coming to a head. Of course they're both going to cover it with all they've got. But does that mean he's just going to forget about everything else? He pats the piece of paper folded into his pocket as if to prove to himself that he won't. But something altogether different keeps nagging at him.

'Stay at my back, OK?' Paloma's eyes glitter as she looks up from her camera. 'I need to be able to feel your hand on my shoulder at all times.'

Finally, Jonny is able to smile as he nods, his reaction as visceral now as it was when she first explained this to him. Of course

Paloma needs someone else at her back if she has to keep looking through her viewfinder. Isn't it easier for everyone to move forward if they know someone else has their back? He just wasn't expecting Paloma to want it to be him.

'Don't worry. I know the drill.'

He reaches out for her shoulder but she's already turned away.

Chapter Eleven

They move as one, facing in opposite directions, Jonny looking backward, letting Paloma set the forward pace. Hand resting lightly on her bare shoulder, they rejoin the back of the crowd, staying at its edge, ducking into any doorways they pass to pause and regroup. Further ahead, the mob has escalated to full-blown riot, Jonny can hear the clatter of projectiles landing, the pop and crack of rubber bullets, the unmistakable thunder of mounted police. He squeezes Paloma's shoulder, gestures towards another doorway on the opposite side of the road where he can see some people taking cover. Is that a streak of blood on the road in between them? A single shoe lies on its side in a dark puddle. The clamour is suddenly deafening, a repeating chorus echoing between the tall stone buildings. But she just shakes her head.

'We've got to get closer to the bank,' she shouts over the commotion. 'We need pictures of the damage. And we need to be first there if we can.'

Jonny nods, looking back and forth at the destruction either side of the street. Was the unearthly crackling sound he'd heard gunfire? They skitter forward another few feet before ducking into an alcove at a series of pops in the distance followed by a scream. Jonny hopes it's not spent bullet casings he can hear rattling to the ground. Peering into the thinning crowd, his blood runs cold. There's a pushchair within the group of people sheltering in the opposite doorway.

'We need to talk to some people if we can,' he says, registering the multiple shopping bags strung over the back of the buggy's handlebars. Something suddenly occurs to him. Turning, he scans their doorway. It's barely big enough for the two of them, a standard Argentinian wrought-iron entryway security gate.

Paloma blinks quizzically up at him, gripping her camera with both hands.

'Is it possible this is an apartment building?' Jonny presses the bell mounted on the steel frame in the same moment that he spots it.

'Even if it is, no one in their right mind is going to let us in.' Paloma twists the lens between her fingers. 'Come on.'

But Jonny just leans his entire weight on to the bell. Paloma can get far better shots from higher, not to mention safer, ground. Hell, she can take all the pictures she wants up there. Keeping his shoulder on the bell, he twists round to check the opposite doorway again.

'I knew it,' he mutters, watching the buggy with its precious cargo disappearing inside. 'Those people must live opposite – why else would anyone be caught out downtown with that much shopping?'

'Which people?' Paloma flinches as a crumpled tin can flies past, clattering as it lands further down the street, followed by a volley of stones.

'The ones with the shopping bags,' he replies, stabbing repeatedly at the bell. 'If we can just get someone to—'

The rest of his sentence is caught by the door behind the gate suddenly cracking open.

Jonny starts in surprise. The door appears to have opened by itself. Then he looks down, and has to stop himself stepping backward into the street, praying that the pair of dark, terrified eyes staring up at him from barely higher than his waist belong to someone short rather than an actual child. Another siren screams through the street behind them.

Instantly Paloma is by his side, murmuring softly in Spanish. A burst from a loudspeaker cuts in from somewhere further away – is that the police finally dispersing the crowd? The unmistakable thunder of hooves suggests otherwise. To Jonny's relief, a gnarled hand curls round the crack. A tiny, elderly man slowly comes into view, trembling as he unlocks the security grill. They duck inside and Jonny slams the two doors shut behind him, and immediately finds himself wishing that he hadn't as the squalor within comes into view.

The stairs are steep, narrow and choked with rubbish. Piles of neatly tied refuse sacks have long given way to loose litter – Jonny claps a hand over his nose and mouth at the smell of soiled nappies. He shuffles behind Paloma up the stairs, trying and failing not to stare. The wooden banister has the kind of deep burnish that only comes from years of painstaking care, its elaborately carved spindles at odds with the filth piled against them. A heavy door at the top is standing open into a wide, bright room.

At first, all Jonny can see is the room's high, intricately corniced ceiling, its blinding white suggesting a huge window is close by. Every ascending step increases Jonny's creeping feeling of dread. Paloma pauses at the very top, blocking his immediate view. But by then he's already guessed what they're about to find. The piteous whimpers and cries have given it away.

Children, some still babies, are squeezed into the wide room's every available inch. In between their brown and grubby bare feet Jonny glimpses snatches of a once immaculately laid parquet floor. There are a few thin, grimy mattresses stacked in a corner, some carefully folded piles of faded sheets and blankets. A bucket full of sponges. A broken doll, a child's dummy on a rainbow-coloured twisted rubber string. The detritus of an interrupted childhood.

Paloma is leaning towards the old man, listening and asking questions in Spanish. She edges aside to let Jonny squeeze by.

'These are his grandchildren,' she whispers between sorrowful nods.

'All of them?' Jonny murmurs back, eyeing the watchful faces, the painfully skinny limbs.

Paloma shakes her head. 'Some are his former neighbours' children. Others are children he has picked up off the street. They all come from families who have lost their homes. Everyone who is old enough to manage on their own is out trying to work. That's why he answered the door—'

'Because we could have been children,' Jonny finishes for her, wondering exactly how old is deemed old enough to manage alone.

Paloma nods. 'They've all been squatting here for months now...' She trails off as the old man picks up again, wiping away a tear with a gnarled finger.

Jonny gazes around the wide room, somehow as squalid as it is enormous. The wall to his left is almost entirely taken up by a huge glass picture window throwing light on to the rest of the white walls, their fresh and clean finish at the top fading to stained and streaked at human height. A giant marble fireplace is set into the wall opposite, its mantle peppered with plastic bottles holding some dried and long-dead flowers.

He follows Paloma and the old man picking their way towards the window, mind racing. The room has been as carefully kept as possible under the circumstances. Hunching against the sill, Jonny can see the spike of the old man's shoulder blades through a well-worn cotton shirt, the faded blue of the Argentinian flag. Talk about wearing their hearts on their sleeves, he thinks. The intensity of Argentina's national pride makes every fall so much more painful. He steps forward, rests a hand on Paloma's shoulder, prompting her to translate.

'It's as I said,' she murmurs as the man keeps talking. Below the window, the carnage is still raging. 'The government has frozen all bank accounts. He heard it on the radio. People are only allowed to withdraw two hundred and fifty pesos per week.

Officials say international aid depends on it. That they have to do whatever it takes to stop a run on the banks. An international bailout package is all that's left that can get Argentina out of this.'

Jonny gazes around the room again as if he's seeing it for the first time, meets pair after pair of agonised brown eyes.

'But hardly anyone has money left in their bank accounts anyway.'

'Right.' Paloma nods again. 'His own savings ran out months ago. Over half the country is already living below the poverty line. People are dying of starvation in the provinces – and they're living on some of the world's most fertile land. These massive apartments have been standing empty for ages. Even the super-rich have fled to their *estancias* in the mountains.'

'To Little Switzerland,' Jonny finishes bitterly, remembering their earlier conversation about Paloma's holidays by the lakes. He recently read a desperate article in a local magazine, equating that tiny part of the country with Switzerland, as if that was going to be enough to encourage international investment.

Paloma has another exchange in Spanish with the old man, pausing to take a few pictures of the street below the window.

'The government has also seized whatever is left of people's pensions,' she continues after a moment. 'And why not, he says, when children are starving to death? But the problem is this government isn't trying to save those children. It's just interested in doing whatever it takes to secure foreign aid. So all the mountains of food that Argentina produces are being exported instead of being used to save hundreds of people from starvation. They're just collateral damage.'

Jonny gulps, peering out of the window, a wide-angle lens on the carnage in the street below. The police are starting to disperse the mob but the damage is already done. The glass frontage of the bank a few doors down may still be closed, but is riven with livid cracks. Much like Argentina itself, Jonny thinks. This nation's scars run deeper than the ocean floor. How many more shocks can it withstand before its legendary national pride finally shatters? Beside him, the man wipes another tear from his eye as Paloma's shutter clicks and whirrs. Jonny rests a hand on her shoulder even though she doesn't need him at her back to take any of these particular pictures. Suddenly he feels like an interloper of the very worst kind. The memory, regret and loss these babies have unknowingly brought with them into this room is threatening to overwhelm him.

'Have you got what you need?'

Paloma murmurs her assent. They leave quickly, but not before Jonny has folded the banknotes left in his pocket into a crack between the windowsill and the glass.

Chapter Twelve

The street below is an assault course. Every step requires careful consideration to avoid fallen projectiles. Even though the immediate area has been secured, the air is still humming with tension – every door reinforced, every window implacably closed. The air reeks of burning rubber – a pile of tyres is on fire a few blocks further down. They hurry away from the lines of feebly strung hazard tape. But no sooner are they out of trouble on one street than they run into a roadblock on the next, mounted police blocking their exit.

Jonny almost crashes into Paloma as she pulls up short, gasping in awe at the sight of the huge horses parked horizontally across the street. Oiled-brown stallions, immaculate livery, muscles rippling with tension as they are reined in tight. Her hand twitches in his.

'Don't even think about it,' he says before she can reach for her camera. 'Pictures of horses from the land of gauchos are definitely not what we need to tell this particular story.'

The nearest one gives its perfect mane a little toss. He looks away with irritation only to find more mounted officers taking up positions in the opposite direction.

'Whoever thought the apocalypse would arrive with only four horsemen had clearly never been to Argentina,' he grumbles. 'What the hell are we going to do now? They've blocked every exit.'

Paloma turns to him, eyes bright. 'Let me just try something.'

Jonny regards her in horror. 'Like what? This country isn't

exactly known for a relaxed approach to maintaining order. We can't tangle with mounted police.'

But even as Jonny asks, he knows they'll have to. There are more huge horses appearing everywhere he looks. He thinks of the instantly recognisable blue flak vests that broadcast journalists wear in combat zones with the word *PRESS* lettered in bright white across the front, suddenly grateful for Paloma's bulky and conspicuous camera case. Will that be enough to indicate they're journalists rather than troublemakers? No average Argentinian is likely to be carrying one. But before he can ask if that's what she is thinking, she starts walking towards the horses, waving a placatory hand at him.

'Trust me, Jonny. I know what I'm doing. There's nothing to be afraid of. Horses are the gentlest animals alive – look, aren't they beautiful? And these aren't stallions, they're geldings – see?' She slows, gesturing towards the nearest horse. 'They'd run wild otherwise. They'd be impossible to control.'

Jonny shakes his head, trying to slow her down. 'What the hell is a gelding?'

'Do you really need me to spell it out?' She makes a snipping motion with her fingers. 'Put it this way. It's only the policemen that still have their balls.'

Jonny winces as the penny drops, somehow feeling even more intimidated by the thought. 'Well it's only Argentinians that ever seem to think you need a pair of balls to do any damage. Their machismo is as legendary as it is deluded.'

'Funny,' Paloma replies, without laughing. 'Just wait here. It's better they think I'm alone.' She adjusts her top, pulling her customary long sleeves down into her palms to reveal bare shoulders before walking away.

'Of course it is,' Jonny mutters to himself, watching her sashay up to the nearest rider. Aside from the country's legendary and deluded machismo, there's something about this spectacle that isn't sitting right; but he can't put his finger on exactly what. After the briefest of exchanges Paloma turns around with a broad smile, waving him over, tossing her own mane for good measure. Jonny despairs at the blush heating up his neck. Trudging on, he tries to make himself as small as possible as he nears the horses before following in Paloma's exact footsteps as she makes her way through police lines.

'See?' Paloma turns around with a grin.

'See what?' Jonny can't bring himself to smile back.

'They don't bite, after all.'

'Not when you're around, apparently.'

'They don't bite at all, is the truth. You should try riding one. There's no other feeling like it in the world. It's like flying.'

'You've tried that too, I take it.'

Paloma rounds on him with the most curious of expressions, caught somewhere between fury and distress. 'Stop it. You don't understand.'

Jonny is floored. Her behaviour is becoming increasingly baffling. 'What? About how much you love horses?'

She pulls the ends of her sleeves down hard into her palms and shaking her head. 'It's not that.'

'So what is it, then?' Jonny asks, reflecting again on how little they really know each other. It's becoming more and more obvious.

'It's just ... it was all I could do to escape,' she replies after a moment, a single tear snaking down her cheek, turning her scar a livid, gleaming red. 'When I was growing up, I mean. I felt so alone in New Mexico. My parents were never around unless it was in church. Riding felt like running away.'

She starts to walk again. Jonny follows her in silence, trailing behind a step, suddenly struggling to suppress memories of his own dislocated past.

'I'm sorry,' he says after a moment. 'I get it now, at least I think

I do. And you're right, I've never ridden a horse. Maybe ... maybe you can show me the ropes one day.'

But Paloma just speeds up rather than reply. Jonny keeps step, wishing he'd settled for silence and a sympathetic nod. After all, does he really get it? He's not entirely sure he does. By the time she says anything else, they are almost back at her apartment.

Jonny scans the empty street. The normally bustling Congreso neighbourhood is deserted, save for a couple of bicycles abandoned on the pavement beside a defaced phone box. It's not quite business as usual.

'Have you got any change?' Paloma is rooting around in her pocket. 'We need to call this in. That phone box better still work.'

Jonny shifts from foot to foot. 'I left what I still had with me in the old man's apartment. I couldn't not. And it wasn't much, anyway.'

Now Paloma is balking all over again. 'You can't just fix things, Jonny. You have to stop acting like you can.'

Jonny frowns. Her reactions aren't making sense. Their earlier exchange can't be all that's bothering her. 'I don't understand. I'm just trying to do my job. Like you're just trying to do yours. Aren't you? I'm not trying to fix anything.'

'Yes, you are. It's all you're ever trying to do. Find the answers to the questions, even when they aren't your problem. Sometimes things are just better off left alone. Our other story has already nearly got you killed—'

He holds up his hands to try and quiet her only for her to start shouting and gesturing maniacally around the deserted street.

'Look around you, Jonny. There's no one here. Now you think the birds have ears? Even they've all flown away. Just forget about everything else, would you? Forget about it all. We can't afford to get distracted. We've got to stay on top of the financial crisis. Widespread chaos, economic meltdown, international implications – that's what's going to pay our own wages. We'll never find out what really happened to all those missing people in time to make a living out of it. And don't you dare mention the missing babies, either.'

She digs feverishly around in her other pocket, groaning. 'Great. Finally we have some serious breaking news to report and we still can't move fast enough.'

Jonny eyes her yanking at her clothes. By now his unease at the unpredictability of her behaviour is so pronounced it is difficult to hide. 'But you know we can just reverse the charges. All we need is a working phone line. We don't actually need any change.'

'*You* can, you mean. *You* can just reverse the charges. You get to just call your editor. You don't even need to pay for it. All you have to do is file down the line and the job's done. You've even got someone waiting on your call. But I've got nothing until I get this film developed. I'm absolutely nowhere without pictures to show for it. And no shops are going to open in a hurry. I'll have to develop it myself, and by then who knows how many other photographers will have got their first?'

The thought that she's been able to develop her own films all along disturbs Jonny even further. 'You can do that? Develop your own film? You've not done it before.'

'Of course I haven't. Not in this country, anyway. I haven't needed to – but what other choice do I have? I can't wait for a professional darkroom. Pictures are my only currency. They're literally all I'm worth at the moment.'

'That's ... that's not true,' he says pathetically. 'And before you say it, I'm not trying to fix anything. I'm just – I'm sorry that it's harder for you than it is for me.'

Paloma straightens, visibly pulling herself together. 'It isn't harder, it's just different. At least we have a solid news story to work with now. Which is a relief.'

Jonny nods even though his instincts are willing him to do the exact opposite. Does Paloma honestly think the story they've been slowly piecing together for the last two weeks is anything other than a dynamite scoop? The sort of news story that journalists dream of breaking? The definition of holding power to account, of giving voice to the voiceless, of shining a light into the darkest of corners. Even the journalism-school clichés don't ring hollow in this story's context. Jonny runs a hand over his head as he tries to make sense of it – still unmistakably sore and tender. Still ringing with the evidence of last night's ambush.

'I'll … I'll leave you to it then,' he replies hesitantly. 'Unless I can help you with developing the film.'

Paloma shakes her head, stabbing at the bell mounted on the speaker unit next to her apartment block's security grille. 'All you can do now is pray for someone to let me in. Obviously I haven't had time to get new keys yet. But I will. Just as soon as I can afford it.'

The intercom crackles. Paloma gabs something in Spanish. The gate buzzes open a second later. She's through before it's fully open, it's as if she can't wait to get rid of him.

'Good luck,' he calls half-heartedly after her, even though she's already disappeared.

Chapter Thirteen

Jonny rattles the shiny black security grille with its knowing gleam. He should go and file on the financial crisis immediately. He should head straight for that fucking phone box across the street and place a decisive reverse-charge call to *Trib* HQ. Filing some short sharp copy down the line should be his first – no, his only – priority. Full of the kind of urgency and gravitas that befits a pivotal moment on a fast-developing news story. Full of the kind of perspective and analysis that only a reporter who has spent the best part of a year following the same story can deliver. Except all Jonny seems to be able to do with any kind of focus is stare at the abandoned bicycles lying on the pavement next to the phone box. And think about where they could get him.

A cover story, he thinks, scanning the empty street. And a distraction. He needs both to get himself inside the ESMA. And he's got himself a distraction right now, that's for sure. Riots like these are excuse enough for the Argentinian military to hit the streets and start herding people around. This is a country with a military that still barely needs an excuse to do anything. A wholly disproportionate show of force is routine around here. And the closest military base – which is hopefully emptying out right this minute – just so happens to be exactly where Jonny wants to be. Getting inside the Dirty War's most notorious prison and torture complex felt almost impossible when Jonny first thought of it. But now?

With that he makes his decision. The financial crisis isn't going to disappear. It'll still be around when Jonny gets back. Whereas he might not get a chance like this again. And judging by Paloma's most recent emotional outburst, she isn't going anywhere for a while.

Crossing the street, he grabs the nearest bicycle, hunching his shoulders as if it will somehow render the theft invisible. Slinging a leg over the saddle, he pedals away and around a corner as fast as he can. He pored over the map for long enough before to know exactly where he is going now.

Bustle is starting to return to the streets. With every block that Jonny covers, he sees shops reopening their doors, trestle tables clattering optimistically out on to the pavement, and the distinctive sharp and bitter smell of *yerba mate* is starting to disperse the tension in the air. But Jonny is already out of breath. The unmistakable clatter of a bus approaching in the distance is the push he needs to keep moving. One last desperate burst of speed later and he's got just enough time to stash the bike on a rack before flagging down the bus and jumping aboard. The vehicle itself is mercifully deserted. Collapsing into a seat, Jonny passes the last few miles to Belgrano in a haze – trying by turns to bring his heart rate down and to figure out how the hell he is going to get himself past the guards at the gates to the ESMA.

The building looks so at home on one of the city's most palatial avenues that he misses it at first, its extravagant stucco columns and intricate naval insignia flashing past in a blur of wedding-cake white before he can fully register their significance. Stumbling off the bus at the next earliest opportunity, Jonny finds his legs are still shaking. Set back from a wide, almost Parisian-style boulevard in one of Buenos Aires' most upmarket suburbs, the ESMA's incongruous location makes it almost impossible to imagine that torture of the worst kind went on behind its gates for years.

Jonny recalls last night's car journey with the pilot. They were speeding along a wide, smooth highway for the part that he can remember. Is it possible that Jonny has already been here? His pulse quickens at the prospect of finding more clues to the man's identity inside the black iron security gates just a few metres away. Gates that, right at this moment, are opening to let a fleet of gleaming Ford Falcon sedans out into the street, one smooth manoeuvre after the other.

Jonny freezes, trying to remember the exact details of the car he was bundled into the previous night. He takes a step towards the gates, squinting at each vehicle's darkened windows. There are nine – no, ten – cars in total, sliding seamlessly on to the tarmac of the road, turning and heading in the direction of the city centre. To help with crowd control? Or to secure the banks? If the point is to put on a wholly disproportionate show of force, are ten carloads of military officers even enough? Jonny starts to panic as the gates begin to close again, casting around for anything that he could possibly say to the guards at the side that won't result in getting himself arrested almost immediately.

And then it hits him.

That's exactly what he's going to have to do.

That's exactly how he can get himself between those gates – maybe even inside the former cells themselves – without having to say much at all.

Hiding in plain sight, Jonny thinks, staring up at the ESMA's impassive façade, a pristine white cover for the dirtiest kind of warfare. Jonny is going to have to fight just as dirty. The plan is still building in his mind even as he begins to carry it out.

Launching himself towards the gates, Jonny arrives with seconds to spare before they close. Playing dumb, he edges between them, gazing wide-eyed to his either side. Two military guards rush over immediately.

'*Disculpa!*' Jonny gabbles, holding his hands in the air, noting, with a little jolt of adrenaline, the gates closing behind him. '*Turista! Ingles!*'

The men manhandle him over to the guard post. Jonny goes limp, lets himself move like a rag doll, for once grateful that he doesn't have to feign ignorance of the rapid-fire Spanish being shouted over his head.

'I made a mistake,' he says, keeping his hands in the air. 'Isn't this a stately home? I thought ... I thought this was a stately home ... I'm from England, you see...'

He trails off as one of the guards barks something unintelligible into a radio. The other pushes him down on to a small wooden stool, shiny silver handcuffs dangling at his belt.

'I made a mistake,' he repeats. '*Ingles*. I'm English. *Turista*.'

The guards exchange a look.

'I have money,' he adds, then makes a show of dropping his hands to dig around with purpose in his pockets. The guards react instantly, each grabbing an arm, hauling him up and out of the guard post towards the building's imposing entrance. Jonny gibbers incomprehensibly in broken Spanish, all the while noting the absence of any other visible military presence around the building. A wholly disproportionate show of force, he thinks, fresh burst of adrenaline firing. He lets himself be manhandled up the wide steps and into the foyer.

Inside, Jonny feels the chill immediately. Other than the entrance doors, there are no windows in the building's thick stone walls. The domed ceiling is cavernous, alien-yellow lights mounted haphazardly on the walls. Jonny is led through a side door and up some dank, steep stairs to an equally dank corridor. His breathing quickens as he notes the small, empty rooms set off to either side – are these former cells? The guards lead him to the end of the row, depositing him inside one at the far end. He doesn't complain, just lets them seat him on one of two long, thin bunks propped against either wall. Both are made up with flat pillows, thin white sheets and sky-blue blankets.

There the guards pause, regarding him with suspicion.

'I made a mistake,' Jonny ventures again. 'I'm from England. I just thought this was a stately home.'

One guard says something to the other before turning to open a small wall-mounted cupboard. Jonny notices an identical one tacked on to the wall opposite. He takes in the rest of the room's sparse furnishings – the two cupboards, some frayed and tattered paperback books, a small, stainless-steel sink.

'Is this your dorm?' Jonny asks, pointing at the guards one at a time. 'Where you sleep?' He pats the bunk on which he is seated. 'You sleep in here?'

The guard at the cupboard closes its door with a scowl, muttering something to his opposite number.

'You are partners?' Jonny tries, finger moving between them. 'You work together?'

Two blank stares. Jonny takes the respite to absorb as many details of his surroundings as he can. An identical dorm room is visible opposite through the still-open door. The doors themselves are solid, conspicuously lacking the small, barred hatches found in cells. Low down beside the bunks, the clammy white walls are covered in etchings and scribbles.

The guards exchange another look.

'Is this a police station?' Jonny asks, letting a note of indignation creep into his voice.

'*No*,' one of the guards answers with an emphatic shake of his head. '*No policia*.'

'*Policia*,' Jonny echoes. 'Yes. *Si*, I mean. You are *policia*?'

The guard's brow furrows. He mumbles something unintelligible to his colleague.

'I haven't done anything wrong.' Jonny folds his arms. 'You can't detain me against my will.'

He stands, and instantly the guards react again. A meaty hand lands in the centre of Jonny's chest, dispatching him back down on to the bunk. Then both men turn on their heels and walk out, slamming the solid door behind them.

'Wait!' Jonny shouts, seized by a curious mixture of relief and panic. He's inside the ESMA, he's even got himself inside the guards' quarters by the looks of it, but he's still not entirely sure he's going to be able to get himself out quite as easily.

'You can't just leave me in here,' he adds half-heartedly, turning to the scribbles on the walls. *Marianna*, he murmurs to himself, running a finger over the name scratched into the plaster. *Tamara*, says another. *Natacha*, says a third. He leans closer, takes in the myriad of names and numbers marked on the walls above the cots. And then – Jonny gasps as he spots some Spanish he understands. *Forgive us*, Jonny translates under his breath, staring at the words. *Disculparnos:* we are sorry.

Then the heavy door flies open again.

Jonny flinches. A different man is framed in the doorway, the two guards standing just behind him in the corridor. Short and sturdy, filling out his pressed military uniform, displaying an impressive battalion of medals and badges on his barrel-shaped chest. An officer of senior rank, without doubt.

Jonny raises a shaky hand to his temple in an approximation of a salute.

'Now I understand,' he says, sounding as clueless as possible. '*No policia*. You are army.'

A shiver runs down his back as the officer replies in perfect, if heavily accented English – a cadence Jonny has heard from another military man just a little too recently for comfort in the back of a locked sedan.

'Yes,' the officer says. 'This is an army facility. It is not open to visitors.'

'I'm sorry,' Jonny replies earnestly. '*Disculpame*. Please forgive me. I did not realise. I am from England. Our army buildings are not so grand.'

The officer's expression darkens. Jonny instantly regrets the comparison.

'Come with me.' He motions that Jonny get up. *'Ya vamos.'*

Jonny keeps gabbling: 'Of course. *Gracias*. You have such a beautiful city.'

The officer steps aside to let Jonny out. He follows the guards back down the corridor with the officer at his back until they reach the door at the end.

But the guards don't head for the entrance hall. They turn in the opposite direction.

Jonny pauses. *'Donde vamos*? Where are we going?'

The officer pokes him hard in the shoulder. The guards have already started to climb the stairs.

Jonny stands his ground. 'What's up there?'

'You are trespassing,' the officer growls into his ear.

'No, I am not.' Jonny tries and fails to keep the tremor out of his voice. 'I made a mistake, that's all.'

This time the poke is more of a solid shove. Jonny stumbles, banging a shin on a step. Before he can say anything else the guards have turned back and are grabbing his arms to haul him along. A little cry escapes him. Jonny can't help himself – the stone steps are sharp and steep. A flight up and they're in an identically dismal corridor. But this time the small rooms are crammed with quadruple bunks stacked impossibly close together and instead of doors they have gates made of thick iron bars.

The cells, Jonny thinks, assailed again by that curious mix of relief and panic. The setup is exactly as the pilot described – the guards' quarters directly below the cells. They would pass each other on the stairs. Living in those rooms, they were prisoners too.

Jonny readies himself for a fight but instead of depositing him behind the first available set of bars, the guards hustle him down the corridor and into a bigger room at the end. Two desks, a good few chairs, and – Jonny's breath catches in his throat – two smart, black and decidedly shiny telephones.

He turns to find the guards stationed either side of the open, and thankfully solid rather than barred, door. The officer clomps past and sits down at the bigger desk, pulling a clipboard from a drawer.

'What is your name?' The officer looks up, pen poised.

'What's yours?' Jonny replies, folding his arms to stop them shaking.

The officer glares at him.

'Jonny Murphy,' he adds just a little too quickly. 'But I haven't done anything wrong. If you'll let me make a phone call I can prove it.'

The officer's pen scratches across the clipboard, scribbling randomly.

'The penalty for trespassing is one thousand pesos,' the officer states. 'This is a military facility. You have twenty-four hours to pay. Then it doubles. Again and again if you do not pay.'

Jonny balks. 'That's ridiculous. I don't have that kind of money. No one does around here. You know that. You've just sent most of your men out into the city to help control people rioting about exactly that.'

The officer's pen stills. A long, slow beat of silence passes between them.

'What exactly are you doing here in Buenos Aires?' the officer finally asks.

Jonny takes a deep breath. 'I work here,' he answers simply, watching the officer's jaw slacken as he continues talking. 'I'm a journalist for the *International Tribune*. And I have been covering the financial crisis in your country for the past year now. I have been doing everything I can to draw as much international attention as possible to the crazy decisions your government is making, to how desperate things are getting for your people. I know the military is in need of as much money as everyone else in this country – and would manage it better, too. My newspaper is American. The officials in charge of international aid read it every day. My reporting is going to help your country get the money it needs.'

By now the officer is staring at him open-mouthed, clipboard lolling in his lap. Jonny has to fight the beginnings of a smile as he notes that the piece of paper the officer has been scribbling on is otherwise completely blank – not even a semblance of an official form. So much for the penalty for trespassing being a one-thousand peso fine, doubling into oblivion.

'Just let me call my editor,' Jonny adds, eyeing the shiny black telephone on the desk. 'I can prove it. Money is all the *International Tribune* cares about in Argentina.' *For now*, he adds silently to himself, thinking about the names scratched into the walls directly below.

The officer recovers himself, shouting angrily in Spanish to the guards behind Jonny, waving a hand. Both men mutter back, hanging their heads and shifting awkwardly from foot to foot.

'You said you were a tourist,' the officer grumbles.

Jonny shrugs. 'My Spanish isn't very good.'

Chapter Fourteen

Jonny can't bring himself to sit down even though the bus is empty, excess adrenaline at an improbably lucky win still coursing through his body. His sore head throbs as he shakes it in disbelief. He's managed to get himself both inside the ESMA and back out again in one piece. It shouldn't have worked but it did – and without needing to call in support from the *Trib*. What would his editors have said if he had? 'Follow the money, Jonny.' Because money always talks, he thinks, simultaneously trying not to panic about how he's going to account for an outlandish fine the ESMA officer obviously made up on the spot. That's one thing he'll definitely have to call in support for from the *Trib* if any serious attempt is made to enforce it. Jonny grips the metal bar overhead with renewed determination. This story better be worth it.

Forgive us, he says to himself, picturing the scribbles on the guards' quarters' clammy white walls. *Marianna. Tamara. Natacha.* There were other names too – *Laurita, Florencia, Julia.* Who are they? Military wives? Daughters? Female prisoners the officers used to pass on the stairs? Jonny shudders at the thought, wondering if the ESMA's torture chambers are still standing as memorials in the building's basement in the same way the former cells are a few floors above. He pictures stone rooms full of metal shackles and electrical rods. He thinks about the guards still living in quarters where torturers and murderers once slept. *We were prisoners too*, Jonny ponders, recalling the thin bunks, the squalid rooms, the conspicuous lack of any natural light. Suddenly he can imagine how it must have felt on both sides of those clammy walls

– the same sense of claustrophobia and oppression, the same lack of any meaningful routes for escape. The total absence of any form of autonomous control. *Marianna. Tamara. Natacha. Laurita, Florencia, Julia.* The bus lurches and sighs all the way back downtown.

Jumping off the bus at the spot where he stashed his stolen bike, Jonny is mortified and resigned in equal measure to find it already gone. He trudges the final few blocks to his apartment, trying to convince himself that even if he hadn't commandeered the bike, chances are it would have been stolen anyway. At least he took it in pursuit of a higher goal. The thought makes him wince far more than the tender patch on his head.

Finally back in his own apartment, Jonny pauses directly in front of the closed door, confirms everything is exactly as he left it. Bookcase in perfect line with the wall, a few stray shards of broken glass, bed covered in a tangle of sheets. As expected, the red button on his answerphone is flashing with a volley of phone messages. Pressing and listening, Jonny wills for a different voice on the other end – that just for once, someone other than his news editor might be calling, maybe even someone just calling to say hi, better still to check on his well-being. But every single message is from Lukas, Jonny's editor, distinctive South African accent getting increasingly more clipped with each one. Jonny places a reverse-charge call to the news desk in London with a rising sense of dread.

'Jonny? Is that you?'

'Yeah, hey, Lukas, I'm sorry I missed your calls but—'

'Are you alright?'

Jonny hesitates. 'Yes – why?'

'The protests, man. Local channels are reporting that three people have been killed. And you've been AWOL all day.'

'Killed?' Jonny echoes. 'What, here? In the riots? That's what other reporters are saying?'

Lukas fills him in. Riots in other major Argentinian cities – Rosario, Cordoba, Mendoza too. A run on banks nationwide. Reports of three dead after police fired into a crowd. His? Jonny wonders. The sweat on his back turns from hot to cold.

'We got caught right outside a bank downtown. That's why I missed your calls,' he tells Lukas. 'It came out of nowhere. The crowd built in seconds. We were right in the middle of it. I'll have photos for you too, shortly. It was carnage—'

'The more you can file the better,' Lukas interrupts. 'I can get you top billing.'

'Really?' Jonny tries to keep the doubt out of his voice. After more than a year of freelance work he is inherently mistrustful of whatever his editors promise.

'*Ja*, of course. This is just the beginning, hey? Banks won't be able to open with a mob outside. What then? The story will run and run.'

'Too right,' Jonny replies, eyeing the floorboards in front of his bookcase. 'Can I dictate down the phone directly to you? It will be far quicker and easier than trying to put copy into an email. So many shops are damaged, I doubt I'll find an internet café fast enough.'

'For sure you can. And the more eyewitness the report is, the better, hey? Make the most of being in the right place at the right time.'

Jonny nods as if Lukas can see him. 'Give me two minutes to get my head straight and I'll call you right back.'

'Two minutes,' Lukas echoes before hanging up.

As soon as he does, Jonny launches himself towards his bookshelf.

'Screwdriver, screwdriver, screwdriver,' he mumbles, upending a chair as he yanks the bookcase away from the wall and grabs the screwdriver hidden behind it. Fumbling with the newer screws below, he hefts away the floorboard. And there it is – his iridium

– a state-of-the-art satellite phone, unbuggable, untraceable, top of precisely no one else's most-wanted lists except his.

Jonny runs a reverent finger over its black plastic casing, trying to conjure how he felt in the exact moment it was given to him. The most precious of gifts from Allen – a childhood friend of his mother's, who was also his former boss in Jerusalem. A boss he'd begged to keep after she was promoted to an executive job in Washington DC, while he had to start again in South America hoping no one ever found out about the hidden story he'd left behind. Wouldn't it be easier for his editor to be in a similar time-zone? Isn't there far more synergy between North and South America than Buenos Aires and London? Every time Jonny files a story on the economy he feels like he's being proved right, the International Monetary Fund in DC in control of all possible meaningful financial aid to the South. But Allen declared a conflict of interest as soon as she found out the extent of her personal connection to his past – and what his mother had done before she left Israel for good. By then Jonny needed to put as much distance between them as possible too. And that's why she gave him the phone. 'Now you know you can still call me anytime and anywhere,' she had said. If only Allen really was the sister he's never had.

Jonny tries to bundle that thought under the floorboards, resting the loose panel in position and shoving the loose screws into his pocket. He'll secure it properly when he's finished talking to Lukas. Heaving the bookcase back into place, he unlocks his front door and heads up the fire escape to the roof, snapping open the iridium's chubby aerial and pointing it at the sky. The light at its tip starts to flash immediately.

'Lukas?' Jonny is talking into the iridium's receiver almost before he's finished punching in the number. 'Can you hear me alright?'

'Loud and clear, buddy.'

'Sorry. I just had to change phones.'

'Never a problem if it means you aren't reversing the charges.'

But the irritation in Lukas's voice is growing, every word a little more clipped.

'It's just there's something else I need to talk to you about before we start.'

'To do with the financial crisis?'

'Not exactly.'

'Come on, man. Follow the money. That's all we need you to be doing out there.'

'I know, I know.' Jonny pictures Lukas, knows he is pushing himself to standing, running a hand through his sandy hair, squinting out of the window through his black-framed glasses to see if the Friday evening crowd is already spilling on to the pavement outside the pub next door to the office. 'But we got a tip from local police—'

'Local? You're filing for the *International Tribune*. The clue is in the name.'

'A headless torso washed up on a beach south of Buenos Aires a couple of weeks ago.' Jonny is suddenly gabbling, the words falling out of him like a torrent. 'But it hasn't hit even the local headlines. Which, given the historical precedent, is interesting, don't you think? So we—'

A volley of static suddenly bursts into his ear.

'Lukas? Are you still there?'

'Yep, I'm listening, although you nearly lost me at historical precedent. A body on the beach, you said? Like the ones that showed up during the Dirty War?'

'Exactly. We've been looking into it, on and off – in between covering the financial crisis, of course. Meeting relatives of the missing, trying to find out if there could be any sort of a connection there. I've been constantly looking over my shoulder the whole time expecting it to hit the local press. But there's been nothing. It's not even been written off as a drug cartel killing or business deal gone wrong. It's been buried, literally and figuratively. But then my notebook was stolen and some of our photos mysteriously disappeared. And last night I was abducted—'

Lukas's exclamation cuts him off this time.

'Listen, I know it sounds bad, but I'm OK. We'd been talking about what we knew—'

'We? What do you mean, we? Who? What happened, exactly?'

Jonny tries not to sigh directly into the receiver. 'Me and Paloma. The photographer I've been working with. We'd just come out of a restaurant, it was about ten p.m. We were standing on the pavement and some men suddenly surrounded us. It all happened so fast. Before I knew it there was a hood over my head and I was being dragged into a car—'

Another exclamation.

'I'm OK, though. I promise. I was only snatched so someone inside the car could talk to me. It was a military pilot; he was even in full uniform – medals, insignias, the lot. They took off the hood once we were on the move and he was just sitting there, ready to talk. About the Dirty War death flights, and about the body on the beach. But he wouldn't tell me who it belonged to, or how he knew about it, or even tell me his own name. Just said that I would have to find that out for myself and that he wouldn't have found me without it. The body is a message of a sort. I just haven't figured out what kind yet. But now I know it's connected to the Dirty War. And that elements of the military junta must still be operational underground.'

Lukas whistles, so piercingly clear through the direct satellite connection it sends a shiver down Jonny's back in spite of the heat. Suddenly he feels nothing but implacable relief that someone is reacting to his investigation in exactly the way he's expecting.

'Which is why I had to call you back,' he finishes. 'It's massive.

We can't talk about it on my normal phone line. Not now I know I'm not imagining the whole thing.'

'So who is this guy? And why has he come to you? Is he willing to go public and speak out against the military itself?'

'That's the problem. I don't know. I didn't get the chance to ask. They knocked me out before I was even close to finishing.'

'What? They beat you unconscious?'

'I actually think they drugged me. I came to on the pavement outside my apartment a few hours later. Which is something else I can't figure out. I get wanting to be anonymous and moving around in secret. But going to the trouble of bundling me into a moving car just so we can talk and then not telling me everything?'

'So what did this officer actually say? Walk me through it.'

'Well he spoke in English, which I also wasn't expecting. There was something strange about it though – he inverted everything in that weird way Americans do sometimes—'

'Get to the point, man.'

Jonny catches himself. 'Sorry. He said he flew some of the so-called death flights. Confirmed the months of torture that went on beforehand. Claimed he regretted it, and has regretted it every day since. He even said they were prisoners too, if you can believe that.'

'Who were prisoners too? The officers themselves?'

'I'm pretty sure that's what he meant. Especially since I just managed to get a look inside the former prison complex. It's right in the city and still operating as a military training facility. The pilot said the officers' quarters were directly below the cells. That they would pass prisoners on the stairs on the way to the torture chambers. That they were all imprisoned together, just on different floors. He made it sound like some subverted version of Stockholm Syndrome.'

'You saw this layout for yourself? How did you pull that off?'

'The riots were so intense that I was counting on the place emptying out to help with crowd control. And I think the current military command may be impressed with our coverage of the financial crisis. Money always talks. You've been schooling me on that yourself for long enough.'

But his compliment doesn't quite have the desired effect.

'The *Trib* does not pay for information, Jonny,' Lukas reminds him crisply. 'Don't tell me you bought your way inside a military facility, of all places.'

'Of course not,' Jonny exclaims. 'Quite the opposite, in fact...' He trails off into clearing his throat rather than reference the ginormous fine he managed to incur in the process. 'When I arrived, the place was emptying out exactly as I'd suspected it might. I squeezed through the gates just before they closed then pretended to be a tourist who'd made a mistake. I knew I'd be detained immediately and be able to scope the layout for myself.'

'How the hell did you get back out again?'

'It was clear pretty quickly that they spoke English. So I told them I was a journalist and mentioned our coverage of the financial crisis. That's what I meant earlier.'

'I thought you told them you were a tourist?'

'I did, but then I told them my Spanish isn't very good. I made out the whole thing was just a massive misunderstanding.'

Lukas snorts. 'That's ridiculous.'

'Maybe so, but it worked,' Jonny says, a little too defensively, reflecting again on the amount of money he might still have to pay. 'And the point is, the layout is exactly as the pilot described. More importantly, though, he told me this recent body on the beach was deliberately staged to look like an attempted disappearance. But when I asked why or how he knew, or who the victim was, he just talked about machines breaking.'

'Machines? What do you mean?'

'It was in the context of how the army was operating as a killing machine at the time. I pointed out this machine was made up of human beings, so mechanical failure was hardly the point, but—'

'Aha.' Lukas cuts him off. 'So this is a crisis of conscience.'

Jonny nods. 'Or something like that, anyway. He's full of regret. He was a prisoner too. But I still don't know who he is or have him on the record.'

'Think about it, man. Your pilot must have turned over something. It's been, what, fifteen years since the end of the Dirty War? And only now is he repentant, or willing to talk about being repentant. So it has to be about the body, right? He must be connected to the victim in some way.'

'But how am I supposed to figure that out without his help? And why wouldn't he just tell me the whole story? Who benefits otherwise?'

Lukas thinks for a moment.

'Who's your source on the body itself?'

'Local police in La Plata, like I said. Paloma got the original tip.'

'So that's your next step.' Lukas is brightening. 'Your pilot must be connected to your source, too. How else would he know about it otherwise? It's either that, or he's the person doing this most recent killing and staging. Which would make his decision to come to a journalist all the more curious, unless it's about fingering someone else for the crime as quickly as possible—'

'—and all he kept talking about were machines,' Jonny finishes softly. Something else is bothering him now.

'Forget the fucking machines, Jonny. You just need to go back to your original source. The one who leaked the whole thing to you in the first place.'

Jonny pauses. He sees it now. It's been right in front of his face the whole time. Except it isn't what he expected. Not even close.

'Jonny? Are you still there?'

'Yep, yep, I'm here.' But Jonny is suddenly miles away. He's asked himself before what else a woman like Paloma could possibly want from an inexperienced idiot like him other than work. Now he's feeling like his instinct has been right all along but in a way he could never have anticipated.

'You got tipped off to begin with, right? So that's where you start again.'

'Right. Yes. Thanks.' Jonny tries to sound as business-like as Lukas.

'And you update me every step of the way, hey? Use the internet. You won't believe how fast that thing is springing up…'

A few more instructions about the internet and its associated resources follow but Jonny's mind is stuck on a loop about Paloma, the police, the pilot and the victim. About how they must all be connected to one another.

'Now, let's get the financial crisis squared away,' Lukas finishes. 'You're our man in Buenos Aires. It's inconceivable that you don't deliver—'

'I'm ready,' Jonny interrupts, desperate to get the conversation back on surer footing. 'Like I told you before, we were caught right in the middle of the mob downtown.'

'We'll need those pictures in time for the first edition, hey. Almost more important than the words.'

Jonny tries not to let thoughts of Paloma put him off his stride. 'I'm on it, I promise. I don't even need to look at them to know they're amazing. We had a better view than anyone else there.'

'*Ja*, OK.' Lukas suddenly sounds far away, equipment humming and clicking in the background. 'Let's get this done, then. Are you ready?'

Jonny nods and nods until Lukas has to prompt him to actually start talking. And by the time they are finished, he has a plan for his investigation into the body on the beach too. There is finally purpose in Jonny's steps back down the fire escape and into his apartment. Packing the iridium carefully back below the floorboards, he screws the panel down tight, heaves the bookshelf on top. Sighing, he makes for the tiny fridge, suddenly so hungry he can almost taste the contents.

It's only then that he sees the envelope.

Chapter Fifteen

Jonny freezes on the spot, screwdriver pointed at the closed door like a weapon. Has the envelope been there all along? Did he miss it on his way to the roof? He squints – there are no footprints or signs of disturbance. Could the messenger still be outside the door? He cocks his head, listening as he drops silently to his knees, using the tip of his screwdriver to lift an edge of the manila envelope from the grubby floorboards.

Plain, rectangular, unaddressed. Bigger than an average letter. So flat it could be empty. Jonny forces himself to assess the envelope as a foreign object rather than an unexploded bomb. Is he absolutely sure it wasn't there when he first arrived? What difference would it make if it was? It's just an envelope, isn't it? Just a simple note pushed under the door? He reaches out with his screwdriver again, prods the front, yep, definitely an envelope, definitely made of paper, even if it is the thick, luxurious kind that usually comes with a letterhead.

Jonny's screwdriver moves to the back of his head this time, scratches gently at his hair. Usually what little post he gets is left in the mailboxes just inside the security gate downstairs. But wasn't there once an invite from the students on the floor below? A grill sizzling on the roof, warm cans of Quilmes beer, a cooler full of sickly-sweet ice lollies. Jonny's stomach suddenly twists. Hell, he is starving. And now all he's got is this fucking envelope, only paper and card, when in actual fact, all he'd wanted was a freshly made *choripan* – actually a proper English hot dog with mustard, and an ice-cold lemon squash.

Jonny's guts suddenly twist again in an altogether different way. Because he's pretty sure that there is no way this envelope is just a fucking envelope.

Tucking his screwdriver behind his ear like a pencil, Jonny leans over and opens it. The piece of paper inside comes out face down. A stiff, thick and glossy sheet of paper, still redolent of the chemicals used to print it. He swallows, hard, last vestiges of his hunger curdling to dread, only realising he is shaking when his screwdriver clatters to the floor.

A photograph is sitting in his lap. And it's not the sort of picture Jonny ever wanted to see again.

A body.

Another body.

Mutilated and staged in the same unmistakable way as the first. The only identifying mark a tattoo on the chest. A tattoo Jonny is sure he has seen before. Along with the medals purposefully arranged alongside it.

The glossy sheet slithers off his legs as Jonny wobbles upright, staggering to the open window, gulping great draughts of humid air. He knuckles his eyes as if he can physically wipe the image from his brain. Who delivered this message? And are they still watching him? Could they still be inside the building? Panicked, he spins round, only to confront the snapshot of horror on the floor. Reaching for his screwdriver, he uses its tip to flip the picture face down again. The patent shine on its back gives off a knowing gleam.

There's been another murder, of that there is no doubt. But why? And when? Jonny eyes the pristine freshness of the white gloss on the floor. All it means is the photograph was recently developed. It doesn't necessarily mean the crime took place just as recently. Standing, he returns to the window, gulps another draught of air, starts again.

The body on the beach was a female. With the same tattoo on

the chest. Connected, Jonny has now established, to the pilot, who confirmed that the similarities to Dirty War atrocities are not at all coincidental.

This body is most definitely male. With an identical tattoo on the chest. And this photograph has been delivered directly to Jonny's door. So the messenger must have knowledge of, or be connected to, Jonny's existing information. Sticking a photo of a dismembered body under his front door just because he's a journalist would be one grisly coincidence too far.

Jonny turns back into the room, tries not to look at the photograph itself as he picks up the thick manila envelope. His gaze snags on his bookcase, mentally reaffirms the scribbled notes stashed below. What was it that Abuela had said – that there would always be too many to bring to justice? That it takes an entire army to perpetrate elimination on this scale? Jonny traces a fingertip over the embossing on the corner of the envelope, needing to physically feel it for the conclusion to take shape inside his head.

For in the corner, invisible to all except those physically looking for it, is the embossed crest of the Argentinian military. An insignia Jonny saw for himself, gazing up at the crown in the centre of the ESMA's pristine white façade.

Jonny's finger stills. This particular message is suddenly clear and keen as the outline of the emblem itself. He flips over the photograph, stares as dispassionately as he can at the medals laid alongside the faded tattoo on the mutilated chest – the same tattoo he first saw on a different mutilated chest two weeks ago – and draws the only possible conclusion he can.

He knew the pilot and the body on the beach had to be connected. And now he knows he's right.

The pilot's dead. Jonny is one of the last people he spoke to. He could be next.

Chapter Sixteen

Jonny screws his eyes shut. Time slows as his stress response spins, veering wildly between fight, freeze and flight. He's suddenly nine years old again and asking what it means for someone to take their own life. His own mother has killed herself and he can't make sense of it, no matter how hard he tries. The only emotional impulse available to try to stop time moving on from the moment before everything changed forever. But by now Jonny's adult brain has processed more than enough to know that time doesn't slow for anyone or anything. Time just ticks on, no matter what agony the future holds. By the time he opens his eyes, Jonny is spoiling for a fight. No photograph, no matter how gruesome, is going to stop him.

He shoves the bookcase away with one hand, wrenches the loose panel aside with the other. Scribbles down a quick copy of the notes he'd made in Hebrew. Grabs a handful of change from his stockpile of cash. Stows the envelope and its horrifying contents alongside the rest. He's back on his feet and listening at the door in a matter of seconds.

Outside, the balcony is deserted. Reassuringly standard sounds lap through the air – the clank of a saucepan, the click of a key in a lock, the distant hum of a radio. He speeds down the stairs, finds reassuringly standard activity under way on the road too. Pavement barbecue: check. Backfiring motorbike: check. Setting off for the internet café a few blocks away, Jonny relives the very end of his conversation with Lukas, the bit he'd zoned out on while his mind was too busy spinning over Paloma – as per fucking usual, then. He grits his teeth as he walks, breathing hard.

There will be clues all over the internet, Lukas had said. The still-nascent worldwide web is springing connections between people and places faster than anyone could have imagined. Websites are promising to reconnect people who are thousands of miles apart and who hardly knew each other in the first place. The internet is already revolutionising all types of businesses, including journalism. The transformation of the traditional news model is happening so fast that consumers themselves can't even keep up. Imagine a live feed of information, accessible from any computer screen. Just imagine, Jonny thinks ruefully. He hadn't been concentrating then, but he couldn't be more focused now. And if there are already clues all over the internet, Jonny can damn well leave a trail of his own behind too. What did Lukas call it? A digital footprint.

Another block down the street and the exaggerated architecture of the Abasto shopping centre unfurls in its jubilant loops and curls. Jonny shivers the moment he walks through its extravagantly huge glass doors. Despite their immaculate reflection, the shops inside are deserted. He takes the escalator down to the lower level, making for the blue-and-yellow frontage of the small internet kiosk in the far corner. Another shop that is deserted despite being open.

Jonny pauses on the threshold, scanning the interior for a staff member. Empty cubicles line the walls on either side, each housing a dark, silent computer monitor. Large maps covered in cartoonish arrows linking islands and continents are pinned up all over the walls. A door opens suddenly at the back of the shop.

Jonny raises a hand by way of greeting. A man hurries forward – short, round, doused in enough cheap cologne to dissolve fabric. A gold crucifix tinkles from a string of blue-and-white ceramic beads looped around his neck. Meeting him halfway, Jonny is ushered to a booth in the far corner. Once the man turns back to the till, he surreptitiously moves himself to the adjacent booth, just in case the first was chosen for a reason.

The computer hums as Jonny flicks it on, sliding coins into the box mounted on the wall alongside it. He is dialled online in seconds, monitor flashing first bright blue, then white, as the connection is established. Pulling the hastily scribbled copy of his notes from his pocket, Jonny smooths it flat with a shaky hand, suddenly stymied by what comes next. A photograph of a mutilated body has just landed anonymously on his doormat, and he thinks he can defend himself by typing information into a search box? But before he has a chance to do anything else, an unmistakable exclamation suddenly rings out behind him.

'I thought ... I thought I might find you in here,' Paloma stammers.

But when Jonny turns around, she looks like she'd thought anything but, shifting nervously from foot to foot, tangling with her sleeves. The air between them thickens, charged with suspicion.

'Me? What about you?' Jonny fights to keep his voice level.

'Photos,' Paloma replies shortly. She avoids his gaze to dig around in her handbag.

He's about to ask how she can have possibly developed this morning's film so quickly when the door in the back wall scrapes open again. In a jangle of bracelets, Paloma motions that she'll join Jonny in his cubicle. The door closes with a tinkle of ceramic beads.

'Obviously I don't have today's film printed yet. But I wanted to have another look at the roll before that. I copied those pictures on to a disk as soon as I realised one was missing.'

She pulls a chair into the booth and sits down next to Jonny. Plugging a thumb drive into the unit below the desk, she grabs the mouse with her other hand.

'Haven't you already filed?' She rattles the mouse.

'Yes, I have,' Jonny answers carefully. 'And yes, of course I promised the best pictures in town. The minute I'd said we were caught in the middle of it I could hear Lukas practically salivating down the phone.'

The start of Paloma's smile fades as she notes his grim expression. 'So what are you doing in here?'

He beckons her closer, looking over both of their shoulders. 'It's the pilot,' he mouths. 'I think he's dead.'

'The pilot,' she murmurs, replacing the mouse on the desk with a soft click. 'Do you mean...'

'Yes.' Jonny's nod turns to a flinch as the coin box pings.

Paloma just stares at him with a pained, questioning expression frozen on her face.

'When I got home someone had pushed an envelope under my door. There was a picture inside. No message, just a picture of a body...'

At that Jonny has to pause, Paloma covering her mouth with a hand.

'It was in the same state as the last one, if you get my drift. It wasn't ... It wasn't a complete corpse. It had exactly the same lack of identifying characteristics other than a tattoo on the left side of the chest.'

'So how do you know it belongs to him?'

'It was delivered in a military envelope. There was even a naval crest stamped in the corner. The medals I saw on his uniform last night were deliberately laid out next to him.'

'So what are you doing in here? It couldn't be more obvious that we're putting ourselves in danger if we keep digging around. What else needs to happen for you to drop it?'

'I could say the same to you,' Jonny shoots back, jerking his head at the thumb drive still plugged into the unit below the desk.

At that Paloma has to look away, a flicker of something else passing across her face. 'Well, I had no idea, did I? Why didn't you ring me first?'

Jonny is suddenly hesitating, stuck back in his mental loop

about Paloma, the police, the pilot and the victim. About how they must all be connected to one another.

'I tried to,' he lies. 'No one picked up. I was hardly going to pace around while I waited for you to answer my calls. And as it turns out, you were already a step ahead of me. I know it's scary. You think I'm not scared too? I went to the ESMA after I left you. I saw inside those fucking cells for myself.'

Paloma gasps. 'But how—?'

'It doesn't matter how. All that matters now is why. The place is set up exactly as the pilot said. They were all held together. Officers and prisoners, one on top of the other, for months and months and months. There were female names scratched all over the walls – wives, daughters, sisters, who knows. All I can be sure of is that the pilot deliberately chose to talk to me because of the body on the beach. Which we know for sure, without putting too fine a point on it – belonged to a woman. And since I just had a photo of his identically dismembered remains delivered to my door, all I can think is that she was one of those prisoners, and they had a relationship of some kind. I have to find out who they were.'

'No, Jonny.' Paloma is shrill with fear. 'Please. This is madness, you have to stop.'

'The pilot's dead and I'm probably one of the last people he spoke to. We can't just let it drop. People can't keep dying for nothing.'

'We'll be next if we're not careful. I was so worried when you disappeared last night, I even found myself calling my parents and telling them everything.'

'Lucky you,' Jonny mutters – he can't help himself. 'Presumably they told you to back off too. Like any sane parent would unless they were addled with grief.'

'Of course they did. We have to. No one has our backs. We've got no leverage at all.'

'And that's what I'm doing in here,' Jonny finishes, rattling the mouse. There will be clues all over the internet, he thinks again, suddenly almost salivating himself.

Paloma balks, looking around the deserted shop. 'In here?'

'Yes, in here,' Jonny replies, bringing up a webpage, using the cursor to highlight the motto running along the top. 'Just look at this. See? The place to find old friends and new.'

'Be reunited?' Paloma reads questioningly back at him. 'What does that mean?'

'Find old friends. Connect with long-lost relatives. Get back together again. Be reunited.' Jonny moves the cursor. 'And here, look.'

'Three million users already?' Paloma is astonished.

'Three million,' Jonny echoes. 'Nearly three million people have reconnected around the world just by using this search engine. And that's just the start – loads more will have made more connections as a result.'

Jonny's breath catches as Paloma's hand closes over his, moving the mouse for herself. 'How ... how does it work?'

Jonny watches the cursor trembling; it's as if she doesn't know where to put it. 'You make an account. You put in loads of information about yourself, click enter, and then see what comes back.'

'The internet can do that?'

'It's not all that surprising when you think about it. The internet is a machine capable of handling unthinkable amounts of information. The only way humans can keep up is to harness it themselves. You can narrow down searches by country – here.' He drags the cursor over to a dialog box marked with flags. 'All of these entries are Argentinian. If we comb through each one, who knows what we might find.'

He starts as Paloma yanks her hand away, shaking her head. 'You said you were in here to protect us. Not to keep obsessing over this.'

'I am,' Jonny answers. 'Because that's not all we're going to do. Just stop and think about it for a second. If we put everything we know on the internet, too, it'll be immortalised forever in cyberspace. It'll never disappear. You think no one has our backs? Three million people from all over the world are looking at these files. That number is growing all the time. And anyone can set up an account. No one is checking to make sure the person who sets it up is who they say they are. We can write up profiles for all the missing people we know about. We might actually find out what happened to some of those babies.'

Jonny's mind begins to spin with possibility. Who's to say his long-lost twin sister isn't one of the millions of people already using this website? *That takes another kind of machine*, he thinks, picturing Abuela's sunken face. *And some of us don't have much time left*.

Another ping signals only ten minutes left on the clock. But this time, neither of them flinch.

Leaning over, Paloma grabs the mouse for herself. 'I'll do it. You know I'm faster. You read, I'll write.'

'Perfect,' Jonny answers, looking down at his notes.

He picks a place to start, but Paloma is already typing. There's not enough time left to wonder about what's changed her mind.

Chapter Seventeen

They speed back through the deserted shopping centre in silence. Outside, dusk is falling, tuning the sky's blue up to purple.

Paloma turns in the direction of her apartment. 'Are you coming up?'

Jonny slows, trying to catch her eye. 'To yours?'

'If you don't mind.'

'Of course I don't mind,' he answers, quickening his step, brain moving in an altogether different direction. The last time he set foot in his own apartment there was a photo of a dismembered corpse lying on the doormat. If it wasn't for what's still hiding under his floorboards he'd ideally never return there. And he's got a whole lot more questions for Paloma. But what is she actually asking him – if he'll walk her home? If he'll come inside and talk? Eat, even? Or share a drink? Suddenly he finds himself having to hurry to catch her up. He's never been inside her apartment before.

'It's just,' she says quietly, 'after everything that's happened, you know…'

'Right, right.' Jonny stares at the sky.

They remain in awkward silence until they reach her apartment building. A neighbour buzzes them in. He's still lagging when Paloma reaches her front door on the top floor.

'Are you hungry?' she asks.

Jonny can't help but snort. He's been hungry for what feels like days now.

'It's only bread and cheese,' she adds.

'Sounds great,' he answers hurriedly.

Paloma shoves open her door. Following her inside, Jonny finds that he's holding his breath.

'Beer?' She kneels to open her fridge; it's in the exact same spot as Jonny's. He eyes the rest of her apartment – laid out identically to his bar a few more books in her bookcase, a few extra cupboards on the walls.

'Are you having one?'

'Sure.' She pulls out a large bottle of Quilmes, puts it on the table between them, followed by a cellophane bag of sliced white bread and a couple of packets of processed cheese and ham.

'*Sandwiches de miga,*' Jonny pronounces, trying to get some sort of conversation going. An Argentine staple – sandwiches made from only the spongiest parts of a plain white loaf. But Paloma just throws him a frown.

'I've always hated crusts,' he adds. 'I just never imagined anywhere would be able to turn it into a selling point when it comes to ham and cheese toasties.'

He waits for Paloma to sit down before following her lead. There's a hiss and sigh as she snaps the cap off the bottle of beer, then takes a deep draught directly from the bottle.

'Ham and cheese or just cheese?' Jonny ploughs on, untying the plastic bag of bread.

'Not for me. You go ahead, though.' She puts the bottle down and pushes it towards him. 'And don't let me drink all this.'

Jonny swaps bread for beer. The ice-cold brew fizzes into his stomach.

'Go on. I told you to, didn't I?' Paloma jerks her head at the food on the table. 'You're doing that weird thing you do when you're so hungry you can't concentrate.'

'What thing?' But Jonny is already reaching for the bread again.

'You can't tear your eyes away...'

'From what? Food?' Jonny crams a piece of ham into his mouth.

Paloma lets out a brittle little laugh. Opening a cupboard, Jonny pulls out a couple of chipped white plates, moving to the drawer under the sink for some cutlery. He hesitates at the sight of a set of stubby-looking knives laid neatly side by side in a black velvet box. Knives of a kind he doesn't think he's ever seen before – short, almost dart-like blades with gleaming porcelain handles.

'These look nice,' he remarks lamely. 'Where did you get them? Are you sure I can't make you a sandwich too?'

'From home. And no, thanks. I'm not hungry.'

Jonny eyes the box. Are these steak knives? He's sure they're usually slim and elegant. And why would anyone bring their own to Argentina, whatever their shape and size? Steak and its accompaniments are even more common here than the bread he's slapping together into a sandwich. He decides to pull the crusts off with his fingers like he usually does rather than chance the knives.

Paloma pushes the beer bottle towards Jonny again, motioning that he drink up. 'There's more in the fridge if you want it.'

Jonny alternates between beer and food rather than ask any more questions. The growing silence takes on an almost physical quality, settling into the chair between them.

'You can stay.' Paloma's voice echoes abruptly around the small room. 'I want you to, I mean. Stay. If you wouldn't mind. I'm just so tired, and I don't think I'll be able to sleep at all unless someone else is here.'

Jonny drains the rest of the beer to stop his mouth from dropping open. Stay? Here? With her? Where? His head revolves on his neck like some sort of brainless automaton, taking in the single bed, the linoleum floor, the two grubby cushions turning the top of the low bookcase into an extra seat. Paloma suddenly gets up, pushing back her chair with an uncomfortable clang.

'Of course I can stay,' Jonny answers hurriedly. 'I'd, well, I'd prefer it too, to be honest. I mean, who wouldn't? After everything that has happened today.'

He swigs pointlessly from the empty bottle, tries to swallow down the urge to keep talking, to just keep rattling on like some verbally incontinent fucking idiot. *After everything that's happened today?*

Paloma can't even look at him as she turns around. 'It's just all so hard to believe.'

'Try and rest,' he says, pointing with the bottle at her bed in the corner. 'I'll be here, don't worry. I'm so tired I could sleep anywhere.' He lets out an awkward little laugh.

When he looks up, she's disappearing into her tiny bathroom without another word.

Moving over to her open window, Jonny scans the street below, registers its comings and goings in a trance, suddenly with no idea what he's looking for. Behind him, there's a click as Paloma turns out the light. When he finally turns around, she is lying face down on her bed, still fully clothed.

Setting his bottle gently into the sink, he collects up her stray cushions, fashions himself a nest on the floor beside her. Only when he lies down himself does Paloma let out a soft sigh.

Jonny blinks into the dark, lying on his side, tries to find the words to formulate the question. What is she hiding from him? And more importantly, why?

'Are you scared?' Paloma's voice is muffled by her pillow.

'A bit,' he answers after moment. 'I know, I should be terrified. But the thing is, and I know it sounds crazy, it's the thought of all those people and the way they died that's stopping me being scared myself. It's the thought of all those families that still have no idea what really happened. What right do I have to be scared in the face of that?'

The silence sharpens its elbows between them.

Jonny tries again. 'Look, the fact that I'm not terrified enough says far more about me than it does about you. But I just can't let it go. Is there anything worse than withholding information about where people are? Or about what really happened to them? The thought of being trapped in limbo, of not knowing the truth or having any sort of closure. And people not knowing who they really are? Or where they really come from? All those babies that might be living as other people? I don't think even physical pain comes close to the thought of any of that.'

'Neither do I,' Paloma finally answers, her whisper floating in the space closing between them. An inescapable instinct twitches in Jonny before he can tamp it down.

Paloma sighs again, this time so long and deep that Jonny knows she's sitting up – is she reaching out for him? But the sound that follows is so unmistakable his own breath stills in his throat.

Squinting into the dark, every fibre of Jonny's body realigns itself in an altogether different direction.

A key is turning in the lock.

Chapter Eighteen

Time slows again. But by now Jonny is primed to seize the illusory extra seconds, prolong every last one. Locate escape routes – Paloma's tiny balcony beyond her wide-open window. Identify defensive weapons – the pointed corners of her bookcase, the chipped edge of a heavy china plate. Assess threat level – these are the short, sharp, deliberate clicks of a key fitting into the lock, not the frenzied jab of a mismatched coat hanger or a pin.

There Jonny tenses. Because the only sound that is conspicuously missing from these illusory extra few seconds is any kind of sound from Paloma herself.

All the possible explanations for why it doesn't seem to be coming as a surprise to Paloma that someone else has a key to her apartment and is unlocking the door in the most covert way possible coalesce into a single, inescapable one.

That she must already know who it is.

And then those precious extra seconds fold.

The apartment explodes into commotion.

Jonny's already on his feet as the door flies open. A yank at his arm and Paloma is in front of him, feet planted, hands out. A chair crashes over, a dark shape materialising in the door frame. Spanish, too frenzied and rapid for Jonny to identify a word from the next, ricochets between them. The door closes again with a thump, more shapes whirling in the dark – outlines, shadows, reflections – and the ghostly gleam of white porcelain.

Jonny lunges, but Paloma gets there first. The steak knife lands with a dull thud. The dark shape slumps, heavy as a felled tree. The commotion falls away almost as quickly as it arrived.

Jonny wills time to slow again, for the shadows to languidly warp and shift, but there's nothing except white porcelain, shimmering insolently up from the blackness on the floor.

'Fuck.' Jonny sags, staggering backward. 'Fuck, Paloma. What did you do?'

Between them, the shape lets out a hiss like a deflating balloon. Somewhere on the street below, a motorbike backfires before zooming away.

Jonny fumbles for the switch by the door, flooding the room with light and immediately wishing he hadn't. The body on the floor is an unidentifiable heap clad in black from head to toe save for the gun complete with cylindrical silencer on the end falling from a slack, gloved hand. He stares at the chest – muscular, barrel-shaped – willing that it rise and fall a fraction enough to confirm Paloma hasn't just killed a man before his eyes. But all he seems to be able to focus on is the gleaming china handle protruding at a grotesquely jaunty angle from the man's side.

Jonny curses again. 'I don't … I don't think he's breathing. Is he breathing? Fucking hell, Paloma. Did we – I mean, did you…?'

'Shhhhh.' Paloma lifts a finger to her lips. She opens a cupboard, the one he was sure held nothing but a pathetically mismatched set of crockery. Instead out comes a roll of paper towel and a plastic bottle of bleach.

'What the fuck are you doing?' Now Jonny sounds like he's being strangled. When he looks back, Paloma is already wiping off the porcelain sticking out of the body on the floor.

'I don't understand,' he mutters, propping himself against the wall.

'I think you do,' Paloma replies softly, rocking back on her heels.

Jonny's heartbeat accelerates up his throat like vomit. For all he thought he was finally starting to understand about Paloma, he now knows for sure she is capable of stabbing someone with a steak knife at a moment's notice. Tears are suddenly leaking from her eyes, their tracks shining in the dark.

'What the hell is going on, Paloma? Did you ... did you set me up?'

'Of course I didn't. You have to believe me. I could never do that, not in a million years.'

Jonny laughs suddenly, high and mad. 'Well, I've just watched you do a whole lot fucking worse.'

'I saved your life. And I had to. You didn't stand a chance.'

'Why? Because I didn't know what was coming, and you did?'

'No. I mean, I suspected, but—'

'Suspected what? That people were coming after us? Like it wasn't already obvious?'

'They told me I had to,' Paloma is suddenly whispering. 'That we were getting too close.'

'*They* told you? Who are they? Too close to what?'

'You tell me what.'

Jonny hesitates again. His eyes flutter closed for a moment. He's trapped in a liminal emotional space, the blessed relief that he can still trust his instincts jostling with the terrifying consequences of them being right. When he opens his eyes again, Paloma looks like a completely different person. The one he's gradually but inescapably started to suspect as having a different agenda to his.

'I don't know,' he begins, acting on another hunch. 'Not least because someone stole my notebook. A notebook full of fragments and scribbles that would only make sense to one other person in the entire fucking world. That's you, by the way. In case it wasn't already obvious.'

She has the grace to look uncomfortable. 'I didn't plan to steal it. I thought you'd assume you'd just lost it, or someone else had taken it, and then I could return it without you realising what had really happened. I just panicked—'

'About what? Why didn't you just talk to me instead of paying some random woman to tell me I was being followed so I wouldn't suspect you? How stupid do you think I am? It was crammed in next to a wallet with actual money in it – of far more interest to everyone else in this city except us. What was so important to you that you had to go to such absurd lengths to steal it from me?'

'I didn't even know myself until I realised one of my photos was missing too.'

Jonny shakes his head. 'You paid someone to fabricate a conspiracy only to discover there actually is one. Great. You should have just listened to me to start with. Would have saved you a whole lot of trouble.'

He flinches as Paloma suddenly gets to her feet, finger stabbing between them.

'How about you answer my questions for a second? Like everything you've been hiding from me too, for a start.'

'I haven't hidden anything. You're the one who's wanted to drop the story at practically every turn over the last couple of days.'

'Don't lie to me. Why else would you start writing notes in Hebrew – a language I can't even read?'

'Because by then I didn't think I could completely trust you. And it turns out I was right. You were already insisting on translating rather than letting me ask any questions myself. You were arguing over taking any more pictures – as if that was ever going to make any fucking sense coming from a photographer almost totally out of work. You were lying about where you were going, what you were doing. What were you really hoping to achieve in that internet café before you discovered I was already there? And never mind all the banging on about dropping the whole thing. I'm still not sure—'

'Of what?'

'Of anything!' Jonny can't keep the panic out of his voice. 'You think I've been hiding things from you? How about what you've been hiding from me! There are more than two sides to this story. We're supposed to be the journalists not taking sides, but you're nowhere near neutral are you? You're part of this. I know you are, but I don't know...'

'...why?' Paloma finishes his sentence.

Jonny's hand trembles as he gestures at the unconscious body on the floor. 'You also don't seem to care about the fact you might have just killed someone.'

'He's not dead.'

Jonny blanches. 'How do you know? Who is he? And who the hell are you?'

'That's just it.' Paloma is suddenly mumbling, hanging her head. 'I don't know.'

Another piece of the puzzle clicks nauseatingly into place inside Jonny's mind. His hand drops to his side. Paloma continues in little more than a whisper.

'I've always known I was adopted. A longed-for only child. My parents even kept my original name. They said it was to respect my heritage. That it was in honour of my roots. But that was the only part that made sense. Nothing else did. Nothing else at all.'

Jonny reels.

They know babies were stolen.

They know these same babies were given to so-called suitable families, to supporters of the regime, to military couples struggling to conceive.

Of course it is equally conceivable that some of those families were Americans. That some of those babies might have been trafficked across international borders. At the time, there was no greater or more powerful supporter of Argentina's military regime itself than the United States.

Jonny eyes the motionless shape on the floor. The rest of his questions dead-end into the inescapable reality that this particular body should, in fact, have been his own. 'We need to get help,' he mumbles.

'No.' Paloma straightens up, whites of her eyes flashing in the dark. 'We need to run.'

Chapter Nineteen

Retiro bus station. A terminal so gigantic that even the Spanish word for the place is *Omnibus*. Jonny loiters in the shadow of a kiosk, watching dead-eyed hawkers at work, jaws grinding with amphetamine zeal, pouches strapped tightly around their waists, bulging with a whole lot more than money. From one end of the plaza to the other, giant coaches are pulling in and out of bays, loading and unloading with rampant efficiency. Ticket vendors are streaking up and down the main concourse, yodelling out what they have to offer. The Trans-Andean Express will get you to Chile before noon. Tierra del Fuego, gateway to the Antarctic, is only two days of driving through the Patagonian wilderness. Jonny checks his watch for at least the eightieth time. Nearly two a.m. Not long to wait now.

The man on the floor would be fine, Paloma had insisted. She hadn't stabbed him, not even close. It turned out those fancy knives weren't knives at all. Just state-of-the-art stunning darts, no wonder the so-called blades looked blunt as lead. Stunning is supposed to be humane. The animal in question is supposed to wake up in perfect health a matter of hours later. Paloma had just knocked the intruder out. For how long, she couldn't be sure, but if he was a horse, she'd have been able to time it to the minute. Jonny pictures mounted police falling back at just the sight of her – some of the world's finest horses literally bowing their implacable heads, glossy manes swishing like giant curtains on the most epic of performances. Jonny had known then, hadn't he? He just hadn't understood.

Paloma, on the other hand, had suspected the story of her own origins long before coming to Buenos Aires for work. Why did her family spend so much time in Argentina, and not Mexico, her so-called land of origin? They kept her birth name to maintain links to her heritage but never took her to visit a country less than a hundred miles away? Why did her parents, who both worked for the US government, only have maps of South America on the walls – not even Central America, where their beloved only child supposedly originated? And why were they so alive to the twists and turns of Argentinian politics?

Because, as it turned out, they were both former advisers to US Secretary of State Henry Kissinger himself. Both were in on Operation Condor and the enabling of the Dirty War from the ground up. And, as it also turned out, both were incapable of conceiving naturally. That's why they had adopted her. From Mexico, they had always said. That's why they moved to New Mexico from DC, they'd also said – abandoning their jobs at the State Department in favour of occasional big consultancy contracts for the US Treasury. They did it all to be as close to her cultural heritage as possible. Paloma's voice had cracked then. Jonny flashes on the image of Paloma as a baby, decked out in an Argentinian football kit, posing outside the Boca Juniors stadium sometime during the Dirty War itself – a photograph he doesn't need to see for himself to understand its significance. When she told them about their investigation the night that Jonny was abducted, they almost gave themselves away. They told her we were getting too close, Jonny remembers. Now he understands exactly what they meant.

But how can she be sure, he went on to ask, but was met by a violent shake of her head. Not now, she answered as the shape on the floor wheezed. And when she opened up that stupid cupboard again, part of Jonny still hoped she was going to pull out some fucking spoons and hand him a pot of *dulce de leche*. Part of Jonny was still fantasising about spending endless days and nights walking the fascinating cobbled streets of this intoxicating city arm-in-arm, stopping only to watch pavement tango in a blaze of violet jacaranda blossom. Part of Jonny was still picturing a sepia snapshot of a life he should have known would never, ever be his own. Instead out came a rucksack, long-packed and bulging, he presumed, with everything she'd ever need to make a quick getaway.

And what about Jonny's own long-packed rucksack, stuffed into the dark cavern under his floorboards? A cavern hollowed out to hide not only his scraps of evidence and emergency cash, but the precious few possessions that he actually values. Suddenly these treasures are all he can think about, even in the blaze of noise from the vendors all around him brandishing their impossible promises of escape and redemption in faraway lands. You either have to leave all your stuff behind or let me go and get it for you, Paloma had said. You're in more danger of being spotted out and about than I am. So either you tell me exactly what you need and where to find it, or you let it go. I'm trusting you with all my stuff, she'd added, handing over her own backpack and promising to take the same care of his.

But her bag just hangs off his back like a dead weight. Because now someone else knows he's the kind of person who goes to the trouble of carving out his own personal safe. Now someone else knows he keeps hold of things that to the uneducated eye will look like the work of a crazy person, a total madman.

Forget the notebooks, the scribbles, the clues on different bits and pieces of paper. Even his prized fucking iridium. It's the cardboard box, papered in gold, containing the clippings from the first time Jonny cut his fingernails after his mother died. He would have grown them forever if he could. They were a part of him from the moment before everything changed forever. He didn't want to move on. He still can't move forward without unspeakable pain and loneliness puncturing his every solo moment. Same for the hairs he'd pulled from his comb and stored along with the bundle he'd pulled from hers. An unwashed handkerchief, fusty with dried tears, rich with her scent, a pain frozen in time. Pieces of himself he can keep from a time that he's forever lost. And now he's had to share them with someone else to have a chance of keeping hold of them at all. He peers out from the shadow of the kiosk, a single tear rolling treacherously down his cheek. Paloma is nowhere to be seen.

The only choice they have left now is to prove everything they know, Jonny thinks, tugging at the straps fastened like a clamp across his chest. Paloma deserves to know who she really is. And finding out will prove that babies were kidnapped during the Dirty War and trafficked with international impunity. It's a massive global news story, and that's before getting into how elements of Argentina's former military junta are still operational underground. The pilot went to a whole lot of trouble to tell Jonny the body on the beach was deliberately staged to look like an attempted disappearance. One that still conspicuously hasn't hit any kind of local news headlines despite its inflammatory connotations. Why? Jonny tries to concentrate on the mechanics of where they can go and what they can do next rather than reflect on the pictures of two identically dismembered bodies still scorched into his mind. Telling the world the truth is the only way to definitively save him and Paloma from the same fate.

But there is another option. Jonny starts at the little voice chiming in his inner ear, suddenly back at his perennial clifftop, teetering on the edge of his emotional precipice. Surely the only sane choice left is to drop the lot and walk away? For Jonny has been in this position before. And back then he chose the most unprofessional path of all. He willingly chose to bury the twisted truth of what he'd discovered on his first foreign assignment in the Middle East – the literal job of a lifetime – because the personal stakes were too high. Is that why he can't even conceive of doing it this time? Even when, this time, it's drop the story or most probably die trying to get to the truth of it?

Jonny shakes his head, tries to send that little voice flying, but the cold, hard reality of his position just becomes clearer and clearer. His choice should be obvious. He should step away from the edge. He should consider himself warned for the final time. And he should encourage Paloma to go home and confront her parents. To get on the next available plane and fly safely away from the storm. But it's the one choice he can't bring himself to make. Two years after burying the truth of how far people will go in the name of peace, he still hasn't salvaged enough peace for himself to have any real choice at all. The job is all he's got. The job is his life. Two years later, he still has nothing else to speak of. His only real choice is to find out the truth and then tell the world about it, hoping it will make the difference he craves.

A low boom chiming from the clock overhead sends a flock of birds skittering from the rafters. Jonny only realises he's screwed his eyes shut when they fly open as he feels a nudge to his side.

'You made it,' he whispers, the sight of his rucksack on Paloma's back wiping his mind clean of everything except checking through its contents. 'Did you—?'

She silences him with a nod. Jonny unbuckles her backpack, swaps it for his own. Weight lifts from his shoulders even as he refastens the straps. Meeting her gaze, understanding passes silently between them. They've already discussed where they're going to go next. They just don't know what they're going to find at the other end.

Stepping from the shadows, they move purposefully down the concourse. The bus pulls into its allotted stand in the far corner, right on cue. Quickening their step, they're in front of the doors as they open, up into the vehicle's dark, cavernous insides as they close. They sit next to each other across an aisle, positioning their backpacks to their either side so there's no view from the window seats, either inside or out.

Jonny feels the tension in his body disengage with the brakes. The bus is already on its way.

Chapter Twenty

Jonny steals a glance at Paloma; she's barely blinking as she stares straight ahead. They are long out of Buenos Aires now, miles slipping past on the fast, smooth expressway heading north. He stands, confirming for the final time exactly where everyone else on the bus is sitting and anything they might be doing other than sleeping, before pushing his backpack into the footwell and shifting over to his window seat. Paloma follows his lead, comes to sit beside him with her own backpack at her feet.

Jonny hesitates. What now? Their frantic, panicked planning had only got them this far. Get on the bus due to stop at Retiro for the shortest amount of time. Preferably on a route heading north rather than south, where their journey only needs to pause when it hits the Brazilian or Paraguayan border some thousand kilometres away, rather than dead-ending into the frigid sea separating the southern tip of Argentina from the Antarctic. On the face of it, they're on the most ideal route of all, hugging the border with Uruguay almost all the way to the northern Argentinian city of Posadas. It was only after the bus had pulled out of Retiro that Jonny remembered that this particular part of the Uruguayan border is demarcated by a rushing, swollen river rather than an unpoliced no-man's land of pampas grass. But by then they were committed to sitting separately and silently in the dark for at least two hours until the first stop on the route, watching and waiting to see who else was also on the bus that might be doing anything remotely unusual during the dead hours before dawn.

'We can get off at Concordia,' Paloma mutters.

It's as if he's asked his question out loud. Jonny nods back. The same possibility had occurred to him when he'd studied the map and noted the sleepy city of Concordia, an obvious transit point a few hours along the way. Of course they weren't going to go all the way to Posadas, especially with no other scheduled stops on the eighteen-hour route. But after that? He sighs, reaching down, hefting his backpack into his lap. Paloma wordlessly does the same, flipping open the front pocket.

Jonny pauses at the sight of his missing notebook emerging from its depths. He thinks of the unmistakably frantic expression in the Bolivian woman's eyes, of how urgently she had warned him about *subversivos*. Paloma must have been just as desperate to beg a total stranger to stage such a distraction.

'I needed to put the pieces together for myself,' Paloma says, presumably by way of further explanation. 'And you had some of them written down.'

'So why didn't you just ask me yourself? Or at least tell me what you suspected?'

'I didn't work it out until we met Abuela.' Even in the dark, Paloma's anguished expression is unmistakable. 'And then I didn't want to believe it. I still don't know if I can. And now look where we are. Both running away because some assassin broke into my apartment with a gun to stop us from finding out anything else. We don't even know who we're running from or even where we're going. Just that we have to.' She fiddles endlessly with her sleeves, yanking the hems between her fingers and palms.

'Maybe so,' Jonny whispers. 'But we're not giving up. Not now. How can we? There's still time. It's like Abuela said.'

Paloma's voice hitches. 'That there's still time for the babies? And you think that makes me feel any better, knowing I might be one of them?'

A beat passes between them. Outside the bus, the cloak of

night is lifting, the first hints of dawn shimmering in the sky. Jonny takes a deep breath.

'I mean there's still time to make a difference to some of those families. To some of those mothers who still don't know what became of their children. If we do our jobs right, there's still time to bring about justice of a kind. And there's still time to find out who you really are. To understand where you really come from.'

'There's no time for any of that,' Paloma replies. 'There are people out there who are trying to kill you, Jonny. The truth implicates some unthinkably powerful institutions—'

'I know,' he interrupts. 'Which is why we need to prove it, and then publish it. You just said it yourself. There are some very powerful people on our tail. We can't run from them forever. The only way to fight them is to expose them.'

'But how? The Mothers of Plaza de Mayo have been trying for twenty years.'

'They don't know that a former military pilot went on record with me about the death flights because of a body washed up on a city beach two weeks ago...'

'Only to die himself a few hours later,' Paloma finishes in a raspy whisper. 'We can't connect any of it. I don't even know if I can try anymore.'

Jonny sighs. 'Believe it or not, I understand how you feel.'

'No, you don't. No one can.'

'I do. I really do.' Jonny unclips the top of his rucksack, instantly sees a gleam of gold. 'Even the happiest of individuals has lies hiding in their past somewhere.'

'Not like this. It's not that my parents never told me I was adopted. They were always upfront about that. And they made it sound so simple, too. That ultimately love is what makes a family, and not DNA.'

Jonny is suddenly lost for a moment in his own memories. Of the Hammersons, the elderly couple that took him in after his mother died. Of Hero, the dog they rescued shortly afterwards. The loving companionship – previously inconceivable – that sustained Jonny through an unimaginable period. Until all of them died too.

'I suppose that's one way of putting it. It would make sense to a child, anyway. It would have made sense to me.'

'What do you mean?'

Jonny stares at his gold box, a sliver of light in the dark. 'My mum died when I was nine. My dad left before I could crawl. I was brought up by strangers who loved me regardless somehow.'

Paloma stills. 'That's ... that's awful. I'm so sorry, Jonny. You didn't ... you didn't have any other family?'

Jonny roughly pulls his rucksack closed. 'It's complicated. I asked a bunch of questions. Never got any straight answers until it was way too late. Sometimes I wish I'd never started asking.'

Paloma shakes her head. 'I know what you mean. Sometimes it felt like my parents weren't even trying to hide it – I started overhearing allegedly classified calls, reading paperwork that was demonstrably confidential. Maybe the guilt became too much? Or something like that anyway.'

'They love you, though.' Jonny can't help but sound wistful. 'You must know that. All those holidays here – *parilladas* on the beach, *dulce de leche* for pudding, horse-riding with gauchos across the pampas. I know you say it was all just so confusing and lonely. But what else were they really about other than love? Maybe your parents didn't actually do anything other than love you as honestly and truthfully as they could. Maybe that's the truth of it all. That all they are really guilty of is silence.'

Beside him, Paloma wipes an eye. Jonny gazes into the lightening sky, thinking about all the different ways in which silence can be guaranteed.

'We have to find out who the pilot was,' he says after a moment. 'He had a point to make, and it was about that body on the beach, and he chose to make it to us rather than anybody else. That's the only place we can start, and hope it leads us closer to the babies.'

'I don't think I can, Jonny.' Paloma is suddenly whimpering.

'But just think about what will happen if we can prove that elements of Argentina's former military junta are still operational underground. That fifteen years after the so-called end of the Dirty War, after an apparently successful transition to democracy, that former military commanders are still able to commit murder with impunity. There will be an international outcry that can't fail to come with intervention of some kind. And now think about what will happen if we can prove babies were stolen from pregnant prisoners. Hundreds of bereaved families might find out they still have living relatives. Hundreds of adopted children might find out who they really are, where they really come from. And exposing the extent to which the United States was complicit in the whole thing? The international community will go ballistic.'

'But I can't implicate my parents.' Paloma's voice breaks. 'They are all I've got. And you're right, they loved me, they still love me. More than anything. I've never wanted for a single thing. Other than to know where I really came from. And to understand, somehow.'

'I know you still don't believe me, but I get it. I get it more than you can possibly imagine. But going over it isn't going to get either of us anywhere new. Let's just concentrate on the pilot for a moment.'

He opens his rucksack again, tries to ignore his gold box in favour of ferreting around through various bits of paper. 'Did you get everything?'

'I think so. I didn't exactly have long. And it was dark. I just grabbed whatever I could that wasn't in the rucksack to start with...'

Paloma fades as Jonny tries to inventory the contents of his bag. Lists of names, both missing and military. Photos, both copies and originals, some too gruesome to look at again. Mind maps of where the internet might lead them. There his brain sticks.

'The map,' he mutters, sifting through the scraps in the bag. Why the fuck didn't he think to show it to the pilot at the time? It was crumpled deep into his pocket then, wasn't it? He leans against the window, holding pieces of paper up to the dawn light slowly filtering through the sky.

'The map,' Jonny repeats again, turning back to Paloma. 'You found it in your photo sleeve, remember? Someone obviously put it there deliberately.'

'Oh yes. But—'

'Bollocks.' Jonny crumples the scrap of paper in his hand, hopes the next is what he's looking for.

'Even if we've still got it, how are we supposed to work out who sent it? Or figure out where it's actually supposed to be? You said it yourself when we were looking at an actual map before we went to the protest yesterday morning. That it was all loops and circles, crosses and dashes.'

Jonny scrabbles in a different pocket. The exclamation that follows comes out a lot louder than he'd intended. Hunching reflexively, he pincers out a small, folded piece of paper. He frowns down at the scribbled drawing in his hand. All loops and circles. All crosses and dashes. Just as he'd described to Paloma.

'He knew he was going to die,' he mutters to himself.

There the paper stills, his mind turning over a much older and far more fragile sheet of paper, folded just as neatly under the nail clippings and hairs inside his precious gold box. A note of an entirely different kind. More loops and squiggles, broken promises and excuses, that even decades later he'll never completely understand. The letter his mother wrote to him before she took her own life – and with it, Jonny's future.

'What are you talking about?'

'The pilot,' Jonny repeats. 'He knew he was going to die. He as good as told me.'

'And?' Paloma prompts. 'You think we can speak to him and he'll answer from beyond the grave?'

Jonny shakes his head, squinting out of the window. The answer is blurring with the dawn haze shimmering higher and higher in the sky. 'Maybe that's it. Maybe it's an unmarked grave.'

'What is?' Paloma stiffens beside him, right as a shaft of light illuminates the symbol Jonny should have registered for himself when he first saw the map.

And then Jonny has it. Between his fingers. The map trembles as he connects its clues into one coherent whole. The loops and circles. The crosses and dashes.

The cross. The universal symbol for a church.

There Jonny wavers. He's a journalist. He's a believer in proof, in reason, in fact. Blind faith is the one thing he's always ignored whenever he's marvelled at the intoxicating qualities of this vast, irresistible country. As for all Argentina's worship of gauchos, *asados* and football, its sky-blue heart beats with zealous devotion to a power higher than any of that.

He turns to Paloma. 'He confessed to it all. The pilot did, I mean. He confessed to everything – to flying the planes, to shoving the bodies out, to covering the whole thing up.'

'So?' Paloma stares at him, creeping dawn light illuminating the haggard hollows of her face.

'He confessed,' Jonny repeats. 'Don't you see? He confessed. I'm not the only person who spoke to him right before he died. I think this map might be telling us where we can find the other person who did.' He points to the cross scribbled on the piece of paper in his hand.

Paloma gasps. To the east, the sun is snaking above the tree line, mercilessly burning through the last obstinate fronds of cloud.

'It's impossible,' she whispers. 'Even if we find the right church we'd need a miracle to get any priest to confirm anything that was actually said.'

Jonny turns back to the map, tracing out its cross with a determined fingertip. 'Of course it's impossible,' he answers, blinking away the light. 'Like all matters of blind faith. But we're just going to have to count on it.'

Chapter Twenty-One

Concordia at dawn. Jonny can't fight a yawn as the bus pulls away, barely idling for long enough for them to stumble off. He checks the tattered guidebook Paloma also had the foresight to shove into his rucksack, along with the single other book on his shelves. He doesn't bother suppressing a snort at the city's full name. San Antonio de Padua de la Concordia. Practically everywhere in Argentina seems to take the name of a saint. He snaps the book closed, tucking it under his arm.

Think about it, Jonny had continued explaining to Paloma on the bus, her expression caught between disbelief and amazement. The pilot will have confessed properly multiple times. Over and over and over again. He will have been begging for absolution for years. Jonny pictures the tears that fell down the pilot's surprisingly young face, of the regret distilled in every spoken word. The military had its own chaplains on hand to grant its generals absolution day after day, year after year. But this was a man who was still begging for forgiveness right till the end. They have to find the church labelled on the map. It must be the reason they've got it.

But how in God's name are they going to do that? They walk quickly down the nearest street in search of fortification. A coffee shop beckons with a finger of rich aroma.

Jonny settles at a small table in the corner while Paloma places their order. She returns to the table in a waft of coffee, setting down two steaming cups and a plate of sticky pastries. Caramel sauce oozes everywhere as Jonny crams one into his mouth, sugar rush making him feel doubly giddy. Paloma fidgets as she picks at a flake of pastry, eyes darting.

'I don't think we need to worry about being followed quite so much out here,' Jonny says, swallowing. 'We're in the middle of nowhere. And we have to eat. Go on, you too. We can't do this on adrenaline alone.'

Paloma shakes her head. Jonny raises his eyebrows, next question lost in a shower of flaky pastry. She keeps toying with the crumbs.

'My parents used to confess all the time too,' she says, picking up the conversation they'd had on the bus. 'It sometimes felt like we were in church more than we were at home. And they would both spend forever inside the booth. I could never understand it. What could they possibly have done, or be thinking about doing, that would take up all that time? And now you seem to think we can just find a priest in a country of millions and that he'll happily break the Seal of Confession to a journalist, just as a favour.'

'But given the circumstances, wouldn't he?' Jonny puts down the rest of his pastry.

'According to the catechism.' Paloma's voice takes on a performative edge. 'Breaking the sacramental seal is forbidden under all circumstances. It is the gravest of sins, punishable only by excommunication.'

Jonny ponders the murky depths of his coffee. 'Surely not if the priest is given specific details of a crime.'

'You would think. I was practically excommunicated for asking the same question once. And I was only nine. I just wanted to know what would happen if someone confessed to committing a crime. I couldn't get my head around the idea you could do something bad and potentially get away with it just by expressing remorse to a priest. The best that church guidelines in Las Cruces New Mexico could do was to say the priest must require the penitent to report his or her conduct to the police, or – shock, horror – withhold absolution.'

Caramel oozes nauseatingly on to the tablecloth from Jonny's unfinished second pastry. The idea that the Church can exact a hold that counters even the most grave of crimes sickens him almost as much as the thought of the crimes themselves.

'And what about the fact that the police have their own chaplains,' he answers rhetorically. 'The military too. What have they overheard? The lot, presumably. The whole salad. One of them will probably end up being made pope one day.'

'Irony has no place in religion,' Paloma remarks bitterly. 'New Mexico's finest used to say that too.'

Jonny pushes the plate away in disgust. Paloma sips at her coffee, gazing out of the window. Beyond, the street is quiet, many of its shops demonstrably closed for good. Eyeing the frontage of a beleaguered bank further down the street, Jonny nods at the leftover pastries.

'We should probably take those with us.' He rummages in his rucksack, pulling out his iridium. 'Maybe they'll give us some napkins, or something – do you mind asking? I'm going to make a call.'

Paloma's eyes widen. 'Where? You don't think marching around on the street talking into a black plastic brick is going to attract any attention?'

Jonny nods towards the back of the café, where he's spotted a door hanging ajar into the ubiquitous small internal courtyard.

'I'll just be in there. Don't worry.'

He walks purposefully towards the bathroom, doglegging at the last minute into the squalid outdoor space, trying to ignore the trepidation prickling up his back. Rubbish steams in the heat from two overflowing bins by the opposite wall. Snapping open the iridium's chubby aerial, Jonny's nerves settle at the sight of the equally ubiquitous wrought-iron fire escape curling up from the courtyard, giving access over the building's roof and down the other side if necessary. He punches in Lukas's direct line, staring into the square of brilliant blue sky overhead. The satellites beyond suddenly feel close enough to touch.

'Jonny?' Lukas answers almost immediately.

He starts. 'How did you know it was me?'

A long, deep sigh bristles down the line. Jonny tenses. What has he missed?

'I've been calling and calling.'

'What? Where?'

'Your apartment. I must have called, I don't know, twenty times.' The tingle on the back of Jonny's neck turns cold. 'You're after our pictures of the riots, right?'

'Right!'

Jonny flinches as Lukas shouts back. There's no escaping the fact, even across who the hell knows how many satellites, that his editor is furious. And why wouldn't he be? Jonny realises, in another cold wash of sweat. It's nearly lunchtime on what is no doubt a freezing winter Saturday in London, the morning after the night before. Missed deadlines on big breaking news stories are the only reason Lukas would be at his desk answering his phone on its first ring. And of course Paloma hasn't developed her pictures of the riots. They've been on the run since they got back to her apartment.

'I told you, man. I got you top billing. You cannot imagine what those column inches cost me.'

'I can explain.' Jonny glances over his shoulder, checks Paloma is still sitting undisturbed at their table. 'You won't believe it but—'

'You're damn right I won't believe it. It's over for us, Jonny-boy. You've shredded my reputation one too many times.'

Jonny's heart starts to race. 'Wait, Lukas. You don't understand—'

'Of course I don't fucking understand. If I was a contractor scratching around at practically the ends of the earth, I sure as hell know what I would be doing with my time if I found myself on top of a news story.'

'That's just it. Remember what I told you when we spoke yesterday?'

But Lukas is still raving. Jonny lets him finish. It takes at least another minute for him to dry up. Jonny's financial-crisis story is, as it turns out, still on the front page. But it contains none of the colour Lukas had promised. None of the wide-angle lens Jonny had described, both literally and figuratively. The analysis that he promised to deliver later that evening? Vaporised into his pre-dawn escape from Buenos Aires. Those snapshots of a city disintegrating, seen from on high, a vantage point that no one else in the world had? Non-existent. Because not only did those photographs not arrive on any meaningful schedule, they were yet to arrive at all – and the best Lukas could get from any other news agency was a wide shot of the aftermath. Which could have been any street in any poleaxed city in the fucking world, were it not for the ubiquitous Argentinian flag. Which was still flying high, by the way.

Jonny shakes his head. He thinks of Paloma's undeveloped rolls of film, of what else those little black canisters are hiding.

'We had to run,' he begins. 'The other story I told you about turns out to be far bigger than I could have imagined—'

'It doesn't matter now,' Lukas interrupts. 'We're out of time.'

'Just let me explain. Everything I told you about is coming together and it's massive, it's almost unthinkable, that's why I'm calling.'

'You could be calling me from the moon and it wouldn't make any difference. This is about you and me, buddy. We're the ones that are out of time. Editorial operations on the right side of the world are picking up from here. Like it ever made sense to run news coverage of the entire South American continent from London. You've been long making that argument yourself, hey.'

'What do you mean?'

'You need to call into the DC news desk from now on. That is, if you can get anyone there to answer the phone to you. Everyone still cares plenty about what's happening in Argentina but no one trusts me to deliver it now, much less trusts you.'

Jonny starts to panic. 'But I need your help. You've no idea what I'm really dealing with here.'

'I tried, Jonny. I really did.'

Jonny reels. For a profession that lives and dies on its objectivity, the actual management of news is anything but. The whole damn enterprise is as political as politics gets. 'So what am I supposed to do now?'

Lukas sighs heavily back down the line. 'You'd better hope your new editor isn't the pit bull everyone says she is. She's probably already got a load of new contacts on the case. A freelance reporter disappearing for hours during a massive news story is never a good look. You've been gone long enough that I thought I'd find you hiding in the mountains with some disgraced former Nazi commander.'

Hiding in the mountains. Jonny is suddenly picturing the map stuffed into his rucksack, then punching the air to stop himself from shouting out loud. Where is the one place in Argentina that has already shown itself capable of harbouring for years those guilty of the most grievous of crimes? Where is the one place in the entire country they might find a church that's already heard confessions of the most unimaginable kind? Little Switzerland, Jonny thinks, heart racing. Nestled in the foothills of the Andes, surrounded by snow-covered peaks and crystal-clear mountain lakes. One of the most breathtaking places in the world, not least because it harboured escaped Nazi war criminals for decades. And this 'she' must be the one person Jonny wishes he had been calling all along.

'You can still radio me anytime, though,' Lukas is saying, but

Jonny is miles away, not just picturing the Andes mountains, but remembering another time and place where he stood shoulder-to-shoulder with the only person left on Earth he feels like he can trust. The closest person Jonny's got to a sister.

'Allen,' he breathes, to himself rather than to Lukas, who answers anyway.

'*Ja*, that's what she calls herself. Use her given name at your peril. I've given her the background on both your stories.'

Suddenly Jonny can't help but laugh.

'I'm serious, buddy,' Lukas adds. 'She's bigger than any story you've got for her.'

'That she is,' Jonny replies before clearing his throat. 'I'm sorry I let you down, Lukas. You'll see why soon enough. Thanks for everything you've done for me.'

The fact the dial tone is already sounding from the receiver as Jonny cuts the call does little to dampen his enthusiasm. He snaps the iridium's aerial closed and charges back inside.

'Let's go,' he says to Paloma. 'Can you drive?'

She gets to her feet, frowning. 'Of course I can drive. But where are we going?'

'Switzerland,' Jonny answers, heading for the door, plan solidifying with every step.

Chapter Twenty-Two

Jonny gazes out of the car window at the vast, intractable pampas. Mile upon mile of flat grassland has passed since they left Concordia, punctuated occasionally by a cluster of secluded farm buildings and the undulating shapes of horses cantering in the distance. He's travelling a road he's most definitely never travelled before, but where is he going? Strangely, Jonny finds the fact he still isn't totally sure of their final destination somehow comforting. And he knows, without needing to ask, that the same can be said for Paloma – hands fixed tight on the steering wheel, wind whipping through her dark hair. The landscape around them is as wild as his theory, but they both seem energised, and not just by the heady thrill of the wide, open road.

What was Jonny expecting? That Paloma remain catatonic with disbelief forever? He traces a finger over the pencil drawing smoothed over his knee. It's been nearly fifteen years since his mother died, and Jonny is still waiting for the passage of time to lessen the pain. The shock and denial, the crushing guilt, the loneliness of a kind so profound it has hollowed out his soul. No, Jonny knew full well that the moment he gave Paloma a course of action, she would take it, however wild and crazy it may have sounded, however many hours of driving it would entail. Because how else are people like them supposed to move forward?

He turns to Paloma, feels the determination radiating from her in waves. The road ahead is as flat and empty as the vast landscape stretching limitless to their either side.

'I saw it, don't worry,' she answers before he can point at the clearing on the edge of the deserted highway up ahead, nothing but pampas grass in all other directions.

'I'll just be a minute,' Jonny says. The car slows into the clearing. He climbs out of the passenger seat, unsnapping his iridium's chubby aerial and pointing it to the sky. Instantly the unit starts to vibrate in his hand. It's never rung before, Jonny almost drops it in shock before he realises why. The smile that follows practically blooms across his whole body – opening his chest, lifting his head, animating his entire face.

Only one person has this number. He filled her in on the basics while Paloma was hiring their car. And by the time he gets the phone to his ear, she's already talking.

'I think you're right,' Allen is saying, rapid-fire American English coming down the line as piercing and sharp as the midday sun beating down overhead. 'I can't believe it, but I do. The Switzerland of Argentina. The official map looks exactly like the drawing you described.'

Jonny's grin starts to make his cheeks hurt. Having Allen officially at his back again makes him feel like he's wearing armour. After dropping the ball on the financial crisis so spectacularly with Lukas, having to prove himself to someone new would have felt almost insurmountable – were it not for the fact that person was Allen.

His heart rate ticks up a notch. The last time Allen and Jonny worked together was in Israel, where everything didn't exactly go as planned. Her new senior editorial management position at the *International Tribune*'s executive headquarters in America is a long way from running the newspaper's tiny outpost in Jerusalem. This time it's Allen with a whole more to lose than him.

'Right, and I checked it myself against the small diagram in my guidebook too. I'd be happier though if I had a full official city map to compare it to. Is that what you're using?'

'Of course it is.' Jonny pictures Allen's determined nod, her glossy dark hair swaying along too. 'And I'd prefer it if I could see this so-called map of yours for myself, but from everything you've described, it sounds like we're talking about the same place. I can confirm I've become a lot more familiar than I ever thought I'd be with cartography since our last conversation.'

'You've double-checked?' Jonny has to ask again. He hadn't had time to labour the point in those first furtive minutes hiding behind the back wall of some budget car rental.

'Yes,' she replies testily. 'V-shaped peaks are the universal sign for mountains. Just as a cross is the universal sign for a church. Circles, preferably ones coloured throughout in blue, show lakes. Wavy lines or dots can indicate an intermittent lake or pond. I could go on. I've matched every part of your description to the actual map of the province in question. And it's exactly as you said.'

Jonny sighs into the receiver. He hadn't known for sure his hunch was right until now.

'The Switzerland of Argentina,' Allen says again. 'I guess we shouldn't be surprised. It's where the Nazis went into retirement, after all. How long is it going to take to get there? Are you sharing the driving?'

Jonny scans the horizon both up ahead and behind them, picturing the city of San Carlos de Bariloche, capital of this so-called Little Switzerland, with its alpine echo of glimmering mountain streams flanked with snowy Andes peaks.

'It's at least twenty-four hours on the road from Concordia. We need to avoid going through Buenos Aires. I suppose we could take an internal flight but—'

'Not if you're trying to stay under the radar.'

'I know.' Jonny nods.

'Where are you now?'

'Only halfway to Rosario.' Jonny peers into the vastness around them as if the harder he looks, the faster the city of Rosario will materialise from its depths, the first big city they'll encounter on the way.

'OK, I'll arrange for you to pick up some supplies there. I've already got people working on it. Write these phone numbers down. Jorge is first, Pancho is second. You shouldn't need to call Pancho but he's the back-up just in case.'

Jonny fumbles in his pockets for a pencil. 'Jorge, you said?'

'Yes. Call Jorge's number as soon as you hit the city limits. He speaks some English and I trust him. That's all you need to know. He's putting together some food and water. It won't be anything fancy but it'll get you through twenty-four hours without having to stop. He'll also have fuel—'

'Fuel?' Jonny wonders out loud.

'Yes, Jonny. Fuel. You're the one who has been reporting on the financial crisis, am I right? Has it escaped your notice that petrol isn't exactly gushing freely from every fucking tap? Don't expect gallons of the stuff, by the way. Just enough to get you out of a spot, is all. And he'll have a proper printed map of Bariloche city centre itself – don't worry, he doesn't know why you need it.'

'And I call Pancho if I can't get hold of Jorge?'

'Exactly. But you shouldn't have to. When you see the signs directing you into the city, that's when to call Jorge. He'll tell you where to meet him. Then try not to stop again until you have to.'

'Who are they?' Jonny eyes Paloma, already back in the driver's seat. 'Who's Jorge, I mean. And who's Pancho?'

'My people. Field security operatives. The best in the business. You'll have to trust me on that.' Allen's voice takes on its famous sharp edge. 'Now get going. Jorge will let me know when you've made contact.'

'So you think we should drive through the night?' Suddenly Jonny doesn't want to let the line drop, desperate to prolong a conversation with someone he feels he can trust absolutely.

'Make sure you make contact again before dark and we'll

discuss it. I'm not going to give you exact times to call in. The last thing I want is you getting off the highway just to find a phone at a certain time. And don't even think about using the iridium too publicly.'

'I won't,' Jonny answers, instantly wishing he had waited to get on the road before calling her the first time instead of choosing a spot in the arse end of a car park.

'And Jonny? Remember what I've always said.'

Which part, he wants to ask, even though he already knows. *No story is worth dying for*, he repeats to himself, again and again.

'Now get going.'

Before he can reply, Jonny finds himself listening to the dial tone. He reluctantly folds down the iridium's chubby aerial.

'What did she say?' Paloma asks as he climbs back into the car.

'Just that she thinks we're right,' Jonny answers. But his mind is still stuck in the past. He'd agreed without question when Allen first told him no story was worth dying for. Back then Jonny had never thought he'd encounter real danger in the line of duty, even in the heat of his first ever frontline news assignment. He felt completely insulated by the rigours of the news reporting process itself, convinced that the truth would always save him in the end. That is, until an unimaginable scoop also became the story of an unimaginable betrayal.

There the anger buds, coarse and hot in Jonny's chest. The lies he unearthed about his family. The sense of betrayal and loss that he's been left with ever since. The search for his twin sister, who could be almost anywhere on Earth by now. The feeling he's condemned to be forever alone. For the briefest of moments, Jonny finds himself considering whether dying over that particular story would have been preferable to unearthing the truth.

He turns to Paloma, but there's nothing left to say. She's already driving, eyes fixed on the distance, powered by the exact same force.

Chapter Twenty-Three

Jonny waits in the driver's seat, hands on the wheel, engine running. They'd agreed Paloma wouldn't be around for the pickup. If Allen's man, Jorge, seems suspicious in any way at all, Jonny is to gun the engine and fly. Paloma will be at a safe distance and will find a way to flag him down again. *You can't expect me to trust her just because you do*, Paloma had said. *What's to say this isn't just another trap?*

Jonny sighs, eyeing the recessed doorway up the street, the only sign betraying Paloma's vantage point a tell-tale curl of smoke. Can he really blame her for not trusting anyone? He's found out enough about her to suggest she'll probably have trust issues for the rest of her life. And hasn't Jonny felt the same himself for days too? And about Paloma herself – he thinks of his notes scribbled down into Hebrew, copied literally into a different alphabet. But now he feels even more exposed without her by his side, unease slinking down his back.

Looking into his rear-view mirror, Jonny spots a tall, fair-skinned man approaching with two loaded carrier bags. He curses himself. Why the fuck didn't he ask Allen what Jorge looked like? Or asked Jorge himself, when he'd got details of where to meet? He squints, the man's decidedly shorn head coming closer, so tall his head is already out of the mirror's frame. He looks completely different to any native South American Jonny has ever met.

A little of the tension leaves Jonny's chest. What had Allen said? *Field security operatives. The best in the business.* He wasn't sure how he felt about it when he first heard that private security was used to support news crews operating in frontline locations. An extra pair of hands is all well and good – help with operational details like food, water and fuel in places where they are often in short supply. But an extra pair of eyes on his every move? What if they aren't necessarily focused on the same goal? He turns in anticipation, but the man is already walking past, too swiftly for Jonny to examine him more closely.

'Damn,' he mutters under his breath, white porcelain gleaming up at him from his lap. Jonny tells himself it's the jolt of adrenaline that's making him feel slightly sick, and not the prospect of potentially having to use one of Paloma's stun-gun darts. He looks up just as the passenger door opens. Before he can blink, the man is inside and closing it. They definitely hadn't agreed Jorge would just get in without so much as a by your leave.

'What the fuck are you doing?' Jonny surveys his unexpected passenger with what he hopes is his most threatening, intimidating expression. 'Get the fuck out of my car! *Vamos!*'

But the man just laughs.

'What's my name, buddy?'

Some more tension drains away at the unmistakable cadence of the man's accent. Still, Jonny finds himself clinging on to the steering wheel for dear life.

'I'll eat my fucking hat if it's really Jorge,' he mutters, trying not to look at the dart in his lap. Its presence is suddenly making him feel worse rather than better.

'Now we can do business,' the man answers, strapping on his seat belt. Jonny hesitates. He's becoming increasingly sure of the man's true origins with every word of his deep, heavily accented English. He's Israeli. Who else would Allen call on, with her history in the Middle East? And any private security agency she knows in this part of the world is almost certainly going to involve agents from Mossad – Israel's shadowy and brutal intelligence agency, revered and feared in equal measure the world over. But no Israeli ever routinely wears a seat belt.

'Hang on a second,' he mutters. 'What actually is your name?'

'Jorge,' the man answers, Spanish accent suddenly impeccable. '*Vamos*!' He motions at the traffic scudding past.

'No,' Jonny answers as emphatically as he can manage. 'I can't. My friend...' He trails off, instantly realising his mistake. In the same instant he sees Paloma emerge from her recessed doorway up ahead, only to pause almost immediately.

'Shit,' he mutters into his lap, willing her not to jump to the wrong conclusion – that this man isn't Jorge at all.

'Listen, buddy,' the man continues like they're just two old friends chuntering back and forth. 'I've got everything you need. But handing it all over on the street isn't a good look, you know what I'm saying?'

'Where are your bags?' Jonny pictures the plastic carriers he's sure he saw the man carrying as he walked past.

'In the trash. And they were stuffed full of it to start with. I picked the right car because you were gawping at them. Your boss wouldn't tell me anything else about you.'

'Still,' Jonny mutters. Putting the car into gear, he wills that Paloma stays where she is. Steering with one hand, Jonny makes a thumbs-up sign with the other, waving like an idiot. He can only hope that she sees him.

'Make a right two blocks up,' the man says.

Jonny holds his breath, he's about to drive straight past Paloma. On cue, her unmistakable outline appears in his peripheral vision, staring purposefully into the car. Jonny turns the allotted corner into a quiet side road. If the man notices, he doesn't say anything.

'Over here.' Jorge waves at the kerb.

Jonny stops but keeps the engine idling. Paloma reappears in the rear-view mirror, hovering on the corner. Jorge gets out of the passenger side as smoothly as he arrived. 'Two minutes.'

Bracing himself on the steering wheel, Jonny streams all his breath out in one go. If Allen can mobilise a Mossad agent speaking fluent Argentine Spanish in some suburban corner of Rosario on a matter of hours' notice, then Paloma and Jonny are very far from being alone on their quest. In fact it suddenly feels like there are eyes on their every move all over again. A germ of a thought begins to seed somewhere in Jonny's mind but he can't quite surface it clearly.

'Open the trunk,' Jorge commands, back by the passenger door. Jonny makes a show of getting out, unlocking the boot. Surely Paloma won't attempt to tangle with a situation that looks under control. Out of nowhere, Jorge lets out a belly laugh.

'I can see her. Don't worry. No one is going to get hurt.'

Of course you can, Jonny thinks, watching uneasily as supplies are loaded into the boot – food, water, petrol. Everything they could possibly need to travel below the radar for days. He doesn't bother asking where it all came from. Jorge slams the boot closed.

'*Suerte*,' he says, throwing a thumbs-up to Paloma for good measure. Jonny resists the urge to reply with good luck to him too, and settles for a nod. But Jorge has already disappeared.

'What the fuck?' Paloma is back by the car just as quickly.

'Doesn't matter,' Jonny answers, walking round to the passenger seat. 'We've got everything we could possibly need, and more.' He stops short of telling her about the two pistols he also saw Jorge loading into the boot. Much like the stunning darts, their presence is making Jonny feel worse rather than better.

'But we agreed.' Paloma flings herself into the driver's seat. 'And then you go and let a complete stranger into the car.'

'I know what we agreed. And he wasn't suspicious. That's the point. We are going to get nowhere fast if we don't trust each other. You can't do this alone, and neither can I. The sooner you accept that we are in this together, then the faster we'll get somewhere—'

The car squeals interruption as Paloma accelerates away. 'How can you expect me to trust you if the second we agree on how to approach something you go ahead and do the exact opposite?'

'What would you have had me do? Kick him out of the car? Throw a punch? Scream bloody murder? Nothing actually happened. And now it's over. We've got everything we need. We're already on the road. We're already on our way—'

'You are, you mean.'

Jonny blanches. 'Me? What are you talking about?'

'You know what's waiting at the end of all this. To you, this is all just about landing the ultimate scoop. About breaking the news story that's finally going to make your name. "The United States stole babies trafficked during the Dirty War". But it's my life, Jonny, don't you understand that? I'm running from everything I've ever known with no idea where I'm going to end up, at all. But to you, it's still just a story. Just a job you've got to do.'

Jonny opens his mouth, closes it again, considers the hundred different things he could say in response before settling for the cowardliest of all. The silence takes root, thickening between them even as fresh air roars through the open car windows. Allen did well, Jonny thinks, focusing on the practicalities of the situation to avoid the emotions that are rising within him. She told Jorge to deliberately pick a spot that got them on and off the main highway with a minimum of fuss. The *estancias* are already spreading out on either side into more limitless horizon.

'I know you think I'll never understand,' Jonny finally says, watching Paloma's grip tighten on the steering wheel. This isn't what she'd been expecting him to say. 'It's unimaginable. It's almost unbearable to even conceive of it. But doesn't how hard I'm trying count for something?'

'If you want me to trust you, that's what I need you to explain. I know why I'm so upset and angry. But why the hell are you? Why are you really doing all this?'

Jonny hesitates. Doesn't she mean the exact opposite? That he isn't nearly angry enough? Wasn't she expecting a far more aggressive response to a complete stranger climbing into their car out of nowhere? Wasn't she expecting him to fight back too, when that masked man leapt towards him from her fucking doorway? And what about when he failed to react fast enough for her during that riot outside the bank? But Jonny's reply just sticks in his throat, thickening and hardening with every passing mile.

For the truth is, Jonny knows exactly what she means. He knows his obsession with this particular story goes far beyond anything that can be explained away by investigating in the public interest.

And can he blame her? Why should someone like Paloma, betrayed in a way that no one could possibly imagine unless they'd been through the same thing, trust someone like him? This is the thought that finally propels some words out of Jonny's mouth.

'Because it happened to me, too,' he replies softly, staring at the limitless horizon. 'We all have lies in our past. I told you. I still don't know my full story either. You probably wouldn't believe me if I told you the bits I do know.'

'Try me.'

'I had…' But the words stick in Jonny's throat, so he has to start again. 'I once had a twin. Still have a twin, I mean. At least I have no reason to believe she's dead. Then again, I had no reason to believe I ever had a sister, let alone a twin, before.'

'I don't understand. You're a twin?'

'Apparently.' Jonny hangs his head. 'I don't remember her. And I have no way of finding out where she is now. My dad took her when he left. Just upped and disappeared. My mum never told me she even existed. I only found out years after Mum died and I met my grandparents. Turns out she'd let my dad take my sister and my grandparents had disowned my mother over it – although that was never the reason I was given when I asked what had happened to the rest of our family. Like I said. It's complicated. And right now there's nothing more important to me than finding out the truth about your past, not mine. It matters to me so much that I'm putting myself in more danger than any sane person would consider doing in a million years...'

He trails off, holding his breath, heart fluttering in his chest. Has he said enough? He casts around for more mechanics but comes up blank as the acres of pampas grass stretch into oblivion all around them.

'That's ... that's pretty messed up,' Paloma replies after a moment.

But Jonny can't bring himself to say anything else, suddenly completely spent.

The miles scud past. Jonny's eyelids flutter, consciousness hovering between dream and reality. Beside him, Paloma accelerates, squinting every so often into the rear-view mirror. Is she looking forward or backward? The thought ripples in for the briefest of moments before finally, Jonny's eyes close, the sunlight too dazzling to resist. Finally, his dreams are only of vacant, blissful dark.

Chapter Twenty-Four

The foothills of the Andes. Watercolour-pink sky, knife-sharp mountain air. Jonny leans down, palms a handful of crystal-clear water from the glacial stream running below the bank off to the side of the highway. He practically had to wrestle Paloma out of the driving seat after their final call to Allen at dusk, confirming their next steps. She only agreed after tucking Jorge's pistols into the rucksacks at their feet. Despite not being the one to drive through the night, he still doesn't think Paloma has slept at all. But Jonny isn't surprised. He's long past referring to anything that happens in the dark as sleep. He can only ever manage it with the lights on to keep his subconscious mind at bay.

'You can take it from here,' he says. A stone scuds past, leaping quicksilver across the water's glossy surface.

'Was that you?' Jonny twists round to find a small smile on Paloma's face. 'Where the hell did you learn to skim stones as well as that?'

The realisation that it was in a probably identical spot a few miles away lands with the same finality as the stone finally plopping and sinking without trace. Paloma shakes her head, sighing. When the car engine starts up again, it sounds like the low roar of a lion. They follow both the official and unofficial map through the city of Bariloche to the cross marked in the exact same place on both.

The church itself is unmissable in the way that certain churches are – regal spires and stained glass surrounded by verdant grounds and tinkling fountains. The whole spectacle is positioned right on the edge of a huge mountain lake, dawn light shimmering transcendentally off the water as if daring anyone not to believe in a higher power. Jonny is momentarily cowed until he spots the moon's faded disc, the sky's ghostly single eye, luminous behind a frond of cloud. That's the real beauty of nature, he thinks. The fact that scepticism is never far away.

Paloma locks the car, tucks the keys into a pocket. A priest is already walking out to greet them on their approach to the church's huge, arched entrance. Jonny tries to play the part, to look penitent, head bowed, hands folded, shoulders slumped in a posture of supplication while Paloma does the talking. They are quickly seated in a wooden pew at the back of the building's cavernous insides. The priest whips away in a flourish of white robes.

'Well?' Jonny whispers out of the corner of his mouth.

'He's just the curate,' Paloma mutters back. 'But we're in luck. Confession opens in a few minutes. You can show up at the same time every day around here.'

Jonny nods. Their next steps are the most tentative they've taken so far. And Paloma is going to have to handle them on her own. He curses his inability to speak fluent Spanish for at least the thousandth time. Glancing round the church, he takes in their surroundings, absorbs them into his mental map – a long central aisle flanked by rows of polished wooden pews, depictions of pain and sacrifice looming from every stained-glass window. Weighty quiet hangs in the air, the kind of atmosphere that the devoted describe as holy but just sounds hollow and empty to anyone bothering to actually listen to it.

'Where are the confession booths?'

'Up there.' Paloma nods towards a black curtain towards the front and off to one side, a shadow behind the giant crucifix that is set centre stage. 'There are reconciliation rooms behind it, apparently.'

Reconciliation, Jonny thinks bitterly. What kind of reconciliation can be promised to those confessing to some of the worst sins of all? He swallows; that's exactly what he and Paloma are counting on finding out about.

'You're going to stay as close as possible, right?'

Jonny nods. Still Paloma cannot relax, gripping the ends of her long sleeves in her palms. Jonny gazes around the church again, dares its stupid, weighty silence to find a way to speak to a heathen like him.

The curate materialises by the pew, quiet as a ghost. Jonny follows Paloma down the far side of the rows of pews to the black curtain. Behind lies a small, dark anteroom almost completely panelled with wood. They pause for the curate to retreat behind the curtain again. A slightly fudgy, overly floral smell of incense winds through the air, a too-heavy-handed attempt at disguising the unmistakable notes of decay creeping in beneath aged and peeling varnish.

The booths themselves are rendered in dark, elaborately carved wood, a dense lattice at their centre separating their opposing compartments. Beside him, Paloma hesitates, rooted to the spot. Is she as sickened as Jonny is by the notion that something as flimsy as a wooden grille can demarcate the difference between good and evil? Or has she, like him, suddenly lost faith in the idea that they can simply show up in a church and demand answers from men who only ever answer to a higher power? A small cough from the curate, waiting for Jonny to retreat to a safe distance, brings him back to the present. 'Forgive me, Father, for I have sinned,' Jonny mutters as he backs away. It hardly matters if the sentiment is missing from words uttered into a silence this hollow and empty. The curate seems satisfied enough to leave Jonny hovering at the gap between curtain and wall. Paloma disappears into the nearest booth, intricately engraved wooden door creaking behind her.

The seconds tick by. Jonny leans against the wall, fighting the drowsiness licking at his edges. By now the church is alive with sunlight, its many glass insets refracting a full-spectrum kaleidoscope. The whole effect is dazzling, but to someone like Jonny, who can only rest in the brightest of lights, it is inescapably narcotic. The colours are dancing now, their shifting shades a hypnotic shimmer – blue to indigo to violet, red to orange to yellow – Jonny squints; he's fighting to keep his eyes open so hard it's almost painful … Finally he slumps, sliding down the wall behind him, blissfully vacant darkness descending. That is until a hand curls determinedly around his bicep, tugging him back into the light. When he opens his eyes, there is no mistaking the exhilarated expression on Paloma's face.

Jonny rubs his eyes. Paloma's own are shining. She gestures behind her. The curate is sitting alone in a pew, rocking back and forth and muttering. The rest of the church is deserted.

'He's been confessing,' she whispers. 'He is. Look. He's still doing it now.'

'You mean you were confessing?' Jonny replies dumbly. 'What happened?'

'No, the curate is. I heard every word.'

Jonny twists round, peers behind the curtain. 'But haven't you been in there?'

'Just follow me.' She pulls him to his feet. 'Hurry up. We don't have long.'

The curate stands, hands folded, head bowed. Paloma tugs Jonny behind her, scuttling behind the curate, out of the pew and up the central aisle. After a predictable pause and bow at the foot of the cross, they head to the far wall. The curate opens a door on the opposite side of the altar to the black curtain. Jonny hates himself for feeling cowed in the giant shadow of the crucifix. He doesn't realise he's stopped moving until Paloma turns, beckoning that he catch up.

'It's a sin,' she says, holding out her hand. 'Curates are priests who are yet to be ordained and it's only ordained priests who can hear confessions.'

'So?' Jonny prompts as she tugs him over the threshold into a small, plain side room.

'The curate heard the pilot's confession. He's the one who granted the pilot absolution at the end. It was only a few days ago. He's losing his mind with regret. He's just spent the last five minutes begging for forgiveness before God because he wasn't qualified to do it. It's a sin of the worst kind.'

Jonny balks. 'You heard him in the booth yourself? It was that easy? I don't believe it.'

Paloma shakes her head. 'No, out here. When I went in there was no one waiting on the other side. So I came out to find him in this sort of trance, just rocking back and forth and chanting. It's only because of what we already know that what he was muttering made any sense, not to mention why he was doing it out in the open. He can't confess to an ordained official. He'd be excommunicated immediately. It's the only crime the church can do anything about.'

The door closes with a soft clunk. Jonny stares at the curate, who has paused a few feet away, gazing out of a high window at some faraway point in the distance. Paloma switches to Spanish to speak to the man, pausing to scrabble in the bag at her feet. Out comes a fold of banknotes. Instantly Jonny realises what she is doing. They're not in this squalid anteroom for an interview of any kind. They're not here to bear witness to every sordid detail of an unauthorised confession obtained by an over-zealous acolyte. No. This man just wants them to pay more than lip service to the business of forgiveness and absolution. Paloma went into a confession booth. Now she needs to pay for services rendered.

'We have to make a donation,' she mutters, peeling away a few crumpled notes.

'That's what he's calling it?' Jonny eyes the curate – his head is still expectantly bowed.

'Call it what you like.'

The curate reaches out for her money with a sorrowful nod. Jonny doesn't need Paloma to translate to understand exactly what she is saying by return: Thank you, O merciful Father, for lighting my path to God. They open the door and quickly walk away, leaving the curate to ruminate on the weight of his own sins. Still Jonny finds himself quailing away from the giant crucifix bearing down on their backs as they scurry down the aisle to hide in a pew at the back.

'So what exactly did he say?' Jonny begins, hunching reflexively.

'That he was cleaning the booths for confession. A military man came in unannounced. He went into the nearest booth and launched straight into a confession. The curate immediately tried to stop him talking until he heard strange noises too, a scratching of some kind. He thought the man might have been trying to harm himself in some way. By then he felt he had no choice but to listen.'

'Why? Because of what he had already heard?'

Paloma nods. 'This military man confessed to an affair with one of his prisoners. Apparently she was just a student. All she was guilty of was wanting to learn. So he found a way to save her. And that's why the curate granted him absolution. I guess you could say he got carried away in the same way as the military man did.'

'But how could the pilot possibly have got away with saving a prisoner? There'd have been other military officers on the planes too – doctors, in some cases.'

'I don't know,' Paloma replies. 'But we knew the pilot and the victim had to be connected to each other somehow. You said so yourself after you got inside the ESMA. That all you could think was they had a relationship of some kind. So the body on the beach must be hers. And to have appeared after all this time means something must have happened that might reveal they once had a clandestine relationship. We already know the military is furious about the growing campaign for justice. They were acting under orders, is all they'll ever say. Maybe the pilot got a little too remorseful for his own good. Maybe he made it a bit too obvious he was ready to go on the record about the death flights. So the former military command sent him a message that only he would understand. But he must have managed to get to us before they got to him too.' She pauses, tapping a finger on the pew's aged wood. 'But we still don't know why he chose us in the first place.'

Jonny looks around the deserted church. 'We've missed something. We must have. There has to be something else in here. The pilot can't have been expecting us to actually get a priest to break his confidence, even under duress. That's the truly unthinkable part. It's ridiculous. Any priest worth his salt would rather die. It can't be the reason we've been directed to this church specifically. It has to be something else...'

'Like what? All we've got to go on is the map.'

But Jonny is still stuck in his previous sentence. *Would rather die*, he repeats to himself, transporting his mind back inside that sleek sedan, hessian sack in his lap. Why didn't the pilot tell him everything then? Why didn't he tell Jonny exactly what it was that had betrayed his secret affair with a prisoner, and got his lover killed all these years later? Why was the map left for Paloma, rather than given to Jonny in the car? *He would rather die*, he says again, silently. And suddenly Jonny is picturing his mother, reliving an altogether different secret that she took to her tortured grave, the baby that she could never admit to giving away.

He's back on his feet without thinking. Paloma calls after him as he heads to the back wall, pulls back the heavy black curtain. The carved wooden door of the nearest confession booth closes behind him, plunging him into half-light. Nothing but shadows in all directions apart from the yellow glow filtering through the lattice separating him from the shadowy figure of another priest waiting to absolve Jonny of all his sins. The pilot saved her, Jonny thinks, running a hand up and down the wooden walls to his either side, remembering Paloma's description of strange scratching sounds and the names etched into the ESMA cell walls. But how? He can't have been flying the plane alone. Others must have witnessed him bringing a solitary prisoner back to dry land. *How do you keep the essential parts of a machine operating day in, day out?* And there his mind snags as one of his fingers catches against a deliberate curve notched into the wall.

Jonny pauses. He feels his breath start to come in little gasps. On the other side of the grille, the priest lets out a small sigh. Leaning down, Jonny squints into the dark, tracing out an inescapable engraving carved into the grain of the confession booth itself. A name he has come to know as well as his own.

You give them whatever they want, he thinks, staring into the dark as the name etched into the wood comes into focus at last. *And our babies paid the ultimate price.*

Jonny gasps as the complete picture takes dizzying shape in his mind. He's suddenly back in the squalid confines of the ESMA cells, directly above the guards' quarters, running his finger over names on a different set of walls. Put together with the strange scratching coming from a military man in this same seat just a few days earlier, he's becoming surer and surer of what must have happened to one particular baby over all. We were prisoners too, he says to himself. Like some subverted version of Stockholm Syndrome. The priest murmurs back approvingly.

'*Gracias*,' Jonny replies, trying to collect himself as he stands. 'And I am sorry,' he whispers, as much to himself as anyone else. 'I am so sorry for everything I am about to do.'

Chapter Twenty-Five

Numb, Jonny walks out of the confession booth and through the heavy black curtain. Paloma is already hurrying out of the pew by the time he draws level with her. She flicks a worried glance over her shoulder. The curate is coming out of the opposite door.

'Quick,' she says. 'You need to make a donation now, too. Then let's get out of here. We've been way longer than we agreed.'

Still dazed, Jonny digs into a pocket for some change, tossing some banknotes into a basket by the huge arched entrance.

They are speeding back east along the highway out of Bariloche before either of them says another word. Thankfully Paloma is first to break the silence.

'Proving any of it is impossible,' she says with a sigh. 'Everyone involved is either dead or sworn to silence. And it sounds nothing but absurd without proof. I still can't believe it myself.'

And she doesn't even know the whole story yet, Jonny thinks, swallowing. How can he find the right words to explain to her that they *can* now prove it?

'It's the only thing that makes sense, though,' he begins softly. 'Don't forget I saw inside the ESMA for myself. I saw how tightly packed those cells and guards' quarters really were. In that context it's actually not that hard to believe—'

'Of course it is.' Jonny is momentarily distracted by a sudden glimpse of Paloma's wrist, her long black sleeve coming loose for the briefest of seconds. 'For a military officer to have been involved with a *subversivo* while the Dirty War was in full swing? We're not talking about some tiny uprising here. The scale of the repression was unprecedented. Artists, academics, teachers. All were labelled as dangerous as the revolutionary leaders themselves. Even if she was only a student, it's still unthinkable.'

'Not really. Love has been fucking things up for people since the dawn of time. Even your parents have been excusing themselves all along in the name of love.'

Paloma's face contorts. There's that glimpse again as she wipes an eye – a flash of something, is it a silver bracelet catching the light?

'I'm sorry,' he adds hopelessly.

'Is that what you were doing for so long in the booth yourself?' Paloma's sleeve flaps loose again as she knuckles at her eyes. 'Just apologising again and again?'

But now Jonny can only stare in horror. No trick of light can explain away the marks he is sure he can see slashed into the flesh above her wrist. He shies away, leaning down to fiddle with the bags at his feet. Still the memories assail him. For Jonny has seen marks like that before, in another time and place, on the person he cared most about in the world. The person that took her own life by means of cuts like that. Scars tangled like silver latticework. So many they looked like bracelets, some red, some silver, intertwined and tangled all the way up her forearms. A tapestry of pain, hatred and self-loathing.

He gives his head an infinitesimally small shake. Suddenly he's nine years old again, watching through a crack in the bathroom door as his mother cuts herself. She'd thought he was sleeping. Her cries had woken him up. It's the exact opposite of suicidal, she'd whispered around the kitchen table with a friend the next day. It reminds me that I'm alive. Jonny had overheard that too. He just didn't understand what the word 'suicidal' meant until it was too late.

'Jonny?' Paloma prompts. 'What were you doing in the booth? Apologising?' But he is still miles away, suddenly able to feel

Paloma's despair as viscerally as if it were his own. And telling her exactly what he's just found out is going to make it immeasurably worse.

'Not … not exactly,' he eventually replies, digging inside the bags at his feet, instinctively fiddling with the weapons that Jorge gave them.

Paloma sighs, long and deep, just as a beam of light flashes through the car. Finally Jonny straightens. This time there is no mistaking where it is coming from.

'What's the matter?' Paloma asks as Jonny twists around. There's another car behind them, following a little too close for comfort on a snaky mountain pass. He reflexively checks his wrist, notes the time – still early, exactly as they'd planned, when these roads are usually deserted, the only possible obstacles ice and fog. The realisation that the car behind is not just following but purposefully closing in on them starts to dawn with another flash of a headlamp. But the road has already narrowed to a single lane, undulating down the mountainside.

And then the rear car makes its move, smashing deliberately into their bumper. Paloma has a split-second to choose between veering into the mountainside or plunging into a ravine. The sickening crunch that accompanies her decision to take on the slope crumples the car's bonnet so hard that it concertinas up in front of the windscreen. Jonny cries out, but the ambush has already succeeded. There's no time to reflect on whether this is a simple accident, the kind that plagues South American roads at least a thousand times or more on any given day. No time to check whether either of them is OK or discuss what to do next. Because it was time that was the giveaway in the first place. Jonny knew the minute he checked the watch on his own wrist. He is yanked out of the car and straight into a headlock before he's even taken another a breath.

Paloma screams, knife-sharp into the silence.

Then Jonny sees the blade.

And then, there is nothing at all.

Chapter Twenty-Six

The clifftop feels different underfoot. There's no floating, unbound, along the edge of Jonny's consciousness, along that most ephemeral of dividing lines between fantasy and reality. This time every step of the journey feels like a step further towards death. Jonny's reached the spot now. It's so familiar he could never miss it even in this alternate version of his endlessly recurring dream. It's as if his subconscious has pitched into an even darker place, where physical pain is embedded into every movement. And yet Jonny is doing it anyway, of course he is, trying to turn his head to watch the family picnic, trying to stretch out to see if he can feel the love and laughter for himself. But all he finds is pain so intense that his head becomes locked into position, no choice left but to stare endlessly into a malevolent sea.

Until he is jerked back into reality by a surge of white-hot agony, a bolt to his torso that, in the split second he has before his consciousness explodes, he decides can only be explained by a bullet.

But when he opens his eyes, he is most definitely alive.

And in more pain than he's ever experienced.

Jonny grunts through the haze. Every movement is agony. He finds himself completely spread-eagled on a table of some kind, hands and feet tethered tight to each corner. There's no smoking car wreck a few feet away, nor fresh mountain air overhead. Just a clammy white ceiling splotched with flies and glimpses of blank walls to his either side.

Memories clatter back into his head, each more painful than

the last. A vast church, a claustrophobic confession booth. A dazed escape, a hot car, a twisty Andean highway. Until an ambush so short, sharp and straightforward it must have been well planned. Bariloche is a populous city, full of eyes and ears. Paloma and Jonny could not have been snatched in broad daylight. So it had to happen where it did.

But *when* it did? Why wait for thousands of miles of empty roads to pass, and then do it on a treacherous mountain bend? Gingerly shifting his head in the direction of a low hum, the source of Jonny's pain instantly becomes abundantly, agonizingly clear. Jonny can't see how they are administering it, nor exactly who *they* are. But the only energy coursing unearthed through this squalid room is electricity. Lots of it.

Jonny cries out, panic squeezing what little air is left in his battered chest. A face covered almost entirely in a black balaclava appears over his.

'Please,' Jonny begs, teeth chattering in pain. 'Please, don't. What do you want to know? I'll tell you everything—'

There he has to stop as the electricity surges, another bolt of agony so intense that his vision fades at the edges. He screams, no longer knowing the difference between rational and irrational thought. The face reappears as if in pixels, eyes blinking from within tiny holes, lips moving underneath a cover of darkness.

Paloma's is the scream he hears next.

'No,' Jonny cries, straining excruciatingly against his bindings. But the face overhead is still staring impassively at him. He's strapped down, he can't turn his head, he can't see where Paloma is.

'What do you want,' he pants, beseeching the face above. 'Information? I'll tell you everything I know. Please, just please don't hurt her.'

Paloma's voice cuts in – frenzied, pleading Spanish. Jonny cries out again, bindings biting at his wrists as he tries to twist round and look for her.

'The girl,' another voice says. 'Where is she?'

Jonny tenses. That heavy accent. That awkward inverted cadence again. *Where is the girl? But which girl?*

'I don't know what you mean,' he pleads. The face looms unblinking overhead.

'The girl,' the voice says again. Not the sound of a voice that's ever said please and thank you in any language before. A low voice coming from a barrel-sized chest packed with arrogance and entitlement. 'We know there is a girl. We need to know where she is.'

'I haven't met any girl,' Jonny burbles. 'What do you want from me?'

'Stop talking, Jonny.' Paloma's voice is shrill with panic. 'Don't say anything else.'

The electricity surges again in the same moment, radiating outward through Jonny's body. His whole skeleton seizes, jerking excruciatingly against his bindings.

'Paloma,' he gibbers incoherently. 'Help me, please—'

'Don't say my name!' she screams. There's a thud. A burst of static. The unmistakable sound of a scuffle in the corner, of Paloma being restrained in some way. The face overhead comes back into pixelated focus, eyes boring into Jonny's.

'The girl,' the voice repeats. 'We know about the girl. This will not stop until you tell us where she is.'

'The girl.' Jonny is frantic. His heart is beating out of rhythm. 'Which girl? There was a body first. A dead female on the beach. Is that who you mean? I don't know her name.'

Paloma screams again, muffled and desperate.

'Then there was a pilot,' Jonny continues, just as desperate. 'He's dead now too. Because he tried to tell me why she had been killed. But you know that, right? So what do you want with us?'

Another thud, harder this time, followed by a strangulated groan.

'Please don't hurt Paloma,' Jonny begs. 'She hasn't done anything wrong. I'm the one you want. I'm the one who has been asking all the questions. I'm the one who knows what happened to the stolen babies—'

Again he has to stop, gasping as the silver point of a cattle prod appears in front of the face above.

'Paloma,' the voice says, lips twisting beneath the balaclava.

'It isn't her fault,' Jonny gibbers, fixated on the gleam of silver. 'None of this is her fault. She's the only innocent party in the whole thing. Please don't hurt her. She doesn't even know the full story yet.'

'Paloma is the girl.' A statement not a question. The eyes flick to a point beyond Jonny's head. And instantly Jonny realises his mistake.

The girl.

The girl that connects all the dots. The girl whose name Jonny has just found carved into a confession booth of a church marked on a map left for her to find. The girl who is a product of an unthinkable relationship, stolen from her mother at birth and given away to a family who helped enable one of the most brutal military repressions in history. The girl that proves Jonny's whole story.

Paloma.

The silver cattle prod shimmers, mercifully still.

And then things start to happen very quickly.

The face falls away, along with the cattle prod. More scuffling breaks out behind Jonny. He pictures Paloma, held between the men, tape of some kind being ripped off her mouth. The Spanish that follows is incomprehensible, so rapid and fast Jonny can't identify one word from the next, only the emotions behind each one, the unmistakable cadence of a deal being agreed by both sides. One face after another flashes past in a blink – two men, dressed in identical fatigues, wrapped in black balaclavas. And suddenly the pressure releases at Jonny's hands and feet, the relief almost as agonising as the original pain of the bindings. He's bending his legs, arching his back, dizzy with the blood rushing to every compressed joint. Are these men letting him go? More Spanish, fevered and insistent, ricochets overhead. Then there's a change in the air. The silencing of a hum. And finally, the slam of a door.

Jonny rolls on to his side, braces for a different kind of blow, sees it as it lands.

For there, hidden in the corner behind him, is Paloma. But she's not rushing over to him, crying with blessed relief, arms spread wide to sweep around him. She's a wraith in the shadows, the whites of her eyes dead as gravestone marble.

And there's a gun in her hand.

Jonny hunches, holding his head between his arms, curling his body into abject supplication.

'You knew,' he whispers.

'I guessed,' she replies.

'That you're the reason?' he asks.

A bitter snort. 'Reason,' she says. 'As if anyone could honestly apply reason to any of this. This isn't the story of a man and a woman who fell in love and had a baby. Or even the story of a military commander who took pity on a prisoner. This is the story of unthinkable criminality and cruelty. And it's my story. I'm the fucking baby. They've been looking for me all along. And now here I am.'

'I'm sorry,' Jonny whispers pathetically. He flinches as she gets to her feet, waving the gun in the air.

'You've finally got it all. The United States stole babies trafficked during the Dirty War. Elements of Argentina's former military junta are still operating with state-sponsored impunity, silencing anyone threatening to break ranks and reveal the truth of what happened during the repression itself. You've finally got the whole story, from start to finish. I'm the missing piece you've been looking for all along. And when you report it, you get to make your name, whereas I get to spend the rest of my life knowing I've destroyed the only two people who've ever loved me. What do you think will happen to my parents when you go public? There's no priest that can get them out of this. No higher power saving them from maximum jail time on unthinkably horrific child trafficking charges—'

'Stop,' Jonny cries. 'Neither of us could have ever imagined it would end like this.'

'Like what?'

He shrinks into himself as Paloma advances on him. Out of the corner of his eye he spies the full horror of the scars laced all the way up her arms as she waves her gun in the air. So many they look like bracelets, red and silver circles intertwined and tangled. Old threads mixed with new. Ropework made of flesh.

'You said all you wanted was the truth,' Jonny says, fighting to keep his voice level. 'All you wanted was to know what really happened. Now you do, and—'

'No.' Something in her reply turns Jonny's insides to ice.

'But it's not just about the truth. It's about justice, too. You can prove it all, just by being yourself. It's been you all along. You're the reason the pilot was able to save a prisoner. He couldn't have if she wasn't pregnant. You're the reason the pilot came to me in the first place. And you're the reason he couldn't bear to tell either of us the full story himself—'

'Shut up!' Paloma's screeching now, Jonny hunches, he can see her flailing.

'I saw your name, Paloma. I saw it carved in the confession booth. It was unmistakable – just like the names I saw in the ESMA. It's why the pilot sent us to that church. A military officer involved with a *subversivo*? You said it yourself, it's unthinkable. Even more so the idea that he was able to save her with no consequences. But if she had a baby for him to bargain with? That's a different story—'

Paloma lets out a sudden, anguished cry. 'It's not a story, Jonny. It's my life. And I've known it since I remembered those stupid tattoos on their chests. I just didn't understand what I was looking at until now.'

'The tattoos of birds?' Jonny replies idiotically, not understanding.

'Doves,' Paloma answers dully. 'They were both tattoos of doves.'

Jonny gasps, their faded outlines instantly flashing into his mind. Along with the Spanish word for dove. *Paloma*, he thinks, for the briefest of seconds. One of the only Spanish words he's learned that has actually stuck in his mind, because it had something to do with her.

'They loved you so much,' he replies desperately. 'Don't you see? This proves it even more.'

'That's something else you said too,' she says. 'Love has been fucking things up for people since the dawn of time.'

She takes a step towards him. Suddenly all Jonny can see is the gun in her hand.

'Listen to me, Paloma,' he pleads. 'This is the story of two people who loved you so much it got them both killed in the end. This is the story of two people who named you after the universal symbol for peace. And it's the story of two other people who still love you so much they've been driving themselves mad for lying. The pilot can't have been much older than twenty when he flew those planes – I know, I'm the one who saw his face. And she was just a student, didn't the curate say? Guilty of nothing other than wanting to learn. They were our age. They probably just got carried away and before they knew it, the world had changed. The laws of the land were different. Maybe the pilot didn't even know she was pregnant until he found her on his plane. Maybe neither of them ever knew they'd had the same tattoos done. It must have happened long afterwards. We know the government's amnesty laws mean these former commanders are largely free to live as they please. Maybe they came across each other somewhere, years later. Maybe she tried to find you, and that's what gave them both away. All we know for sure is he saved her in the first place. And think about your adoptive parents, everything they've done for you your whole life. They chose to keep your birth name, memorialise it all in a small way – why? Because of love. The real truth here is you've never wanted for anything.'

'And that's the whole point,' Paloma replies with a voice as dull as stone. 'I can't lose it all now. Which I will, if we tell anyone else the truth.'

And when Jonny looks up, it's into the barrel of a gun.

Chapter Twenty-Seven

Terror kicks at Jonny's chest. Paloma has both hands wrapped around a gun that Jonny is sure he has seen before. Its barrel is so close he can smell the sharp tang of steel, the inescapable chalky edge of gunpowder.

'That's why those men left? Because you convinced them you'd finish the job? Silence their last remaining threat? As if you're not still a potential loose cannon too.'

'Shut up,' Paloma replies, trying to stop the pistol shaking. 'I have to do this.'

'And they bought it too, because of who you really are,' Jonny continues disbelievingly. 'Somehow what your parents did all those years ago is still protecting you even from thousands of miles away.' Head still bowed, his gaze snags on something in the corner behind her.

'Stop talking about them. You don't know my family and you never will. You'll never be able to prove what happened here without me.'

'I know how lucky you are, though.' Jonny is suddenly gabbling, squinting at the shapes in the shadows behind her, praying he's right about where she's got her gun from. 'Even people with stories far less fucked up than yours don't feel the same love that you have. Trust me. I'm one of them.'

'Nothing compares to this.' Paloma is still trying to level the pistol at him. 'Don't try and convince me otherwise. I know what I have to do next. It's the only thing left that I have any control over. And it's the only way I can protect my parents too.'

Jonny squints at the shapes again, at the unmistakable outlines of their backpacks in the corner, still lumpy with possessions save for the gun that Paloma must have pulled from hers. The tiniest seed of hope starts to bud in his chest, the most agonising gamble of all.

'But this is just the beginning,' he tries again. 'There's still time—'

'...for the babies,' she finishes, finally returning his gaze with dead eyes. 'The problem is, none of us are babies anymore. All we've got left is the horrific truth about who we really are. About what the people we thought were our parents really did. About how some of us have realised we've colluded in it all too somehow, just by being ourselves. The truth is all that's left, and it's fucking unbearable. And that's the problem with people like you. You think the truth is enough. You think that's where it ends. You think the facts bring closure – worse, you think they bring justice. Like there is ever any kind of justice that can be dispensed to address crimes as monstrous as these. You can't see past the truth, even when the only option some of us have left is to live with the lie.'

Jonny screws his eyes shut. Instantly he's nine years old again, quivering with disbelief and confusion, repeating the same question to anyone who will listen. What does it mean to take your own life? And doesn't he wish he didn't know the real answer – that it means you can't live with yourself? In that moment Jonny can almost hear his mother sobbing that he forgive her. For the facts of this particular matter are the truth hollowed Jonny out till there was nothing left but betrayal to fill the void.

'People like me,' he repeats. 'Don't you see that we're made for people like you?'

'Journalists who want the truth at all costs are the ones who'll never understand its consequences. And the truth is, there's nothing to fear from dying if you're already dead.'

Jonny's eyes fly open. And this time all he sees is the palm of

Paloma's hand, long sleeve yawing back around the latticework of desperation scarred all over her arm.

Because she's turned the gun on herself.

Time slows, turning their surroundings into a wormhole, prolonging the click of Paloma's trigger to a single, agonising note.

And then there are two screams.

One from Paloma, the soft flesh of her cheek catching the sharp edge of Jonny's metal table as she falls to the ground in shock.

And one from Jonny, laden with blessed, incredulous relief. The most deranged of gambles has come together with the mechanical precision of the electrical unit still live-wired in the corner. He scrabbles in his pocket for the bullet he removed from Paloma's gun in the car the moment he registered the true depth of her scars. He only had the briefest of moments to do it in. But for someone like Jonny, it was more than long enough. Anyone with scars like that is safer without weapons of any kind.

And then the clock ticks inexorably forward. Jonny's next steps become painfully, instantly clear.

Suffused with adrenaline, his tortured body twitches as he moves at speed. Sliding on to the floor, he clamps a hand over Paloma's mouth before she can scream again, jerking his head in the direction of the closed door ahead, willing that she understand. They need to make use of every second. Jonny is supposed to be dead. Any more screaming will just signal a scuffle that needs immediate attention, and they won't stand a chance then. The bullet twinkles under the grimy overhead light as it rolls between the fingers of his other hand.

'I didn't want you to hurt yourself anymore,' he whispers, dropping the bullet to take hold of her wrist, running a thumb over its bracelets of scar tissue. 'And I knew you would, once you understood everything. I've … I've seen scars like yours before. I wish I didn't know what it takes to … to make them.'

Above his hand, Paloma's eyes fill with tears, dark pools of sorrow. Years flash past in the seconds Jonny stares back, seeing himself reflected in the tortured abyss, feeling the most curious of emotions prickling in his chest. How strange it is to feel grateful. How strange it is to see value in such depths. For Jonny only appreciated the depths of her pain because he's borne witness to similar pain himself.

And then he feels something else. Racing, just below his thumb. Paloma's pulse. Unmistakable even under the layers of knotted flesh. His breath stills in his chest, energy coursing between them both, a live circuit that suddenly feels infinitely more mighty than the one humming in the corner. He lets her go, taking his last chance.

'The only way out of this is together. If you die, then I'm finished too. I'll be shot the second I step into the corridor and leave your body behind. But it won't end there. Because the story will come out either way. Both our names are printed all over a major international newspaper. We've put clues all over the internet. I've told my editors almost everything we know. Neither of us can just disappear. And what do you think will happen to your parents then? There are thousands of people out there who still don't know who they really are. There are thousands of bereaved families who aren't just going to stop looking for them. You aren't the only one, Paloma. You know that. You've known since we started looking into this whole mess to start with. Both of us need to get out of here alive to stay in control of the whole story. And we can only do that together.'

He reaches for the bullet on the floor, reloading it into her weapon with a soft click before rocking back on his heels and holding his hands above his head.

'I trust you, Paloma. I know you can do it. Don't you see that you can trust me too?'

He holds his breath as Paloma reaches for her gun, slowly raising it from the ground.

And then – a burst of sound. Ricocheting round the squalid room.

Along with the bullet. That she's deliberately fired into the wall.

When she looks up at him, she's lifting a finger to her lips as she nods, the dark pools of her eyes filling with something other than despair at last.

Then Jonny understands. For he's supposed to be dead. But he's not. Which tells him the only thing left that he needs to know for sure.

She finally trusts him too.

Chapter Twenty-Eight

They move silently over to their bags. Jonny pulls out his gun, still loaded as Jorge had intended, tucks some stun darts into his cargo pockets. He switches on his iridium, prays its GPS tracker is everything Allen says it is, before pulling on his socks and boots and moving to the wall behind the door. When he looks up, Paloma is at the opposite side, bag strapped to her back, reloaded gun in one hand, the other poised to release the lock and turn the handle. He straightens, feels the weight of his rucksack on his back like armour. Then he nods.

The door flies open but Paloma and Jonny are ready. He's behind the heavy door, completely shielded from the bullets that fly. And Paloma is a good shot. She has the element of surprise. And she's been more than ready to use her gun for a while. They step over the bodies of two men and thunder down the corridor. Adrenaline surpasses the electricity still lingering in Jonny's veins. Because, unlike him, Paloma was conscious for the entire journey inside this fucking building, so she knows exactly how to get them out. And in a matter of seconds, they're in front of a modest single-storey cinder block set deep in a mountain thicket, with no guards in visible range. Paloma disappears between the trees almost faster than Jonny can follow her, threading a path away from the single dirt track leading to the building itself.

Jonny feels his breath coming in raggedy gasps. The bursts of adrenaline are still firing, urging his battered body on, but his tortured muscles are starting to flail. Paloma is running now, the woods starting to slope downhill, twigs and stones rolling underfoot. She turns, spurring him on with an outstretched hand and looping an arm around his waist.

'Watch your step,' she calls, reaching for his other arm with her own. 'It's about to get really steep. Grab my hand, look.'

The ground below suddenly falls away, dropping precipitously. But Paloma is ready even if Jonny isn't, bracing their outer arms together into the point of a triangle, lacing her fingers tightly through his at the tip. Jonny realises what's happening just as it does – she's making them dance a zigzag down the slope, feet so fleeting they're almost skating, borne forth by the soft earth underfoot, so steep that even the twigs and stones have fallen away too. And just as suddenly, they are there. With a small splash. The most precipitous of dances concludes with them ankle deep in water. Jonny rears instinctively, but Paloma dives, making use of the motion propelling her forward, reaching into the depths. She returns with the end of a chain in her dripping, triumphant hand, giving it a sharp tug.

Then Jonny sees it. He laughs, pure and clear as the mountain lake itself.

For gliding towards them across the surface of the water is a boat. Impeccably rendered in camouflage-green, approaching with a jaunty little sway. Accompanied by a smell so acrid and sharp that can only be explained by one thing. A tank full to overflowing with fuel.

Jonny splashes on board behind Paloma. She yanks the starter cord, engine whirring pungently to life. Hand firmly on the tiller, she steers them away from the bank, cutting a path through the water as close to the shoreline as the slope of the bank will allow.

Jonny laughs again, delighting in the smell of petrol, in the whip of cold mountain air. Even though he'd only snatched a glimpse of it, he can suddenly picture that nondescript cinder torture block with its single dirt track for entry and exit as clearly as the water glimmering all around them. He gazes to his either side, reaffirms the jagged peaks of the mountains, the obvious lack of covert, much less straightforward, air escape routes. Of course their assailants were going to have a fucking boat. And of course they were going to make sure it was ready for a quick getaway. He rummages in his rucksack for his iridium, unfolding its chunky aerial and aiming it at the sky. Punching in the numbers, Allen answers almost immediately.

'Jonny! Where the fuck have you been?'

'We got caught out,' he shouts as Paloma accelerates. 'It was ugly. But we're safe for now. We're on a boat and we've got plenty of fuel.'

'I can see you,' Allen shouts back. Jonny pictures his iridium's GPS tracker flashing on a screen thousands of miles away, its technology working exactly as Allen had described. 'What happened?'

'I got it all, but I'll explain later,' Jonny answers, eyeing Paloma's hair whipping behind her. 'Some sources still need more protection. Right now we just need to get out of here, and fast—'

'Don't worry. Jorge is on his way.'

'From Rosario?' Jonny can't keep the note of panic from his voice. 'That'll take way too long.'

'No, he's close. He's been following you from a distance for a while now.'

'What?' Jonny stands without thinking, sending the boat yawing from side to side. 'Jorge has been following us all this time? Why? And why didn't you tell me?'

'Not now, Jonny. I'm sending you a ping.'

On cue, the iridium vibrates in his hand. 'It's a heading,' Allen continues. 'You need to set your GPS to direct you there, OK?'

Jonny shakes his head, suddenly flummoxed by far more than just state-of-the-art technology. 'What are you talking about? Jorge's been behind us all along? He saw what happened to us in Bariloche?'

'I'll explain later,' Allen rasps impatiently. 'Just head to the location. When you programme the GPS, a map should flash on your display screen. Jorge will meet you there. Don't ask any questions, just do it.'

'But—' Jonny starts as Paloma puts in another burst of acceleration. He waves away the noise but she just waves in the opposite direction, urging the boat on.

Jonny turns, iridium still clamped nonsensically to his ear.

And then he sees them.

The cars. Two smashed-up heaps of metal – one damaged at the back, the other at the front. Their car, and the one that ran them off the road. Both gleaming malevolently in the sun on the far side of the lake.

And then, the gunshots start.

Chapter Twenty-Nine

Two men, two guns.

But a whole lot more ammunition.

Jonny ducks, trying to stay level, squinting towards the figures next to the cars on the far side of the lake – two men, their concentration singular, their shadows in lockstep, focused on one target.

Them.

The hail of bullets falls far short of the boat but lands with such force that the lake is starting to churn, maniacal energy coursing through the water. Anger and frustration whips with every shot, both gunmen ripping through whole magazines of live rounds with the kind of velocity that only comes with automatic-fire weaponry. The boat is yawing from side to side, forcing Paloma to slow down to avoid capsizing completely.

Water is sloshing over the bow, white-tipped and menacing, bubbles bursting all over the place. Jonny thrusts the iridium towards her, slipping and sliding as he tries to brace himself with his other arm.

'We need to get to this cove,' he shouts, flinching into another volley of sharp cracks. The wind gusts, laced with gunpowder, acrid and sharp. 'It's our only way out.'

'Stay low,' Paloma screams back, fighting to keep the boat level. More water slops over the bow in a spray of foam. Jonny shoves the iridium into her free hand before flinging himself on to the floor. Instantly his clothes are soaked, there's so much water pooling in the boat that he has to lift his head to keep breathing.

He pushes his body one way as the boat yaws towards the other, trying to rebalance the craft with weight alone. The engine roars as the boat banks steeply, cutting back to the opposite shoreline. Paloma grapples with the iridium, leaning her whole body on the tiller. Still the men keep firing, a merciless thunderstorm of hail into the water.

Jonny watches in horror as Paloma fumbles with the phone, knowing it won't survive being dropped into the water. A deep channel is churning round him in the bottom of the boat, little peaks and waves all of its own. Their pace slows as Paloma wavers, still leaning heavily to one side. Instantly Jonny realises what the gunmen are trying to do – must have already done. The smell hits him as physically as the waves themselves, nausea rearing immediately.

'Something's wrong with the fuel tank,' Paloma shouts. 'It must be leaking. We're losing power too fast to get to the shore.'

Jonny reels, the motion of the boat coupled with the sudden reek of petrol threatening to overwhelm him. Of course the men are trying to disable the craft itself. It'll be a bonus if they kill either of them in the process. But the boat itself is a far easier target. And it's a boat they know far better than Paloma or Jonny do. It's one of theirs, after all.

'But wasn't the tank full?' he screams back nonsensically, even as the engine starts to sputter. And who gives a shit if it was? The waves churning to either side were already gleaming menacingly enough. Now an oily sheen is spreading like a stain through the water.

'I think the tank is in here,' Paloma shouts, gesturing underneath herself. 'The shots must have pierced the side or something.'

Another hail of bullets cuts her off but they are landing further away this time. Jonny can hear Paloma's sigh of frustration as she casts around for the source of the leak.

'We can't do anything about it now.' He kneels up, bracing himself on the tiller. 'We just need to bail the boat out.'

'With what? Our hands?' Water sloshes as Paloma looks around wildly. The boat may have steadied but it's getting heavier every second. Jonny takes a deep breath.

'We can throw the bags over if we have to.' The eerie quiet that descends as the gunmen finally run out of ammo feels as terrifying as the gunshots themselves.

'There!' Jonny starts as Paloma shouts, pointing. And just as he sees it, the engine sputters and dies. The solid edge of a wooden jetty, poking into the water a few hundred yards away.

'Is that where you meant?' Paloma asks, but Jonny is already snapped back into action, emptying his rucksack of everything but essentials. Opening his gold box, he pulls out the plastic bag stuffed with the fragments of his past, with relics of a different time, shaking them into the oily water without hesitation.

And just as instantly, they are gone. Drifting like petals on a current of subterranean wind. In the sheen of the lake, Jonny sees himself, gives his reflection a little nod. For even if they do resurface, one thing he knows for sure now is that he doesn't need them anymore.

He stuffs his cash, notebook and iridium into the empty plastic bag before tying it into a watertight knot and shoving it into his rucksack. There's another splash while he's strapping the bag to his back. Paloma is already in the water. Jonny smiles as he jumps in behind her, gasping at the cold.

The edge of the jetty disappears and reappears with every stroke, but Jonny and Paloma fight on, swimming side by side, understanding passing silently between them. The only way to beat the cold is to keep moving. The outline of the jetty is solidifying now, they're getting closer, a battalion of wooden planks jutting into the water from the thickly reeded shore.

Then Paloma suddenly falters, gulping a mouthful of water.

Ahead, Jonny can see why. A tall, brick-set figure is emerging from between the bullrushes at the foot of the jetty.

'It's Jorge,' he says, slowing as she rights herself. 'We have to keep going.'

But Paloma is still floundering, coughing and spluttering.

Jonny hooks a hand under her armpit to hold her above water, his own teeth starting to chatter.

'Are you sure...' She dissolves into another coughing fit.

'No,' Jonny replies honestly, even as Jorge comes into clearer and clearer focus. If this man was instructed to follow and protect them, why has he let it come to this? The answer is as hazy as the sky above, the sun still beating back the clouds overhead.

Paloma shakes her head, treading water.

'We have to,' Jonny urges her, the cold creeping into his bones. 'We can't do anything from the middle of this freezing lake. We're on our own out here.'

'But we're together. You and me. You said we can only do it if we're together.'

'With nothing but cash and a satellite phone. Please, Paloma—'

A sudden splash makes them both flinch. Jonny peers up and down the lake, squints at the jetty. Jorge has disappeared.

'What the fuck was that?' Paloma starts to paddle in wild circles, creating her own whirlpool of panic.

'I have no idea. But I'll sink if I get any colder. And so will you. Which, by the way, is about two minutes away from happening if the colour of your lips is anything to go by.'

Jonny clamps his jaw together, gritting his chattering teeth. Paloma's lips have been blue for a while now, and not an optimistic shade of Argentinian sky blue either. She starts to swim again, panting furiously, wet tendrils of dark hair sticking to her face. Jonny pushes forward with a fresh burst of adrenaline but it fizzes and dies away almost immediately.

'Where the fuck is Jorge?' he spits through water, grunting with effort. But Paloma doesn't reply. The clouds have clamped themselves over the sun again, turning the temperature down further. It's all they have left to keep their heads above water, jetty inching tantalisingly closer with every glacial stroke.

And then Paloma's scream turns to a gurgle.

A man is suddenly between them, rearing from the depths like an electric eel, water coursing off his shorn head, hooking a meaty hand into each of their armpits.

Jonny is suddenly so cold he can't even blink, his skeleton locking in position and simply refusing to move now someone else is bearing all of its weight.

'Don't worry,' Jorge says, flashing a smile so wide that it almost sends spray off his face. 'You're safe now. Everything is under control.'

Chapter Thirty

Jorge dispenses with the jetty and with a few sharp strokes of his powerful legs has Paloma and Jonny directly in the reeds fringing the steep banks of the lake. By now Jonny is so cold that the outer reaches of his body are almost numb. Even the questions swirling around his mind are starting to slow, fragmenting into single, disconnected words. Rearing from the shallows on his knees, Jorge drags them both through the slippery bullrushes up the riverbank. A few more tugs and he's hauled them both to kneeling, propping their bodies together against a wet tree trunk. The cold is taking root now, mountain air turning their sodden clothes to frost.

Jonny folds a wet arm around Paloma, deathly pale and shivering beside him. While his body shaking uncontrollably, his mind is slowing to a crawl. Somewhere deep inside of him, he knows warmth should bud soon – they're out of the water, they're on unmistakably solid ground. But his core still feels inescapably cold, foggy with mistrust and confusion.

How did Jorge find them so quickly? If Allen told him to tail them all along then what the fuck was he doing while electricity was chasing the blood out of Jonny's veins? More, why was he told to tail them in the first place? What was the point of some covert meet and greet a gazillion useless miles further north?

There's a rustle and a second man materialises from further up the bank – Pancho? Now there are two sets of hands manipulating their bodies – lifting Jonny and Paloma, propping them to standing, dragging them both further and further away from the water. Paloma lets out a weak cry, the surrounding reeds suddenly razor sharp higher up the drier sections of riverbank. Jonny tries to take in the man to his side but can only seem to process the most basic of details – shorter than Jorge but moving with equal strength and deliberation, following the same path, focused on getting them away from the water's edge.

But where are they going after that? What's these men's ultimate goal? Here, Jonny's body flails along with his mind. And just as the question finally starts to form on his numb lips, they are there. The slope levels out into a small, dusty clearing. At last Jonny can feel something, the blistering reflection of sunlight off polished metal catching in his eye with a painful gleam. Because waiting in the clearing is a small car. And when its back doors open, the interior is so warm that by rights, it feels like steam should come billowing out.

Jonny suddenly feels himself moving like a rag doll, the prospect of getting warm and dry making him even weaker at the knees. They are crumpled into the backseat, where there are towels, thermoses, even two balled-up pairs of thick socks lolling ghostly white in the footwell. A sharp gust of mountain air takes his breath away again as more doors open and Jorge and the second man slide into position up front. Beside him, Paloma is gasping, rocking back and forth, seemingly incapable of exchanging the wet arms wrapped around herself for a dry towel.

The second man turns from the front, snakes a thick arm backward between the seat and the door to extract a thermos. Jonny folds his towel around Paloma before reaching for hers to wrap around himself. The car is already moving, scything through the undergrowth. But he can't see anything through the windows, condensation already misted on to every surface. The clearing seems to have narrowed immediately to a dirt track, heavily wooded on either side. The lid of a thermos, steaming with hot liquid, appears in a meaty hand in the gap between the two front seats. Paloma shakes her head as Jonny leans forward to take it.

'Come on,' he urges her, flinching as hot splashes burn his fingers.

She shakes her head again, tendrils of hair finally lifting from her face as they dry.

'We have to get warm,' Jonny whispers, sipping from the cup himself. 'We're no good to anyone, least of all ourselves, if we're half frozen to death.'

He gestures at the supplies in the footwell: clean, dry, appropriately sized shoes alongside the balls of socks. Two fleeces. Two undershirts. All in dark, forgettable shades of green, brown and grey. The prospect of warming even further is enough to snap him into further action. But Paloma just stiffens as he leans down, unlacing their soaking boots.

Jorge grunts approvingly from the front seat. 'Good. Dry yourselves. Get changed. Everything you need is there.'

Paloma clenches her towel, teeth chattering. 'Who ... who are you people?'

A branch snaps off the windscreen, but Jorge doesn't flinch. 'Just get changed. You don't have long.'

Long? Jonny pauses with a sock in his hand. Warmth finally starting to penetrate, he takes in the supplies in the footwell again as if he's seeing them for the first time. Socks, shoes, clothes. Two small, brand-new and neatly fastened document wallets sitting next to his sodden and largely empty rucksack. He pictures his iridium in its waterproof bag, its GPS dot flashing red on a screen somewhere else.

'How did you find us so quickly? Did Allen tell you to follow us from the start?' he asks.

Another grunt from the front seat.

'Does that mean yes?'

Silence, until another branch cracks off the windshield.

Jonny tries again. 'Did you see us get ambushed? Did you see those men snatch us in Bariloche?'

Jorge presses the accelerator. The car lurches forward with a barrage of sharp snaps.

'I need to talk to Allen,' Jonny says, reaching for his iridium, intact below the damp plastic bag. 'And if she's the one who's been telling you to stay close all along, then you need to talk to her too. You need to confirm you've extracted us safely.'

'We don't have time right now,' Jorge answers finally.

'Why not? Aren't we going back to Buenos Aires? That's almost as far as driving to Rosario. If you've been following us all this time, you know exactly how long that takes. We've got hours ahead of us. Time is one thing we've most definitely got.'

Paloma reaches a hand out from her towel to grab his arm. But not even her quicksilver bracelets of scars can distract Jonny now. 'We only need to stop for a minute. I know Allen will want to hear directly from me. She's the one who gave me this satellite phone in the first place. Just stop the car and let me call her.'

'It's not safe yet,' Jorge answers. 'And that is why we are here. To keep you safe. That's all.'

Jonny feels electricity fizzing in his veins all over again.

'Then why didn't you rescue us before? You must have seen us get ambushed. You must have seen where we were taken. You couldn't have found us so quickly otherwise. With dry clothes, too. What are you, mind readers as well as former special forces? If you can't explain that to me, then Allen is going to have to. And she's expecting me to call in. That's the protocol for any *Trib* journalist being extracted from a high-risk location. I've heard her explain it on the phone myself. She'll want immediate confirmation that you've got us safely secured. She's done it a zillion times before.'

'Don't worry. She knows.' The second man this time, staring resolutely ahead.

Jonny pictures that dot again, flashing on a faraway screen. Exactly what else does Allen already know? The cold sweat of betrayal begins to trickle down his back.

'The same way you knew where we were too, huh? So why didn't you help us when we got into trouble? If you've been so close by all this time? Did Allen—' There he has to stop, chest hitching. 'Did she...?'

But Jonny can't get the rest of his question out. Just to give the idea oxygen is enough to take his own away. He thinks about the two years that have passed since he and Allen last worked directly together. How she has been promoted into ever more senior editorial positions at the heart of the *Trib*'s headquarters in Washington DC. How her goals have clarified, how her focus has sharpened, while his has consistently fallen wide of the mark, always distracted by searching for the one thing he never seems able to find. When Paloma takes over, she is able to articulate the obvious in a way Jonny can't.

'You were under orders too.' A statement, not a question. 'You were told not to intervene under any circumstances, unless you got the nod. And now...'

Jonny knows Paloma is still speaking, she's even leaning forward, shrugging off her wet towel, stabbing an accusatory finger into the fetid air. But his ears are shutting down, processing any more of her words is causing him physical pain. Isn't Allen the one who always says that no story is worth dying for? Isn't Allen the one repeating this to him whenever he heads off on a story with the merest hint of risk? Jonny tries to mouth the words but can't seem to make his lips obey instructions either. Is it possible that Allen, the one person left on this earth that Jonny thought he could trust with his life, is now driven by ambition over everything else?

Jorge suddenly hits the brakes, sending them both flying forward. Jonny meets the leather back of the seat head on, instinctively screwing his eyes shut, bracing for the blow. But when he opens them, Paloma is pulling herself straight with the most curious of expressions.

A flick of a wrist and Jorge cuts the engine. Jonny shakes his head. He's sure he can still hear the car running, but there's a keening in his ears. Paloma turns, mouthing something unintelligible. He shakes his head again, mind short-circuiting every time it encounters the idea that Allen might have deliberately let them come to harm just to get the best possible news story of all.

Jorge opens his door into an unmistakable cloud of noise.

Paloma mouths at him again, but it's no use. Jonny's hands are clamped back against the sides of his head. The keening is so intense now that it is almost unbearable. Relentless waves of sound are billowing dust up off the floor of the wide forest clearing.

Jonny sees it now without needing to look into the sky.

A helicopter is coming in to land.

Chapter Thirty-One

The craft is small and as neatly rendered as the boat, its gleaming aluminium curves painted the same distinctive Argentinian blue as the sky. It would be almost invisible were it not for the relentless thud of its rotor blades spinning up bare earth as it hovers into land a little further ahead.

Roaring scuds unbearably through the car as the back doors crunch open, fine clouds of dust churning all around them. Jonny is hauled out one way, Paloma the other, shouting unintelligibly all the while. He feels rather than sees something being pressed into his pocket – the small bags from the footwell, his own sodden rucksack left behind. They are manhandled over to the helicopter itself, Jorge climbing in behind them, leaving the second man on the ground. Jonny knows they are talking to each other, salutes are being tipped back and forth, but still can't make out a word. The helicopter whines, banking steeply as it rears, flinging them around on the cockpit's metal floor.

Jonny watches in a crumpled daze. Paloma is allowing Jorge to strap her in and clamp a pair of ear defenders around her head. He finds himself letting Jorge do the same for him – righting his body into position, deftly placing the soft pads over Jonny's ears too. Only then does Jorge sit down himself and stare implacably out of the window as if he is surrounded on all sides by serene silence rather than deafening noise.

'Hey!' Jonny shouts, clicking his fingers into Jorge's face. 'Are you going to tell me what the fuck is going on? Where is this helicopter going?' But Jorge just sits, impassive, gestures that he can't hear a word.

Jonny turns frantically back to Paloma. He still can't make out what she's trying to tell him, her lips are barely moving. He tries to read her expression instead, her body language – sleeves fastened tight around her wrists, hands wrapped around the leather straps across each shoulder, the rhythmic, unhurried rise and fall in her chest. It's clear that something has calmed Paloma down, but Jonny can only guess at what.

Leaning forward, he taps Jorge on the arm, mouths over the din. 'Buenos Aires?'

Jorge affirms with a little nod. Jonny returns to his seat, mind turning.

Buenos Aires wasn't safe for Jonny and Paloma before. It's even less safe for them now. And they have no control over where they are going. They have almost no leverage left other than information that implicates some of the world's most powerful institutions and Allen, the one person he thought could have weaponised it safely on their behalf, is feeling less trustworthy with every passing minute. Jonny looks out of the helicopter window, despairs at the sky's infinite blue depths. They're trapped on all sides, surrounded by nothing but open air.

He digs around in his pocket only to find a small document case – one of the two he'd spied in the footwell of the car. Unzipping it, he finds a sheaf of dollar bills and a British passport inside – in his name, all details present and correct, newly issued by the British embassy in Buenos Aires. When he looks up again, Paloma is already nodding back. He reaches into her pocket, finds an almost identical set of documents.

Jonny contemplates the passports, the money, the improbable mint-newness of it all. So, as well as positioning reinforcements close by all the while, Allen had also long prepared for their exit? His heart gives a staccato thump as an image flashes before him – being tied down in that squalid cinder block, shock after shock, coming not just from electricity, in so much pain he couldn't tell the difference between rational and irrational thought. And suddenly he finds himself considering exactly what's rational and what isn't about everything that's happened since they were ambushed.

What could Paloma possibly have said to their assailants over the course of those few fevered seconds that convinced them to give her control of a loaded gun? Why would two hardened professionals leave their most precious quarry alone with a deadly weapon and in charge of the most delicate task of all? And by then they knew who she really was – a product of an unthinkable relationship between a former prisoner and a commander during one of the most fearsome and wide-ranging repressions in history.

So they must also have known where she was raised, Jonny realises. He considers what he knows about her adoptive parents. *US government people, in on Operation Condor from the ground up.* How is it that they are still exerting control over the Argentinian establishment years later, control that seems somehow to be extending as far as Allen in Washington DC too? He's fingering the pristine sheaf of banknotes in his hand when he sees it staring him in the face. The story he has been covering since he arrived in Argentina. *Follow the money, Jonny. It's all you need to be doing out there.*

Jonny gasps, suddenly winded all over again. Argentina is in the grip of the most serious financial crisis since the end of the Dirty War. The only way out is with a massive amount of international aid. The means by which Paloma's parents are exerting their seemingly inconceivable levels of control over the Argentinian establishment from thousands of miles away suddenly becomes as abundantly clear as the money in his hand. What else was it that Paloma had said, back in the crazed dark of her apartment, over the body of an unconscious stranger on the floor? That her parents had only been able to move from DC to New Mexico by abandoning their jobs at the State Department in favour of occasional big consultancy contracts for the US Treasury. Does it get any bigger than a multi-billion-dollar international financial bailout package for a country with record-breaking levels of sovereign debt? Her parents – with their previous experience of Argentina – must be architects of the whole damn thing. Influential enough to also hide the fact they're making financial aid contingent on keeping Paloma, their longed-for only child – safe from harm.

The helicopter banks steeply, sending sunlight piercing through the windows. And now Jonny is picturing Allen in an altogether different light, in her seat as managing editor of a major international newspaper headquartered directly opposite the White House. She looks upon monuments of American nationhood from her office window every single day. She herself has just been granted dual citizenship. And she is, without question, one of the best and most fearsome journalists of her age. Here she is with a reporter on the cusp of a horrifying global scoop that incriminates the United States above all. So what is she doing to protect her reporting team on the frontline?

The fact that some thirty thousand people died during the Dirty War is well known. So is the fact that many of those people simply disappeared. And so is the fact that America backed the principals of the repression itself. But the fact that babies were stolen from pregnant captives? Worse, trafficked across international borders with impunity to none other than the United States, the world's so-called bastion of freedom and liberty? Those facts are so incendiary that they are almost unbelievable. Jonny pictures Allen with a phone to each ear, calling all her contacts in double-quick time. She must have set state-sponsored alarm bells ringing at the highest of levels. And now she's under new orders herself, the ones that journalists are paid not to heed. The ones designed to intimidate journalists from speaking the harshest of truths to the highest of powers. *That's* why Jorge and Pancho caught them up. It wasn't Allen deliberately putting them in harm's way just to get the best news story of all. It was Allen rushing to shut their reporting down as comprehensively as possible. A betrayal of an altogether different and even more sinister kind.

Jonny pulls out Paloma's passport, flicks through its pages to confirm it to himself. There's her picture – the dark hair, the even darker eyes. Jonny's heart lurches, the expression on Paloma's face now unforgettable in so many more ways than just the jerk in his chest he'd become used to trying to suppress. How else would Allen have been able to mint passports such as these without government collaboration at the highest levels? How would she have access to all of Paloma's personal information? She must have tipped off people with direct knowledge of her history.

Jonny stares into the sky, finally understanding that something so limitless can only ever give him a completely empty answer. But when he turns back to Paloma, she is smiling.

Why? He frowns, as if his eyebrows can ask the question themselves.

And then he sees it.

The bulge at her belt, under her shirt. Invisible to everyone who doesn't know her like Jonny does.

He looks at Jorge, sees the empty holster at his belt, puts it all together.

There's one weapon left on this helicopter. And Paloma is the one who has it.

Chapter Thirty-Two

Paloma's eyes lock on to his – ferocious, determined. A sequence of images plays through Jonny's mind – the steamy confines of the car, everything still slippery and wet, Paloma pitched up against the driver's seat when Jorge abruptly hit the brakes. The lake's freezing, churning dark waters. The commotion through the reeds and up the riverbank. Cold enough to go numb. Treacherous enough to lose a shoe. But to dislodge a pistol?

Paloma stops him checking out Jorge again with an infinitesimal shake of her head. But Jonny still wonders. Is it possible a man like Jorge, a seasoned intelligence agent of the most mercenary kind, would ever lose his grip on a weapon?

A small smile turns the corners of Paloma's mouth. All around them, the sky beams Argentine pride. And hope, that cruellest and most capricious of mistresses, starts to bud again inside Jonny's chest. Who cares whether it was possible or not? All that matters now is what happens next. Allen's paymasters in DC may think that they'll silence them for good just by helicoptering them out. But by now Jonny knows exactly what they need to do next to fight back with the truth. *Leverage*, he thinks, returning Paloma's gaze with similar conviction. It's sitting there right in front of him. Her parents couldn't be more desperate. She just needs to call them. They'll help her in any way she asks in return for keeping their family together.

Follow the money, Jonny thinks to himself. Things never happen for no reason. Paloma needs to establish beyond doubt that the United States is making financial aid contingent on covering up the true extent of its involvement in the Dirty War. They already know it must be true, but only classified information will confirm it. And Paloma sure as hell has got some inside sources on that. He pushes away the thought it usually takes more than just two powerful people to bring down an army. The hope is still blossoming.

But how will they get their story out? Follow the money, Jonny repeats to himself. Freelance journalism always comes with a price. Especially in Argentina, where the financial crisis is all that has interested Western newspaper outlets for months. Allen may be their current paymaster, but she doesn't speak for every news agency in the world. They can simply take their story to another bidder. Jonny pushes away the fact that the *International Tribune* is one of the biggest news operations going. It has plenty of rivals snapping at its heels. If they're going to convince one of them to take it on instead, Jonny and Paloma will just have to make sure they have watertight evidence that American institutions, at the highest of levels, are effectively holding the Argentinian people to ransom over something so incendiary as atrocities committed during the Dirty War.

Jonny calculates. Bariloche to Buenos Aires is almost a thousand miles by road. Even flying off-grid, they must have at least an hour up in the air, if not more. By the look of the land below, they still have a way to go – miles upon miles of pampas grass flash through his mind before green starts to win over brown and become the more fertile *estancias* within hours of the capital itself. He steals a glance at Jorge, at the man's half-closed eyes, dreaming into the blue. And begins to talk. Rant, in fact. About a load of absolute fucking nonsense.

Has Paloma ever had a cup of real, English tea? Builder's – the same strength and colour as tan leather. The teabag comes out before the milk goes in. It is outrageous to do it the other way round. The teabag must steep, under no circumstances must it ever be stabbed with a teaspoon – doesn't she know that bruises the tea leaves? And no, buttermilk pancakes and maple syrup will never be an equal substitute for a Full. English. Breakfast. Doesn't she know that either? Two bacon, two sausages, two eggs. Beans, mushrooms, tomatoes, bread – also fried. White, not brown. The sauce is brown, not the bread. And while we're on the subject of colours – black pudding. It's essential. It's not a full English without it.

Paloma nods along, smiles, even cocks her head. Jonny unzips document wallets, waves matching passports around, starts up about the London Eye. No, it's not a fucking Ferris Wheel. If she must call it a wheel, then at least call it the Millennium Wheel – and no, of course he hasn't been up in it yet, it's still not finished. Jonny tucks away the passports with a sidelong glance at Jorge, confirms the man's eyes are firmly closed now, though his head is still balanced perfectly straight up. If Jonny had to guess, he'd say the man was faking sleep to avoid talking, especially this kind of mindless babble. On cue, Jonny throws himself into further deranged discussion of London's millennium planning. The land below the helicopter's scudding motor is turning greener by the mile. Jonny squints, they can't be more than half an hour out from Buenos Aires by now. Surely they aren't going to be landing in the unvarnished daylight of a commercial airport?

He leans towards Paloma, mouthing. 'We must be going to a private air field.'

She nods back, eyes glittering.

'You lead, I'll follow,' he continues, eyes darting to the bulge below her shirt. A small frown crosses Paloma's forehead. Jonny sits back. Up front, he sees Jorge has turned around. On cue, Jonny's ears pop, the helicopter starting its descent.

'Are we landing?' Jonny shouts pointlessly, frowning just a little too hard, pointing a finger downward for extra emphasis. Jorge nods, another self-satisfied jerk of his head at a job well done.

Jonny smiles back like a maniac. Anything to ensure Jorge doesn't realise what is missing from the tiny, lightweight holster at his belt. The helicopter banks, descent turning to a corkscrew. Jonny's stomach lurches, the land below feels like it is coming up to meet them rather than the other way around, telescoping a cluster of low-lying buildings around a grey smudge amid the green.

Jonny peers out of the window to his side, no need to disguise his sentiments any longer. Beside him, Paloma's hands tense around the leather straps pinning her into her seat.

The grey smudge is solidifying to a slab. A shadow at its far end is coming into sharper focus.

The unmistakable silhouette of a plane.

Jonny's mind speeds up, rotor blades overhead starting to howl. For Jorge, this is his final step – get his precious cargo on to this plane and back into the sky. Will he have an armed escort waiting to help finish the job? Are they going to have to fight their way past more than just Jorge? Even without his pistol the man will have been trained in hand-to-hand combat of the highest order.

Jonny tries to think as methodically as the thudding rotor. Someone like Allen having ready access to private security agents is one thing. Those same agents putting on a conspicuously public show of force is quite another. Allen needs to keep this operation covert to be sure of getting away with it. Just like the original death flights, he realises, sickened. He scans the scene below as if he's seeing it for the first time.

The plane is small. Much like the helicopter, and the car before that. Five black dots on its side – windows? Jonny counts again to confirm. A cockpit, a tiny passenger compartment, a tail. He considers another dot on the tarmac. A car? And can he pick out any figures moving around? There must be staff of some kind to keep the place operational. As Jonny thinks it, the thin, silver lines of a control tower start to shimmer at the airstrip's far end. The helicopter banks again, curving round to the airstrip's opposite corner. Jonny tightens his grip on the straps over his shoulders, winces at the hum of the engine turning to a roar. Jorge has climbed from his seat in the front to the rear of the helicopter and is opening the door.

Soundwaves scud inside with an almost physical force. Briefly Jonny longs for Paloma to turn, to meet his eye, to silently reassure him that she's going to draw her weapon, she's going to force Jorge to fall back. But then what?

Suddenly Jonny is flailing, the engine roar unbearable. What if that isn't what's going to happen next? What if Jorge is going to disarm Paloma with the simplest flick of his wrist, then hogtie them both in this stupid impassive aeroplane before sending it on a death flight?

Jorge is out of the helicopter now, turning around with an outstretched hand to help Paloma down.

With a far simpler flick of the wrist than even Jonny was imagining, Paloma whips the pistol from beneath her shirt and shoots Jorge's hand off. The spray of blood is dispersed before the droplets can land. The sound of the shot and the screams of agony are borne away by the merciless thud of the helicopter's rotor blades.

'Help me!' Paloma yells at Jonny. His hands are still clutched around his seatbelt. She's heaving Jorge's body back through the passenger portal, no thought to the bloody stump at the end of one arm. The man is in too much shock and agony to fight back. Overhead, the motor is still thundering, fragmenting and dispersing howls of the most tortured kind.

Paloma shouts again but it's the remaining healthy hand curling around Jonny's ankle that snaps him back to the present. Jorge is suddenly flipping around on the floor of the helicopter like a fish out of water. Almost in slow motion he sees the pilot, ear defenders still clamped into place, tinted sunglasses failing to hide the question in his eyebrows, beginning to turn around.

'*Gracias*. Thank you,' Jonny screams, unstrapping himself from his seat and leaning forward in one fluid motion. He grins maniacally, even as Jorge's writhing escalates. It feels impossible the pilot won't notice the commotion. Thumping the pilot's shoulder for all he's worth, Jonny nods, grins and waves all at once before bounding over Jorge's body and ducking out on to the tarmac. Paloma is already heaving the door closed. Ducking, they run from the helicopter towards the car without a backward glance. Paloma is ahead of Jonny, dark hair whirling into a black tornado. Whether the pilot has registered his wounded cargo or not, the helicopter must be taking off again.

The car is idling between the helicopter and the plane. Its driver falls back at the sight of the gun, hands out and quavering in the air. Jonny jumps into the driving seat, flinging the engine into gear, accelerating away with a screech. Beside him, Paloma keeps her weapon trained firmly out of the window. Jonny corners away from the airstrip without a second's hesitation.

Chapter Thirty-Three

Jonny's knuckles whiten on the steering wheel. 'You shot his fucking hand off.'

'By accident.' Paloma closes the passenger window with a thump. 'It was a warning shot.'

'Like hell it was.'

'It was the only way. He was about to bundle us into an airplane, we don't even know where it was supposed to be going—'

Jonny bangs a hand on the steering wheel. 'But he was just following orders.'

'And isn't that what they all say?'

Jonny thinks of the pilots, the generals, the chaplains. The hit squads sent to kidnap, imprison and torture. All still hiding behind the same defence. That they were just following orders. That they had no choice but to comply. 'What?' Paloma asks.

Jonny realises he has snorted back. He waves the question away. But he knows it's because he'd started to think of Allen, and her orders. The ones from the deepest state of all. The ones journalists are paid not to heed. He presses down on the accelerator, forces his mind back to similar matters of mechanics. What Paloma and Jonny need to do next is find somewhere to make a call.

'Never mind. How far out of the city do you think we are?'

'I don't know, really.' Paloma leans forward, pistol still in the hand laid on the dashboard. 'But this road should be a lot busier, either way. There – look. We're right by the airport.'

She points at a street sign coming up on the side of the deserted highway, a picture of a plane picked out in white alongside the rest of its lettering.

Jonny frowns. 'That's strange.'

'Right,' Paloma answers. 'There should be a whole lot more traffic on this road—'

'No. I mean that I assumed a private air strip wouldn't be pitched so close to a major international airport.' The sign pointing to the exit to Buenos Aires' main airport scuds past in a blur. 'You're right, though. This road should be busier no matter what time of day it is.'

Paloma shrugs. 'It's better for us that it isn't.'

Jonny slows to follow the twists and turns of a roundabout, the pistol glinting and catching his eye. 'Definitely. Not least because now we need to find somewhere to get rid of that.' He jerks his head at the gun.

Paloma shakes her head. 'No way. I'm not dumping our only weapon.'

'We have to.' Jonny squints at the road ahead, fighting the image of Jorge's severed wrist, blood spraying into the air being denied even the decency of landing. 'We can't risk being tied to what happened back there in any way. No fingerprints. The only weapons we really need right now are ourselves. And a telephone.'

Paloma blanches. 'What do you mean?'

Jonny fills her in. The financial crisis, the Dirty War, the means by which deals have been agreed and sealed since the dawn of time. 'It was always going to be about money, Paloma. I should have put it together long before remembering what you told me about your parents.'

'Their contracts with the Treasury,' she murmurs, grip finally slackening on the pistol.

'What the hell else would US government people with a background in Argentina like theirs be working on for the Treasury right now if it isn't a massive financial bailout?' Jonny adds rhetorically. 'All you need to do is get them to confirm that they are making international aid contingent on your safe return. They must have panicked when you called them the night I was abducted. You told them about our investigation, right?'

She nods.

'That's when they must have started pulling various strings. Thought they'd lose you for good if you found out the truth. Or worse, that you might come to some harm in the process. They're not thinking about what'll happen to them – only about what might happen to you. So ask them. Say you'll walk away forever if they don't finally tell you everything. They are so terrified of losing you they'll only do it if you're the one asking. We just need to prove beyond doubt that the Americans are holding Argentina to ransom over covering up the true extent of their involvement in the Dirty War. The only way to do that is with classified information. And no news editor worth their salt is going to expose a source that hands it over. Telling you the truth doesn't have to mean they go down for it, too.'

Paloma wavers. 'There's no way of being completely sure of that though.'

'There's no way of ever being completely sure of anything,' Jonny answers, accelerating. 'But I know that no news editor will ask us to name a source, either. We just walk away if they do. And they won't. Because it's a massive story. You said that yourself when you were trying to convince me to drop everything else. Widespread chaos, economic meltdown, international implications – that's what's going to pay our fucking wages.'

Paloma fingers the gun in her lap. 'But you're the reporter. You're putting your name on this whole thing. You took an oath to report a source if you suspect them guilty of a crime.'

Jonny grips the steering wheel, forces himself to keep staring straight ahead. 'That I am. But what would I report in this particular case? I'm not the one calling my sources. You are. I can't prove anything on that score. Only you can. And that part is up to you. Look at it this way. Imagine if at some not-too-distant point in the future the Mothers of Plaza de Mayo get access to their overseas scientists after all. That some of Europe's finest forensic geneticists fly in to help identify individuals unknowingly living a lie. The Argentinian government can't just mandate that hundreds of people come forward for random genetic testing. It has to be voluntary. People have to want to be found.'

Paloma lets out a soft sigh. Jonny tries again.

'We're not them, Paloma. If someone told you to push unconscious bodies out of a plane, would you do it? We're not going to force anyone to do anything. We're just going to state the facts that we have. We've discovered corruption at the highest levels of US institutions in a bid to cover up the true extent of America's involvement in Argentina's Dirty War. The headline alone may give thousands of other people looking for answers access to some more information of their own.'

'But is that going to be enough for you? You don't also want to expose the fact we now know for sure that babies were stolen and trafficked from Dirty War prisoners – because we know that I'm one of them?'

'No,' Jonny replies simply. 'But it's your life. You've saved mine twice. I'm not going to force you to be the international poster child for the Disappeared if you're not ready to be. Like I said. It has to be voluntary. People have to want to be found.'

Another sign shimmers up ahead marking out the slip road to the airport. Jonny hits the indicator even though there are no other cars in sight.

'Where are you going?' Paloma asks.

'We need a phone,' Jonny answers, bearing off the highway. 'Last time I looked the airport had loads of them. Along with security cameras and armed guards. And we've got brand-new passports, too. We'll just look like we're heading off somewhere else.'

He pulls over on a grass verge, stopping just shy of an open drain.

'Last chance,' he says, nodding at the pistol in her lap. 'Just let it go. The water will wash it away.'

Chapter Thirty-Four

Jonny hovers in the airport lobby. Paloma is still in fevered conversation inside a telephone booth a few feet away. Like the highway outside, the departures terminal is largely deserted. Nevertheless, a disembodied voice blasts incomprehensibly from the tannoy overhead. Jonny pulls a passport out of his pocket, flicks through its pages with an air of studied intent. Paloma has been on the phone for a while now. And every second is slowing Jonny down.

His palm starts sweating against the pristine leather. He's in an airport. There's money in his pocket. There's a passport in his hand, a ticket to another life. Escape routes are literally lighting up the departure board. For the briefest of moments, Jonny finds himself considering whether he could do it. Whether he could actually run away. But where would he go? And how would he start again? He already knows that some things are impossible to leave behind. Every painful second Paloma is still talking is a reminder of how he hasn't got anyone left to call himself.

Another disembodied announcement clatters out of the speaker. It's only when the echoes have died away that Jonny realises Paloma has started shouting.

'Calm down,' he hisses, hurtling over to the booth. But she's already hanging up the receiver and turning to him, eyes wild with a curious mix of panic and defeat.

'My dad's disappeared. No one has seen him since yesterday morning. Everyone is going out of their minds with worry. Obviously no one was able to contact me either.'

'Start walking,' Jonny murmurs, taking her elbow. 'All you have to do is follow me, come on.'

He starts steering her back out on to the street and towards the car park.

'He's disappeared, Jonny.' Paloma sounds increasingly frantic. 'My mother said she woke up and he was just ... gone. His wallet is still in the house. His car is still on the drive. And it's all because of us.'

'She said that?' Jonny guides her over the kerb. 'How does she know?'

'Because we're right. We're right about everything. I got it all, just like you said. I knew I would the minute she said she needed to call me back on a secure line to keep talking. Why would she worry about phone surveillance if she didn't have anything to hide? But we didn't see this coming. We didn't think that guilt might have made one of them just disappear themselves.'

Jonny yanks at the car door with dread.

'Everything you said is true,' Paloma continues, voice trembling. 'They wanted a baby so much that when I arrived they couldn't bring themselves to question where I really came from. They convinced themselves just loving me enough would make it alright. Especially if they kept bringing me back to Argentina, even if they never told me the real reasons why. Then the lies became toxic. The shame has been eating them up for years. But not as much as the terror of losing me for good.' She gets into the car, slamming the passenger door closed behind her.

'So we're right about the money too?' Jonny prompts, reversing at a clip.

'Of course we are.' Paloma puts her head in her hands. 'It's the only leverage they had left. And then I disappeared anyway. All the time we've been running they've been calling my apartment. Just calling, calling and calling. Thinking the worst. Planning for the worst. Then assuming the worst. She thinks he couldn't take any more. And now she can't find him anywhere. Oh my God, what are we going to do now?'

Jonny wrenches the car into gear. 'There's only one thing we can do. Which is to tell everyone about it. Report what we know as fast as fucking possible. Make the most amount of noise we can. It's the only way that he'll know you're still alive. We're the only ones with the real story, so we're the only people who can do it. You told her that too, right?'

'Yes. But what if it's too late for him?' Even muffled by her hands, Paloma sounds completely defeated. She twists round in her seat. 'I should go back. We're at the airport. I should just go try and get on a flight out right now—'

'No.' Jonny accelerates, fighting the beginnings of his own panic. 'You think your photo isn't already flagged in some way? And even if you could get yourself on a plane heading in vaguely the right direction you'll just be incommunicado for hours and hours, completely incapable of doing anything at all.'

'But we're in the middle of a city thousands of miles away with no one on our side.'

'That's not true.' Jonny puts his foot down. 'Just think of the mothers.'

'That's all I am thinking about, Jonny.'

'The mothers of Plaza de Mayo, I mean. All the other mothers that can't eat or sleep for all the eternal fucking wondering. They're on our side.'

'But they can't help us at all.' Paloma's voice rings hollow round the car. 'We don't need cheerleaders. We need a microphone.'

Jonny looks at the clock on the dashboard. The white headscarves are suddenly back in his mind, teeming like doves. 'And that's exactly how we are going to get one. If I floor it, they'll all still be there. Hundreds of them. Mothers, grandmothers, aunts, sisters. Marching, protesting, stirring up a storm. Making themselves seen and heard.'

Paloma lets out a small gasp. 'We're just going to show up and tell them everything we know?'

'Too right we are. And it's going to whip up one hell of a storm. Those women won't back down for anything. It's the fastest way to draw cameras, microphones, the lot...'

Jonny trails off, squinting at the horizon as if he can already see the crowd turning to a swarm. But something altogether different is starting to come into focus. A roadblock is materialising across the entire carriageway. Right as the unmistakable drone of a helicopter keens through the air, its patchy green-and-brown exterior anything but camouflage against the bright-blue sky overhead.

Jonny brakes reflexively, the realisation taking hold. The reason they are the only car on the road suddenly becomes abundantly clear.

The army has control of the rest.

Chapter Thirty-Five

Jonny pulls over to the side of the highway rather than stop in the middle. Paloma's hand is already curling around the door handle. He flicks on the radio, turning the volume up to full. Rapid, solemn commentary punctuated with the occasional burst of static fills the car. The drone of the army helicopter is falling away as it flies towards the city centre.

Paloma leans forward, bracing herself against the door handle.

'Riots,' she mutters, listening intently. 'The city has exploded...' She trails off into a gasp. 'They're saying that more than twenty people have died in this latest round of protests.'

She raises a hand to quiet Jonny, but there's no need. She's already answered his question. Follow the money, he thinks, hand stealing reflexively to the wad of banknotes in his pocket. If cash was king before, then it's emperor now. And riots this deadly will guarantee plenty of cameras and microphones if Jonny and Paloma can just get to them.

A megaphone bleats in from the roadblock ahead. Now it's Jonny curling a hand around the door handle, pulling the money from his pocket with the other.

'Hold on.' A note of dread has crept into Paloma's voice. 'It's the Casa Rosada, Jonny.'

'Of course it is,' he replies, eyeing two officers waving at them from the line ahead. 'The army is hardly going to take control of the roads just because of some pot-shots at a bank. It's got to be happening outside the presidential palace.'

'That's where the worst of it is, yes. In the Plaza de Mayo, outside the Casa Rosada. But the commentator is saying they've been told to stop broadcasting.'

'What?' Jonny hesitates. But Paloma is already yanking the billfold out of his hand.

'Now we need to move even faster,' she mutters, opening her door. 'Just wait for my signal.' She walks towards the officers before Jonny can say anything else.

Jonny seethes at the floor for a moment, wishing he could understand the rest of Spanish droning incomprehensibly around the car. When he looks up, Paloma is already waving him over. He shifts into gear, but not before turning the radio off, silencing any evidence of potential dissent. Nodding at the officer who waves him through, he pauses just past the roadblock and waits for Paloma to rejoin him.

'Go,' she murmurs, flicking the radio back on immediately that the car door closes behind her.

Jonny decides to take his chances in the suburbs rather than negotiate another roadblock. Paloma is busy concentrating on the radio commentary. Taking the next slip road off the highway, he recognises his surroundings with relief. They've made it through the hinterlands between the airport and the city.

Paloma twiddles with the knob on the radio.

'Don't turn it off,' Jonny snaps.

'I'm not.' But silence is suddenly the only thing filling the air between them, even as Paloma repeatedly clicks the knob back and forth.

Nothing.

It hits them both in the same moment.

'They've stopped broadcasting,' Paloma murmurs. 'Something must have interrupted the radio transmission, but why...?'

'Why do you think?' Jonny bangs a furious hand on the steering wheel, doesn't even flinch when the horn blares. 'To stop contagion spreading. To disappear any signs of a revolution. To silence evidence of dissent. The fastest way to take control of a narrative is to shut it down. Tactics dictatorships have been using since the dawn of time. And we're not dealing with a democratic government here. We're dealing with a dictatorship in all but name, and we can prove it if we can just get our story out.'

'Slow down, Jonny.' Paloma puts a warning hand on his thigh. The road is narrowing as it moves closer to the city centre, the surrounding buildings getting higher, damaged shopfronts becoming more obvious.

'The last thing we can do right now is slow down,' he replies, gunning the engine into a sickening crunch. Heaps of shattered glass glint off the road ahead.

'No.' Paloma tugs at him, waves at the side of the road. 'I mean slow down, here.'

Jonny shakes his head. 'We're going to have to walk soon enough. We need to at least get as far as possible by car—'

'No, Jonny. Just stop for a second. We need supplies.'

Jonny's objections die on his lips when he sees where she is pointing. He brakes and stops the car just short of an upended trash can, registers the smashed frontage of the enormous shopping centre beyond.

And then Jonny sees the people.

Dozens and dozens of people.

Moving silently back and forth, arms loaded with anything and everything. As much as they can physically carry.

'Looting,' Paloma mutters.

'But where are the police?' Jonny wonders even though he knows the answer. He stares at a man wobbling beneath the weight of a television set.

'It doesn't matter, come on.' Paloma gets out of the car.

'What are you doing? We don't have time for this.'

'They've stopped broadcasting. You heard, I couldn't get the radio to work for anything.'

Jonny bangs another frustrated hand on the steering wheel, instantly regrets it as the horn sounds again, sending heads swivelling in his direction. He holds up a hand, ducks deferentially as he gets out of the car. 'Well we're not going to stop too, are we?'

'Of course not.' Paloma ducks through the building's wide-open façade.

'So what the hell are we doing in here?'

She wrings her empty hands. 'I need a camera,' she shouts over her shoulder as she speeds away.

Inside the building, the carnage is distracting. Every single shopping trolley is long gone, presumably loaded to the brim. People are working silently, shrinking into themselves as if it will somehow distract from the fact they are looting in plain sight. Working hand in glove, ransacking shelves and hangers, running back and forth between aisles with armfuls loaded so high they can barely see. But Paloma seems to know exactly where she is going too, cornering down an aisle to head for the few television sets left in the back corner. Jonny has to run to catch her up, hurdling a plastic high chair lying across the width of an aisle and skidding on a puddle of milk, burst carton bleeding on the floor like a dead white cat. When he rights himself, Paloma is letting out a triumphant sigh.

'I knew it.'

Jonny totters for a moment, finally appreciating the ingenuity of her quick thinking. 'A camera,' he murmurs, reverently watching Paloma wind the thick, black leather strap around her neck.

'No ordinary camera, either.' Paloma holds the compact viewfinder up to an eye, frowning. 'An actual video camera. Loaded with a bonus tape, too.'

She points at an upended discount sign, but Jonny is still shaking his head in amazement. He stares at the row of cameras, seemingly the only items in the entire store to still be lined up, present and correct.

'I was counting on there being at least one left.' Paloma lets the camera hang around her neck as she gazes at the rest of them. 'Then again, I suppose it isn't that surprising. These people aren't stealing in cold blood. Look how mortified they are. They're just taking what they need to survive. No one else except us needs a camera to do that.'

In a different time and place Jonny might have countered – hadn't Paloma just seen a huge television set wobbling on its way out of this beleaguered market too? In a different time and place Jonny might also have pointed out that a local radio station stopping broadcasting could also be down to a transmission glitch, and not a state-sponsored attempt to muzzle the media. And in a different time and place Jonny might have left Paloma on the pavement and carried on driving, so convinced of the fact that so long as he keeps talking, people will be forced to listen.

But in this time, in this place, with perspective of an entirely different kind, Jonny finally says absolutely nothing at all.

He leans down, takes a camera, loops a strap around his neck too.

'Now we're ready to go,' she says.

Chapter Thirty-Six

Back outside the ransacked market, the air is thick with tension. More and more people are arriving to take what they can. Jonny shrinks into himself, quickstepping past the beginnings of a fight over a loaded shopping trolley. Mercifully, the car is exactly where they left it, sticking out into the empty road at an awkward angle.

Paloma winds down the passenger-side window before Jonny has pulled away, motioning that he hand her the stills camera still looped around his neck.

'It's carnage,' she murmurs over a volley of shutter-fly. 'And if it's like this here...'

'Yep,' he replies grimly, throwing the car into gear. Something primal flares in the void in his chest before he can tamp it down. Paloma closes her window with a thump. It still feels like the tension outside is pressing up against the glass. They drive some more, cornering around the inner city's one-way grid system as far as it will let them go. Jonny pulls over just shy of a roadblock.

'*Avenida Independencia*,' he mutters with a snort.

Paloma grunts back in kind. 'Well, if independence was going to catch up with us anywhere.'

She hands back his camera before opening her door. Jonny gets out, leaving the keys dangling from the ignition. From here, they need to be fleet of foot. From here, travelling in any car other than a military vehicle will just hold them up. And Jonny hopes whoever spots this particular car's keys also appreciates the perverse irony of finding a free ride at the blocked entrance to Independence Avenue.

He breaks into a jog, Paloma following suit. The wide, majestic avenue is eerily empty, sky pinking on the horizon. The air is laced with far more than just tension now – the low roar of distant protest is punctuated by menacing hisses and staccato pops. Rubber bullets, Jonny thinks, camera slamming into his shirt front in agreement. Live rounds sound different, unless ... He pulls up short at the sight of a line of mounted police thundering perpendicular across the avenue a few blocks ahead.

'Here!' Paloma is yelling, a foot or so behind him, ducking and cornering a block further north. The horses disappear from view only to be replaced by another burn of lurid pink on the horizon – flares, Jonny realises – and he'd thought he was witnessing another dreamy sunset.

Another corner, another few tense squares on the grid, another few camera thuds to his breastbone, as if to confirm they're running towards the crack of gunfire. Live or dummy, Jonny doesn't care anymore, he just knows they're about to encounter a protest the size and severity of which he has never seen before. These are people who've been mugged by their own government. Paloma is by his side as they are borne forth into the crowd ahead on a wave of tension, anticipation and unfettered rage. They're so close Jonny can literally smell it, the air is spiked with the acid tang of tear gas, infecting every molecule with its silent, invidious grip.

Paloma turns to him, her eyes are streaming. 'I can't see,' she cries, pulling at the camera strap looped around her neck. Jonny turns out his pockets. Nothing but passports and cash. No scarves, or handkerchiefs. No tissues of any kind. He tugs at one of his cargo pockets but can't get it loose from the trouser leg. He yanks at his T-shirt only for the cotton to spring back into his hand. And then he registers Paloma's long sleeves, flimsy material flapping around her wrists, reaching for one almost as soon as he does. Even the full horror of the scars on her arms doesn't slow him. Tears stream down her face as he rips off a length of sleeve to wrap around her nose and mouth, protecting her airways as far as possible, while his own eyes start to sting uncontrollably. Paloma's scars blur as she yanks off her other sleeve to protect him too. And now it's Jonny's tears that are rolling, torching their treacherous path down his cheeks, still seeing scars on someone else. He blots his eyes with the torn fabric before tying it firmly into place. Screams are tangling with the tear gas filling the air.

Round the final corner and they're at the back of the crowd roiling forth into the square. Jonny knows he should stay at Paloma's back, let her camera be both their eyes, but the tear gas is making it harder and harder to focus. Further ahead, security forces on both horseback and foot are struggling to quell the surging crowd, a flood of injustice and rage at their backs. Jonny glimpses the Casa Rosada through his tears and it seems as if the mob's collective fury has suffused the building itself, looming red-faced and impassive over the commotion.

'We have to get forward!' Jonny screams, but even with tears streaming out of his eyes he can see it's no use. There are no white headscarves. Much less fluttering white flags. And now a sudden squall is barrelling the crowd back – water cannons, firing their merciless jets, forcing waves of people back. The ground underfoot starts to fall away, slick with rushing water.

Jonny's legs buckle as Paloma crashes into him, jamming his camera into his chest. Another jet lands, closer this time, spray with the force of a dragon's plume, pummelling bodies out of its way. A small, elderly woman is lifted off the ground, her body slamming into Jonny's before slumping into a soaked heap beneath the crowd. And it's impossible to help her, they're already being swept away themselves, another relentless round of water sending protestors scattering, trampling everything underfoot, no regard to whether it is human or not.

But the crowd roars back, unabated. And the bullets fly again – *crack-crack-crack*, directly at those still trying to stand their ground, even as it slips from beneath their feet, even as the clamour drowns out their screams. The stench of gunpowder suddenly rents the air, a live rather than dummy round's inescapable tail.

And then bodies start to fall.

Blood starts to run.

Panic takes hold, wrapping its adrenalised grip around Jonny's already choked throat. He tries to wipe his streaming eyes, only to have his arm roughly buffeted away by another merciless jet from the water cannon, sending more bodies flying.

And time doesn't slow. Not even for a single second. Not even to spare innocent protestors, guilty of nothing other than emotion, from carnage of the worst possible kind.

Jonny fumbles blindly with the camera around his neck, uses both hands to lift it above the melee. Fastens his finger to the button as if he is firing a gun of his own.

Somewhere beside him, Paloma screams.

He doesn't see it coming until he's already gone.

Chapter Thirty-Seven

There's no clifftop this time.

No floating along a rocky path watching a distant family have a stupid picnic.

No reaching out to try and touch something. No spinning backward and freefalling away from something that never existed in the first place.

There's just vacant darkness. A total void.

Until a tinny rattle – a fan? – starts scraping at the edge of Jonny's consciousness. He sips a breath, air laced with the faintest rim of smoke surfacing his last memory. Burning tyres, battleground streets, live rounds slamming into a baying mob.

'Jonny?' Now a familiar voice is rippling in and out. Along with pressure on his head – a bind, tight and hot. He tries to open his eyes, flails immediately. Blind panic hits him with an almost physical blow. A warm hand comes down to cover what little he can see.

'It's alright,' Paloma reassures him. 'You've got a bandage on one eye. You haven't been shot. Don't worry.'

Jonny reaches up, clutches at the hand on his face, lurching himself to sitting. When Paloma takes her hand away, two men come into lopsided and blurry view beside her. Along with the confines of a squalid room and the outline of a wide, open window. Acrid smoke still pungent on the air drifting inside. The unmistakable clamour of protest still under way below.

'Hey.' One man steps forward, lays an unnervingly solid hand on Jonny's shoulder. 'You gave us a quite a fright back there, buddy.'

Jonny blinks with his good eye, a sudden flurry. Paloma looks as if she is smiling, the men beside her too. Something bright, something unmistakable, flashes across his consciousness but in the one-eyed fog Jonny can't quite make out exactly what it is. Below the window, the crowd is still baying. He coughs gunpowder out of his throat, gingerly touches the patch on his face, tracing the loops of medical tape stuck directly into his hair.

'What happened?'

'You just went down,' Paloma replies. 'It's carnage out there. Security forces are shooting directly into the crowd. But we think you just got an elbow to your head. These guys caught it all.'

Jonny's good eye flutters closed for a moment. In the dark, he sees it all over again – mounted police firing on unarmed civilians, water cannon spraying terror in their wake, skies blushing in shame overhead.

'Caught it all,' Jonny murmurs, still stuck in the mob, shrinking into himself as if the bullets are still flying in front of him. 'Caught me? When I fell? Or did you film me falling?'

'Both.' Paloma sounds amused, even playful. And when Jonny opens his good eye again, he finally understands why. It is written all over the two men next to her. Still Jonny can't bring himself to believe it, even as he reads the unmistakable white lettering on their identical blue chests.

Bright-blue flak vests, printed with uniform-white block letters. *PRESS*.

'Yup.' There's that solid hand again, giving Jonny's shoulder a squeeze. 'How's the head feeling? It's a bit of an emergency patch job, sorry about that. When this is over we need to get you properly checked out.'

Jonny works his good eye some more. Electrical equipment of a sort is littered all over the squalid room and – he gasps at the sight of a large television camera fitted to a solid black tripod, elegant angles positioned directly opposite the open window, as focused as a sniper's rifle.

The second man steps forward, training a pair of keen hazel eyes directly into Jonny's single, disbelieving one.

'Do you remember what happened there? Everything that you saw before you went down? We spotted you with the camera way over your head – nice work, by the way. Seriously impressive stuff.'

And now Paloma is stepping forward too. 'These guys are TV news reporters, Jonny. Cable news, too. It's available round the clock back in America. There's no escaping the stories they tell. And they're about to broadcast live, right now. They've got a satellite dish on the roof.'

'That's right,' the second man adds, a glint flashing through his penetrating gaze. 'It's a lot harder to cut off our transmission – yep, we know all about the attempts to interrupt TV and radio too. And I don't want to rush matters, in light of what you've just been through yourself and all, but you're living proof of what's happening in that crowd outside. State-sponsored authorities are firing live ammunition at unarmed civilians. You don't need to be a fellow newsman to know a story when you see one – if you'll, um, pardon the reference to seeing anything, given we've just put a whacking great bandage over your eye.'

But the man doesn't drop Jonny's gaze, not even for a second.

'Do you think you can tell us all about it?' he says.

And at last time slows.

But those extra few seconds are finally worth nothing at all.

Because this time Jonny knows exactly what comes next.

'Yes,' he replies immediately. 'And it's a whole lot bigger than you think, too. The riots aren't the full story. It's the issues behind them. You have to hear me out on that first, OK? And then we'll need your help getting us out of here safely.'

When he glances at Paloma to check he can go on, she is already nodding back. The reporter frowns at the scars etched silver inside her arm. Jonny's gaze lingers for the briefest of moments. He may only be looking with one eye, but he's sure he can see the silver marks winking at him as they catch the light.

'You see,' Jonny begins. 'When Paloma was a baby…'